The Life and Opinions of Maf the Dog,
and of his friend Marilyn Monroe

The Life and Opinions of Maf the Dog, and of his friend Marilyn Monroe

Andrew O'Hagan

faber and faber

First published in 2010
by Faber and Faber Ltd
Bloomsbury House
74–77 Great Russell Street
London WC1B 3DA

Typeset by Palindrome
Printed and bound in the UK by CPI Mackays, Chatham

A CIP record for this book
is available from the British Library

ISBN 978–0–571–21599–7

2 4 6 8 10 9 7 5 3 1

In memory of
Margery and Betsy

'Faith is the argument of non-evident truths.'

RABELAIS

One

My story really begins at Charleston, a perfect haunt of light and invention that stands in the English countryside. It was warm that summer and the mornings went far into the afternoon, when the best of the garden would come into the house, the flowers arranged in pots and given new life by Vanessa in her fertile hours. She was always there with her oils and her eyes, the light falling through the glass ceiling to inflame the possibility of something new. She had good days and bad days. On good days she set out her brushes and knew the time was right for work when all her memories became like an aspect of sleep.

It was June 1960. The gardener had just brought a tray of foxgloves into the kitchen, the flowers pert but deafened after a week or two of bees. I was sitting in a basket next to the oven when a ladybird crawled over the table. 'He's got the knock, innee?' said the insect, climbing over a breadcrumb.

'He's just tired,' I said. 'He needs a cup of tea.'

Mr Higgens swiped the soil off the table and the poor creature, too. 'Bloody slummocky in here,' he said. 'Grace! Where you want them?'

People have no head for miracles. They are pressed into shape by the force of reality, a curse if you ask me. But never mind: I was lucky to have my two painters, Vanessa Bell and Duncan Grant, a pair who, for all their differences, shared a determination to dream the world they lived in and fashion it into permanence. And what a blessing it was to paddle about on those Sussex flagstones and chase the yellow wasps, turning slowly into lovely me, the sort of dog who is set for foreign adventures and ordained to tell the story.

There are several things every civilised person ought to know about your average dog. The first is that we love liver and think it's a *zizz* and a *yarm* and a *rumph* and a treat, especially when it comes with sausage. The second is that we usually hate cats, not for the typical reasons, but because they show an exclusive preference for poetry over prose. No cat ever spoke for long in the warmth of good prose. A dog's biggest talent, though, is for absorbing everything of interest – we absorb the best of what is known to our owners and we retain the thoughts of those we meet. We are retentive enough and we have none of that fatal human weakness for making large distinctions between what is real and what is imagined. It is all the same, more or less. Nature provides a nice example, but it is no longer the place where men live. They live in a place they invented with their own minds.

This day, my siblings and I were to be found crowded around three dishes on the kitchen floor, while Grace Higgens stood at the table with flour up to her elbows. She was giving voice to all manner of nonsense about her holiday in Roquebrune, which wasn't really a holiday. Grace was clever: she imagined the animals were listening to every word she said and she even grew embarrassed if she said something foolish, which was not only endearing but quite wise. The loudest of the people in the dining room was certainly Mr Connolly, the literary critic, who was visible to us beyond an expanse of sisal carpet and a lilac armchair, the great man munching olives and inhaling dark wine like it was going out of fashion. He made a pinched face every time he drank from his glass.

'You hate the wine, Cyril,' Mrs Bell said. 'Why don't you ask Grace to bring one of the better things from downstairs?'

'Even during the War,' Mr Grant said, 'Cyril always knew where to find a decent bottle of wine. Yes, he could always find wine. And paper for his angry little magazine.'

I licked Mrs Higgens's elbow when she put me on the table. She made a jolly sound and bent down to look at her reflection in the kettle and primp her hair. 'I'd say you're a terrible charmer,' she said. 'A right one for the charm, eh? Not as clever as that last litter. My. That lot were the cleverest dogs. You hadn't seen clever until you saw those dogs. What? A lovely group. You could just tell they came from good people. Walter said it himself. Yes, he did. A credit to the breed he said. The beautiful eyes they had on them.' Like most people who don't say much, Walter was always being quoted for what he did say. She touched my nose. 'But you are the pretty one. Yes you are. The pretty one. Mmm-hmmm. And America! You'll be too good for us once you're in America!'

Mrs Higgens kept the whole thing together, cooking and cleaning, and of course it's a great thing to be among talented people, but all the hurly-burly of their extravagant natures and their sexual lives and everything appeared to quite exhaust Mrs Higgens. Just thinking about what went on in their minds made her want to go for a lie down. Of course she wasn't scared to have her say and when she lifted me onto the table I spied immediate evidence of her tendency to complain: her wee brown diary sitting there open and quite proud of itself. It was Mrs Higgens who gave me sympathy for the household gods; here she was, this experienced rinser of garments, this Helen of failed cakes, who might have ruined her eyes during forty years of enabling those artists to be free. She sat down, wiped the rim of her teacup, and lifted the book. On the inside cover it said, 'Grace Higgens, Charleston, Firle, Nr. Lewes'. As she flicked through the pages she was living all that life over again, what wasn't there as much as what was.* The laughter coming from the dining room seemed an adequate accompaniment to the smell of cinnamon drifting over the kitchen.

Mrs Higgens wasn't the best cook in the world. She always worked out of a box of clippings – things she'd torn out of *The Times* or the *Daily Express*, pages now discoloured, covered in powdered egg, ground spices, dust. (It was the same box she had used to hold the gas masks during the War.) Mrs Bell was forever rolling her eyes at the desperate chore of having to pretend to Grace her dinners were edible. For my own part, however, she was the best feeder of dogs I ever encountered, and I thought of her kitchen long after I'd succumbed to the American way of life.

A supreme effort was being made in the kitchen that day, not for their neighbour Cyril Connolly, a frequent and frequently complaining guest at Charleston, but for Mrs Gurdin, the dog-loving lady from America, a noted Russian émigré and mother of the film star Natalie Wood. I never

* As a diarist, Mrs Higgens was a minimalist. Feb. 5: 'Bought cream buns with real cream.'

4

fully processed the connection, but I think it was that nice writer Mr Isherwood who put them all in touch, knowing from Mr Spender that the Bells' housekeepers bought and sold puppies. Mrs Gurdin, not without grandeur, liked to say that the world's dogs were her life's work and her great hobby.

I passed through the dining room, where Mrs Bell was talking quietly. 'Quentin used to say it was odd how Virginia wanted to know what dogs were feeling. But she wanted to know what everyone was feeling. Do you remember Pinker?'

'The Sackville hound?' said Connolly. 'I remember it only too well. It had Vita's face. I'm sure Virginia's little novel *Flush* was a joke on Lytton. All those eminent Victorians, and here was the little Browning spaniel, the most eminent of all.'

'Pinker is buried in the orchard at Rodmell,' said Vanessa, gently touching her wrists in turn, as if dabbing perfume.

When it comes to pedigree, each dog worth his mutton is a font of expertise. We Maltese – we *bichon maltais*, the Roman Ladies' Dog, the old spaniel gentle, the Maltese lion dog, or Maltese terrier – are suffered to know ourselves to be the aristocrats of the canine world. A great relative of mine was famous as the boon companion to Mary, Queen of Scots; another one gained the ravenous affections of Marie Antoinette. We have known philosophers and tyrants, dipped the pink of our noses in the ink of learning and the blood of battle, and Publius, the Roman governor of Malta, having given house to my distant relative Issa, had a portrait painted of the little dog that is said to have been more lifelike than life itself. That is our habit and also our creed. Once I came to know myself, to know that my relatives in art are no smaller than the story of my own cells, I understood at once that I must be a scion of that contemplative muse, the little dog in Vittore Carpaccio's *Vision of St Augustine*. Nothing is lost on the littlest of all dogs. We served in the heroic narratives of the Mediterranean, in the Holy Wars, we sat on the laps of evil-doers and saints, were passed by marriage across the princes of Europe to lick the tragic boots of Charles Edward Stuart, producing, in our turn, heirs out of the houses of Eduardo Pasquini and the Contessa di Vaglio, the Conte Anselmo Bernardo de Pescara and the Principessa de Palestrina. After princes and pups alike were murdered by Hanoverian agents, the surviving brother prince and brother pups married into the house of Dalvray and later into the house of Claude Philippe Vandenbosch de Monpertigen and the Comtesse de Lannoy. From there, by ferry, a son of that union, married to Germaine Elize Segers de la Tour d'Auvergne, came to Leith with a litter of pups that included my ancestor Muzzy. In good time Muzzy met a full Maltese bitch against the park railings on Heriot Row, right across from the house of Robert Louis Stevenson, whose cousin Noona once patted them both.* It was some of their noble grandpups who were taken from Edinburgh to the Highlands, where the next generations grew up in a castellated mansion at the end of an avenue of silver firs.

Our pedigree was terrifically intact, and our good fortune secure, at the time of my own birth in Aviemore in the kitchen of the tenant farmer Paul Duff. My first owner had

---

* The whole family was kind to dogs. In the first surviving letter written in his own hand, RLS makes affectionate mention of his dog, Coolin. Three years later he is still thinking of the dog when writing to his mother from boarding school: 'I hope that Coolin is all well and that he will send me another letter.'

imagination galore, a really infectious manner of drumming up knowledge and making up words. He was fierce excellent, a noted Trotskyist, terrible with money, and he – the eager-faced Mr Duff of Aviemore and Kingussie – had a wonderful old Stalinist mother with whom he argued until both were purple in the face. She was in fact a great hero of Red Clydeside, but a posh old bird as well. The family all called her Elephant or Stodge on account of her greed for Madeira cake, potato scones, and Paris buns. Her voice was terribly plummy and even in her old age she still scooped up great ladlefuls of bramble jam. Bless her, though: the old lady loved my own great-grandfather Phiz, and was said to have feathered his basket with a red flag the day after Trotsky was attacked in that Mexican villa. I could never have imagined that one day I would see that place, but we'll come to that in good time. The Duffs were the first people I ever knew on earth, and I find their habits pretty much cling to me from when I was a suckling, those evenings of argument, with Duff and Stodge ripping the world's prose to shreds as they spat crumbs across the dining table like bullets at Ypres and threatened liquidation to half the population. I say liquidation, because that was the kind of thing Mrs Duff would say. She couldn't bear to use the word 'death' or 'dead', and, consequently, neither can I. She would narrow her excited little eyes as if about to say something deeply shameful, and then say: 'If anything ever happens to me, the policy book is in the cupboard above the kettle. I've taken to policy books. That's how far we've come down. But you have to be careful. Something happened to Mr McIver over the hill and he had to be buried by the Parish.'

'It wasn't that *something happened*,' said Paul. 'He *died*.'

'Don't be morbid,' she said. 'Those dogs are howling, Paul. I'm sure they're listening to every word we say.'

The Duffs, mother and son, never had any money, but they were quite grand about it, making do in the old way of farming common to Scotland. I am not saying I sprang out of a dunghill, but my origins were not propitious. A muddy kitchen. A stale parlour. The breeder Paul was a complex man with a love of whisky and a passion for the early European novel.* He would work the fields and read a tome at the wheel of his tractor before returning at sunset with colour in his cheeks, ready to begin drinking himself into a stupor. His favourite actor was Cantinflas. He had watched all those old socialist movies when he lived in Glasgow.

But truly I digress. (And digression is another creed.) Paul was short of a few quid in the spring of 1960, and he sold my entire litter to a gardener from Charleston, Firle, in the province of East Sussex, who liked to travel to Scotland on holiday, looking for dogs and plant cuttings. This was none other than Walter Higgens, full-time husband to my great good friend Mrs Higgens. He had driven up to Scotland to buy pedigree dogs and he found us in Aviemore. It wasn't far from the place where Mr Grant was born – we each yelped our first notes in the land of midges. The main thing about Mr Higgens was his capacity for listening. We could all talk, after a fashion, and I suppose the Bloomsbury habit was for the endlessly characterful business of talk, a modern version of the classical love of rhetoric. Talking was a thing I took very much for granted, as all animals do, but the vital talent

---

* He liked novelists who got out of doors. Defoe, Smollett, Orwell. He said novelists who didn't like adventure should take up knitting.

8

was the one for cocking an ear. Walter Higgens listened to everything and he said little: that was my initial inheritance, on the long drive through the mountains, lowlands, and smoky shires.

I sat up and looked at Mrs Higgens. I moved my head in the way they liked, and she clapped my coat and stroked my face. She pressed her lips together as she tried to open an old tea tin. 'Mrs Gurdin told me this morning she comes to Europe a lot of the time, and she always arranges to take dogs from England. She finds lovely homes for them in California.' Mrs Higgens, as she spoke, was looking at me with a brand of self-pity, the kind that imagines other people's lives are always more exciting than their own. She finally got the tin open and took out a collar that smelt immediately of leather that had spent many long hours out in the rain. 'Walter used to look after the dogs,' said Mrs Higgens, 'the ones at Rodmell as well, and this was Pinker's collar. You don't inherit much in this family. Mr Grant is seventy-five. We're not that kind of family. But Vita gave this to Mrs Woolf's dog and now I'm giving it to you.' She made the collar small, taking it down several notches. Then she fastened it around my neck with the great ceremony that English people reserve for moments of minor sentiment, and I was immediately glad to have its story with me.

Two

As the man said, the truth is seldom plain and never simple, but this comes pretty close. Mrs Gurdin took me to London for a night at the Savoy then put me on a Pan-American flight to Los Angeles. With a group of other dogs I was placed in an existential vacuum called 'the hold'. We were then put in quarantine at a new facility somewhere in Griffith Park, close enough to the zoo for us to hear the *wazooms* of the elephants. Years later, when I thought of this time I would recall how Sigmund Freud, on coming to London, had pined for one of his beloved chows, Lun, who was quarantined in Ladbroke Grove while the great doctor was being lionised in Hampstead. In that prison in Los Angeles, I yearned for someone to own me and miss me. I was no horse: I loved the idea of being owned, because, for a dog, ownership sets you free. I wanted someone to love me and I didn't yet know her name.

'Mason, Tommy. Look how cute. This is definitely the one I would take home. The little white one? Sir, can we buy him?'

'I'm sorry,' said the jailer. (It was always him. The crunch of his boots on the gravel was familiar. The whiff of cologne. They were heavy boots. It was heavy cologne.) We were outside, in a little fenced-off area. 'These dogs are not for sale. They are in these cages for a reason. The zoo is that way.'

'You can buy things at the zoo?'

'No. You want a pet store? Los Feliz is that way.'

Apart from his genius in the arts of imprisonment, the jailer made a strong impression with his love of stars and planets, which he talked about incessantly while feeding the dogs. He often knocked off at 2.30 and made his way to the Griffith Observatory, where he liked to fall asleep in the planetarium beneath the whirling cosmos. He was a twenty-six-year-old part-time employee with a good sense of what was visible and not visible to the naked eye. He was especially fascinated by the cool, distant, impervious stars and I'd say he was my first American friend. He worried about proximity, judging everything by how near or how far it was from him. Animals and outer space are excellent hobbies for such a person, for each is useful and comforting to humans with more than a passing interest in loneliness. Much of his conversation was about space animals, the poor beasts regularly sent into the sky as part of the respective space programmes of the United States and the Soviet Union. He enjoyed spending his afternoons thinking about those legions of chimps, monkeys, and macaques floating about the solar system, fulfilling man's need to discover. The jailer's natural patriotism led him to stress the American side of things: it was all happening in those years, so we heard a lot about Able and Miss Baker, the two monkeys who were the first creatures to travel into space and return, but there were many others – Sams, Hams, Enoses, Goliaths – shooting into the sky on *Little Joe 2* as part of the Mercury programme, dozens of profoundly reluctant beasts gaining altitude, going sub-orbital, lost in space.

Mrs Gurdin, Maria Gurdin – 'Muddah', or 'Mud', as her girls called her – displayed all the imperial ruthlessness of her White Russian cousins. Just as the Romanovs at Ekaterinburg had sewn their jewels into the linings of their dresses, gems that the assassins' fusillade soon embedded in their bodies, so Mud sustained an image of herself as a martyr to her riches, a modern Russian icon glittering in pain. When she came to Griffith Park to collect us one November morning, she wore a bright grey turban and extremely rickety peep-toe heels. She was quite different from the woman I'd met in England. In homage to the ravages of American motherhood, she wore too much make-up. No question: she believed motherhood was a kind of martyrdom, the make-up a show of coping. Muddah had what the poet Keats called 'negative capability': in England she had seemed to be the perfectly coiffed, white-gloved business lady, but in California she tottered across the lawn doing Joan Crawford at the apogee of her maternal ruination. You could actually *scent* her lipstick and her general unhappiness at five hundred yards. I would soon come to know very well the depths of anger that lay beneath Mrs Gurdin's efficiency mode: the day we got our release from Griffith Park she came to fetch us in a rented bus which she drove herself, throwing open the back doors and tossing the dogs inside after the paperwork. Me, Myself and I? What do you think? I sprung into Muddah's van like Tom Jones vaulting a garden wall.

Bumps. A great many bumps. And what a wonderful lesson in the price of devotion Her Ladyship offered during the ride into the valley and the township of Sherman Oaks. Let me tell you: Mrs Gurdin was a high priestess of devotion, a fan of fandom, an actor's mother indeed, fully charged up and quite mad with the émigré's love of American possibility. Yes. There she was at the wheel in her blazing turban, shouting her Russian curses out the window as she battled through the traffic with a bus full of British dogs. On the seat beside me, a dark, lugubrious Staffordshire bull terrier was trying to establish a mathematical formula that could prove Mrs Gurdin was happy in her life, despite the obvious. 'If you added her minor portion of talent to her major degree of desperation,' he said, 'multiplying it with the exact quantity of her need for revenge and then dividing it by the standard vanity, I think you could show that Muddah is actually quite content.'

We passed the Greek Theater at the edge of Vermont Canyon Road. Mrs Gurdin was pulling erratically on the steering wheel: she was keen to avoid the freeway and trying to calm the barking. 'I'd say the mammy had anger enough for half the town,' said the Irish wheaten terrier. 'Would you look at her now, the devil couldn't put a mark on her. The big face on it. I'm not kidding: the face would cool soup. Take the thickness of that nail varnish she's got on. Ahh, now.'

'I say,' said an Old English sheepdog sitting in the row just behind me. 'Frightfully nice to be out of the old dungeon, what?'

'I think I'll fair miss your man, the jailer,' said the wheaten, staring into a run of palm trees as we crossed Los Feliz Boulevard.

'Me too,' I said.

'Steady on!' said the sheepdog. 'It's jolly nice to be free. That jailer fellow was awfully strange.'

'I think he was a little paranoid,' said a Labrador with north London eyes. I gather she was bred by a psychotherapist who

13

mainly treated rich ladies who wanted to kill their maids. 'Wasn't there something a little needy about his schmooze?'

'How do you calculate that?' said the Staffordshire.

'Well. It was as if he was asking us to reject him,' she said. 'Isn't it possible that his deep insistence we find him interesting was evidence of something self-hating in him?'

'Ahh, now,' said the wheaten.

'Some people have a deep-seated fear,' said the Labrador, 'a fear that the animals know more than they do. It makes them feel inadequate.'

'Oh, come on,' I said.

'Stuff and nonsense!' said the sheepdog.

'You're all in denial,' said the Labrador. 'Human beings often worry that the animal kingdom, so called, is looking at them and talking about them and . . .'

'Judging them?' I suggested.

'Don't you think that's possible?' she said, pawing the window and then bedding down in the seat. We were now on Franklin Avenue and everybody outside was wearing sunglasses. 'If you take the sum total of a person's paranoia,' said the Staffordshire, 'and divide it by their natural sense of dominance, subtracting a variable amount of humility before adding a stable degree of self-preservation, then you can prove that human beings never really succumb to the truth of what their imagination might tell them. They are never defeated by the truth.'

'Woof!' said a little schnauzer, quite excited and given to acting the fool at the back of the bus. 'I mean, *precisely*.' The schnauzer had spent the first two months of his life in a porters' lodge in Cambridge.

'I'll give you woof,' said the Irish wheaten.

'Be good dogs in there!' said Mrs Gurdin, twisting round with a manic, unhappy smile. 'We're on the Highland, coming on to the Hollywood Boulevard.'

A voice came from the other side of the bus, from a Jack Russell-style mongrel who had kept himself to himself in the quarantine facility. He seemed to know a thing or two about life, and he spoke, when he spoke, with a kind of plain honesty. Most dogs are socialists, but the schnauzer said the mongrel was a workerist kind of dog with a chip on his shoulder, a *New Masses* throwback, one of those pups who go on about the vanguard of the proletariat. It was rumoured that Mrs Gurdin found him in Battersea.* 'The truth is people know we're looking at them,' he said, 'and the smart ones know we're talking about them. People aren't stupid. They only behave as if they were.'

'Golly,' said the sheepdog.

'I'm serious, man,' said the mongrel. 'They worked it out for themselves a long time ago. They just don't listen to what they've already worked out. It's us that got listening. It's us that remember. Every system of exploitation depends on the fact that the exploiters will forget what it was that allowed them to enjoy a natural advantage. That's the way it is. The same way people can tell a lie for so long they believe it is the truth.'

He paused to scratch his ear.

'It's there in Aristotle,' he continued. 'He laid it out about animal intelligence.'

The schnauzer butted in. 'He wrote that we have

---

* The famous home for stray dogs. On her trips to England, Mrs Gurdin was often to be found there, weeping into her kid gloves.

"something equivalent to sagacity". In *Historia animalium*. He said humans and dogs do indeed have much in common.'

'He wrote that we're endowed with memory,' said the mongrel. 'We live on a social footing.'

'Good for the gentleman scholar,' said the Irish wheaten. 'He had the wisdom about him. But he also wrote that the elephant could eat nine Macedonian medimni of barley at one meal. La! It's hardly testimony of our equal powers. Your man also put in that the pig is the only animal that can catch measles. La! Aristotle.'

'Grauman's Chinese Theater to the right!' Mrs Gurdin was shouting from the driver's seat. 'This is where the stars put the hands and the feet into the cold cement.' The bus was still swerving about the road, the dogs growling and arguing while padding about the seats. The vehicle was high with the odour of body heat, saliva, and perfume.

I *frizzled* and *chooked* in my seat as I worked to rootle out the thought I was trying to reach. 'Everything man touches is changed by invention, technique, and artificiality. I think . . .'

'That's what we're saying,' said the Staffy.

'Yet animals are the great subjects and the great appreciators of art in any time.'

'Now yer talking,' said the wheaten.

'Precisely,' said the schnauzer.

'Jolly good show!' said the sheepdog. 'About bloody time somebody threw down the gauntlet.' The other dogs looked at him and he became, well, if not sheepish then sheepdogish.

'People lead the way,' I said, 'and we follow. But *how* we follow. The great leader in this respect was Plutarch not Aristotle.' Some boos and low hisses and general disputatious hubbub and lots of 'come on' followed on from this, quickly

16

broken up by Mrs Gurdin.

'Would you animals pipe down back there!' she said. 'Is very much like menagerie!' The bus crossed Fairfax and seemed to tumble, all its atoms alive, onto Sunset Strip. We could see the cars outside and the sunlight dashing off everything.

'You can say what you like,' I said. 'It was Plutarch, the genius from Chaeronea . . .'

'Down with practical ethics!' said the Staffy. There was now much excitement pervading the bus.

'While Aristotle was benevolent in relation to us,' I said, 'he basically saw us as feeders and breeders.'

'For shame!' cried the sheepdog.

'Here's to feeding,' said the mongrel. 'Here's to equal portions.'

'It was Plutarch who recognised our speech,' I said. 'He allowed us the power of "picturing". Isn't that something? He has us talking and dreaming.'

'*The Interpretation of Dreams*,' said the Labrador, snuggling into her seat. 'Perhaps we should provide copies for the men going into space.'

'Or the people who made the Bomb,' said the Staffordshire. 'If you take the sum total of the world's ambition and divide it by the general happiness of the greatest number, then go on to subtract all ideology and add the maximum quantity of economic fairness, it will quickly establish . . . what?'

'That nobody would be human if they had the choice to be something else,' said the mongrel. He licked his paw. 'Anyhow,' he added, looking up at me with humour in his mismatched eyes. 'You seem to have plenty of opinions.'

'Breeding, old cock. Breeding,' I said.

Mrs Gurdin had taken us on a detour. (Her life was a detour.) Fairly close to the Los Angeles Country Club, she turned the wheel and pressed on the gas in a burst of excitement. She always liked to see the greenness of the lawns. Lucky her. I caught her eye in the mirror and she said, 'How are you, little one? Soon you'll see an English garden as it ought to be done.'

'You know we're in a desert,' I said, looking over at the mongrel for common sense.

'Yes,' he said. 'Water is really the great scarcity here, though you'd never think it. They imagine it's lush.'

'The whole place is an oasis.'

'Or a mirage,' he said, turning again to look through the window, surveying the expanses of dryness that lay beyond the French chateaux and Italian villas. Down in the canyon there was smoke, brush fires, and just as I spied them a helicopter came over the Santa Monica mountains and began spraying water, a ghostly vapour. The dogs' tongues were busy with talk and panting in the heat and I noticed a bead of sweat appearing from under Muddah's turban to roll down her cheek. 'Why is it so hot today?' she said. 'It is goddamn late November.'

You must be able to see Ventura Canyon Avenue from outer space, the street and its swimming pools, the bursts of bougainvillea covering the Gurdin house and the lights blinking on the Christmas tree. I imagine that if aliens converged on Earth they might make Sherman Oaks their base: the place just seemed ready for them, ready for extra-terrestrials, ripe for UFOs; but that was before I discovered Texas. (Don't let me get ahead of my story.) A pair of fat robins were sitting on a telephone wire outside the house when we arrived. 'Ah, poor shmucks,' said one of the robins. 'I wonder how long these ones will last.'

'Jesus,' said the other. 'She looks more broken-hearted than usual. Look. She's all set. Muddah is *on*. And Nicky Boy just went in half an hour ago, drunk as a Russian sailor. I was in that big tree over there, and I saw Nicky Boy falling out of a cab, singing a song and calling for the old balalaika. Holy smoke. Now all these dogs.'

'Why does she do it?'

'I guess she's sick in the head. She wants to give them out to people for Christmas.'

'Poor limey shmucks.'

'Don't talk to me. Don't talk to me about Christmas. I've never seen it any worse than it is around here, the way they torture each other into having a good time.'

The robins shook their heads.

'That little white guy won't last a week.' I looked up and caught the two of them mid-sentence, inclining their little grey heads together. 'Cover your ears, kiddo!'

'I bet you three berries, three berries, he won't last a week. He's got "Christmas Present" written all over him.'

'Oh, boy.'

'Yeah. The lady of the house, the Empress of All the Russias, she keeps a waiting list. A waiting list as long as your wing. She knows people go crazy for these English dogs. Some fat kid with four scooters is gonna be hugging the life out of that white one in no time.'

Imagine the scene. Seven pups are chasing one another round a garden of winter blooms, flowering magnolias and pepper trees with grey berries, the pups peeing and barking and shouting. Mrs Gurdin opens the front door and we shoot through her legs into a house that smells liberally of candlewax. For me, the decor will always be the thing and will always begin with the flooring. Natalie Wood's family home in Sherman Oaks was a vision of interior decoration in a state of distress, the site of a shotgun wedding between American lightness and Russian morbidity, the tone of the carpet smiling hysterically at the frowning pictures, the optimistic ice-box sending breaths of milky freshness into the curtains, heavy with stale cigarette smoke, yellow brocade, and dire memories of St Petersburg. 'Nice digs,' said the mongrel. He looked at me.

'You must be joking,' I said. The little farmhouse touches were making me dizzy.

'What's wrong with your muzzle, prince of Malta?'

'The pictures! The wallpaper!' I padded into the dining room and found a stone cat. The urgent, thrusting ugliness of the place left me panting as I wandered the rooms, avoiding several lifetimes of horror, ornaments in brass, frothing oceans of filigree, and tartan rugs. Tartan! In several of the alcoves, there were little shrines either to Nicholas II or to Natalie Wood, the elder daughter of the house, with por-traits, in each case, surrounded by pots of plastic flowers, icons, and votive candles. In Natalie's shrine – the actress was still only twenty-two – there were a number of plaster cherubs, porcelain eggs, as well as a small crucifix made of ivory, brought years before in one of Muddah's large trunks from Harbin. A nearly invisible, shy Hawaiian maid called Wanika had the job of keeping the shrines going each day and parts of the night.

Up on the landing, Nick Gurdin was already shouting at his wife. I would soon discover that Nick spent most of his time upstairs, where he kept the bottles, and where the television was never off. I'm afraid Nick was a buffoon of long standing. He was always pasty-faced, the sort of man who sweated gently, like a girl crying. Everything in his life was to do with respect or rather its absence: he inspired none and he got none, he didn't know why, and the situation drove him backwards into his deepest hollows, where he drank by himself in San Fernando bars and thought of new ways to deploy his growing hatred. If he'd lived in New York and worked in an office, he might have thrived as the typical, over-martini'd, cheating husband, leaving every night on the 7.14 to White Plains, a smudge of lipstick high on his neck and a tide of lies to see him through to the next day. But Nick was with Muddah and Muddah was in Hollywood. And in Hollywood Nicky Boy was forced to take early retirement. Upstairs, I could hear him berating his wife for leaving him without sufficient funds to see him through the day. She mentioned something about work at the studio. Carpentry work. A candle flickered in the alcove as he shouted again. I pulled myself up with my paws in an effort to inspect the gaudy seats of the chairs in the hall.

'Oh, don't be like that,' said the Staffordshire. He came and lay beside me under a rococo-ish chair that smelt of cheap varnish. 'If you take the maximum amount of nationalist sentiment,' he said, placing his handsome head on his paws, 'and splice it with equal degrees of artistic banality and emotional panic, you will end up with . . .'

He turned to look at me. 'What exactly will you end up with?'

'Home Sweet Home,' I said.

Three

These first homes were temporary: I was waiting for my owner, as people call it, or my fated companion. We picaroons know that waiting and listening and learning by our mistakes will always be the bigger part of our adventures. The great challenges are forever ahead. In the meantime, there was the manic world of Ventura Canyon Avenue and the hourly rounds of crisis. Mrs Gurdin lived her life through her children but also via a huge sense of historical desolation. On this front the poor woman could not be soothed or assuaged. The dogs quickly came to see they had no role in comforting Muddah, so we decided just to skip round the house ignoring her cries for help.

'To thine own self be true,' said the bard. Yet in all the animal kingdom, only humans consider integrity to be a thing worth worrying about. I grew up in the golden era of existentialism, so you'll forgive me for finding the whole idea of a self that one must be true to a little ridiculous. We are what we imagine we are: reality itself is the supreme fiction. Despite years of excellent evidence, humans cannot get the hang of this condition; they live like the people in Plato's cave, never quite believing their shadows are as true as they are.

It was my great good fortune, first in England and then

in the United States, to be among people who were very much of the opposite tendency. These were people who shaped themselves according to the farthest reaches of their desires, finding the most fevered kind of honesty in their invented states. Mrs Gurdin was once called Maria Stepanovna Zudilova: people of her background enjoyed a total immersion in feeling, the sort of thing that would endear the Russian interior fandango to several generations of American actors, Mrs Gurdin's daughter Natalie and my fated companion among them.

Mrs Gurdin came from a line of people who owned soap and candle factories in southern Siberia. Running from the Bolsheviks they stuffed money into their pockets, but they forgot Mikhail, Mrs Gurdin's brother, and when they came out from their hiding place they saw the boy hanging from a tree at the end of a rope. Mrs Gurdin would hate the Bolsheviks for life. The family escaped – she liked to say on a private train – to a house in Harbin, where Maria took ballet lessons and enjoyed the services of a German nanny and a Chinese cook. Mrs Gurdin varied her stories, but they all told of a life made out of adversity. She was forever elaborating, forever covering her tracks. Sometimes she was a gypsy child who was found on the steppe but more often she was a Russian princess escaping the bullet or cheating the hangman. In any event it made California a kind of paradise for her, a place where the bare truth was seldom sufficient and seldom reliable. Mrs Gurdin's husband, Nick, was once Nikolai Zakharenko from Vladivostok.

Early one evening our friend the dog-lover came down the stairs wearing what can only be called a ballgown. She had set her hair and applied her make-up and was bedecked with a ton of costume jewellery. She addressed Nick over her shoulder as if talking to someone high up in the cheap seats. 'Faddah,' she said.

'Cut it out, Muddah. You can exclude me from any goddamn drinks down there.'

'Fahd! You make me sorry about the day I met you. You are not a man.' Nick came on to the top landing carrying a rifle. His hair was mussed up and he was drunker than a Siberian doctor.

'Don't start me, Muddah. Not tonight. I'm staying out of your communist meeting.'

'How dare you,' she replied. 'You hurt my heart, Faddah. Little Mikhail is still lying in his grave and you accuse me of having communists in my house?'

'Sinatra is a communist.'

'He is a friend of the new young President-Elect. We should be proud to know him.' Nick's rifle wasn't loaded; he liked holding it up while watching cowboy shows on the television. He said something about Kennedy being an Irish peasant.

'*Krestianin*,' he shouted. 'Peasant.'

'Mr Sinatra is a friend to Natasha,' Mrs Gurdin said in return. 'You are not a man. You don't look after your family. You are an object to be pitied.' Her husband shouted a curse and turned up the volume on the television set as she continued her regal descent. I hopped out of the basket and parried her hemline. 'Mr Gurdin is a . . . you say, naughty man,' she said, smiling. 'But you do not care much for that, Maltese, do you?' Mrs Gurdin always looked a little desperate even when she was happy. 'It doesn't matter,' she added. 'This is your last night here, Sizzle.'

They had started calling me Sizzle as a tribute to our old friend Cyril Connolly. It was just a family thing: she didn't say it to breeders – she still called me 'the Maltese'. When Natalie said that Mr Sinatra was looking for a dog to give as a present, Mrs Gurdin didn't hesitate to nominate me. She said I had British class, though, in private, her sense of British class had been dented in Sussex. She swept off in her taffeta gown to visit the kitchen, at which point I clambered up the stairs to have a look at Nicky Boy. He was sitting in an old yellowish armchair in front of the television, surrounded by a great variety of Russian dolls peering out with their dead historical eyes. He was slugging from a quart of vodka. This was Nicky Boy's time. He stared at the screen like someone imagining they might at any moment leap forward and disappear into the Wild West. Mr Gurdin was watching *Bonanza* and he pointed the rifle at the screen before resting it on his outstretched legs. 'Mr Cartwright,' said the young man on the screen, 'there's two things I can handle – horses and women. In that order, of course.' Mr Gurdin let go of the gun and slapped his thigh, before holding up his bottle and toasting the show. The guest star Ben Cooper was thrown to the ground by a horse and the music went all strange. Nick leaned forward. 'My legs, Mr Cartwright!' said Ben Cooper. 'I can't move them! I can't even feel them!' Then the titles began and *Bonanza*'s theme tune filled the bedroom.

'This,' said Mr Gurdin, looking across the room at me through tired eyes, 'is a very beautiful show. A very very beautiful show, I tell you that for free, Dogville.' I walked across the carpet and he lifted me onto his knees, the cold barrel of the rifle pressing into my side. Looking at him I felt Nick's face was a small tragedy. 'You are a nice person,' he said in a slurred whisper. 'A nice little dog and I've got one thing to tell you. Watch out for the Reds. They will take your food and leave you out in the rain.'

I nuzzled his hand. Pity can be a fairly civilised way of feeling good about yourself. He wore a pair of dirty white bucks, the shoes of someone who'd seen better days.

'Out in the rain,' he said. 'That is how it goes with such people.' I turned and sat on his lap for a second and we watched an advert for Swanson 3-Course Dinners. 'Disgusting,' he said. 'Khrushchev food for people who want to live in the outer space.'

The doorbell rang downstairs and I jumped off his lap and made my way down. Nick got up and slammed the door behind me. But it wasn't Sinatra, it was Natalie, arriving early to talk to her mother about problems she was having with the new house on North Beverly Drive. 'How perfectly adorable,' said Natalie when I appeared at her feet in the hall. 'Oh, Muddah – is this the one for Frankie? It's got to be, okay?'

'Dah,' said Mrs Gurdin. 'I know he loves an entertainer and this one has been in the world before, I'm telling you, Natasha. Even in England, the other dogs sat in the basket. This one was out. He is the friendly one.'

'Oh, how completely sweet.' Natalie lifted me up and involved me in her beauty for a few seconds. I nuzzled her neck and she smelt of some excellent floral thing, Joy, I would have said, yes, Joy by Patou, jasmine, tuberose, a philosopher's notion of the perfect flower.* Her eyes were so

* As you know, canines are not so hot with the eyes. Not with colour, anyhow. But our ears and noses make up for it. Unlike humans, we can hear what people are saying to themselves, and we can sniff illusion. The latter capacity makes dogs especially responsive to commercial perfumes.

dark you felt they must hold secrets, including the darkest secret, but only a perverse dog could speak of anything but life when speaking of Natalia, Mrs Wagner, Natasha, Natalie Wood, in her prime, only months before she starred in both *Splendor in the Grass* and *West Side Story*. Her lovely face concealed a nest of hostile feelings; I absorbed that as she stroked me and put me down, the daughter preparing for battle with Muddah and all she presumed to understand. Life is a movie anyhow, but no one played it like Natalie, rolling the dialogue in her mind before she spoke.

She took out a holder, lit a cigarette, and gave Muddah the full up-and-down treatment. 'We have frogs,' she said. 'The new swimming pool is crawling with frogs. They're all dying. You argued for a salt-water pool, Muddah. Better for the circulation, you said. Now we have a fucking biblical plague down there. Isn't that just dandy? I tell you we're the talk of Higgins Canyon. It is not a Beverly Hills smell, Muddah. Dead frogs is not a fucking Beverly Hills smell!'

'Don't swear, Natasha,' said Mrs Gurdin. 'It is very common to swear.' Natalie looked down and enlarged her eyes for dramatic effect.

'Not in front of the puppies, huh?'

Natalie spun round and walked into the living room, looking for an ashtray as if underscoring a point. Without pause, she reeled off a list of complaints, about her house and her husband and the new picture she was making, that went from being a litany to being an avalanche. Mrs Gurdin was the sort of mother who allowed her children's strong feelings to trump her own, at least for as long as she was in their presence. And that's how she saw it: not as being with her kids, but as being in the presence of her children. Her relationship with

27

Natasha involved a heady mixture of pride and humiliation. 'That is the most enthralling part of her story,' the Labrador said before she went to a new owner. 'Does she want to be honoured by her children's success, and also martyred by it, allowing it to reveal the chances she never had?'

Natalie went on. The decorators were phonies. The rose-tinted marble didn't match in colour all the way through the ground floor. Her private bathroom was too heavy and cracks were now appearing on the ceiling downstairs. At least half of the chandeliers were fakes. The pipework was amateur and by the time the hot water reached the faucets it was stone cold and, *can you believe it*, dirty. Dirty bathwater and frogs in the pool! It was like living in a swamp somewhere in Bolivia. The head of Fox was threatening to ditch her husband RJ's contract. 'Isn't that just the limit? This busboy from St Louis, Missouri, this Greek guy who is into buying ships. Actors aren't ships! You can't just scuttle them when they get a bit rusty.'

'RJ's not rusty,' said Muddah. 'He's thirty.'

'In this town that's rusty,' said Natalie. 'That's salvage. An actor over thirty is bad news. Some Clyde in a nylon suit from the front office is testing him for the push, I can tell you, I know these guys.' Muddah wrung her hands and dived into the doom. We should never have left Harbin. My poor mother and father. Before you know it we'll all be starving. The Bolsheviks hanged poor Mikhail from a tree. At this point she produced a handkerchief from the sleeve of her gown. Things were supposed to be better and now Robert will be on the scrapheap and life is over. Over, I tell you.

Mrs Gurdin had a tendency to approach all problems with those tears of ecstasy and tender emotions typical of

Dostoevsky's women of faith. No occasion was too small for this awesome trick of unburdening: Mrs Gurdin required almost daily exhortations to the higher authorities that they suspend her portion of misery here on earth, and make sure the milkman comes on time.

'Oh, turn it off, Muddah!' said Natalie. 'I'm having the time of my life because for the first time . . . for the first time it *is* my life.'

'Are you rehearsing?'

'What?'

'Are you running your lines?'

'Don't be ridiculous, Mama. I'm not a kid any more.'

'You're running lines, Natasha. This *Gypsy* role you'll never get. I read the script. They want someone to play a whore. You're too innocent. They remember the baby girl in the Christmas picture.'

'Stop it, Mama.'

'And this Kazan picture, too. You're reciting from it, aren't you, Natasha? These things you are saying to me. You are playing the Deanie girl with me. All these pictures you want to do are mother-hating pictures. Everybody wants to blame the mother.'

Natalie suddenly flushed. 'Don't lay it on me if you can't find the right way to be a mother. Don't blame me if you don't have the lines, Muddah. I've been Maureen O'Hara's daughter and Bette Davis's daughter. I've been goddamn Claire Trevor's daughter. Gene Tierney's. I know all about mothers!* Mothers always looking for forgiveness, mothers

* Natalie was overstating her case. She had never been Joan Crawford's daughter.

always looking for redemption, mothers making out like it wasn't about them all along. Mothers crying themselves to sleep at night. You're right, mother! More than anything I know, oh yes, I know how to play at being a daughter.'

'I'm not asking you to play, Natasha.'

I looked up at Mrs Gurdin with eyes that I hoped betrayed the deepest confusion. She lifted me up and walked into the parlour where Wanika, ever-smiling in a white maid's apron, was laying out sandwiches and cheese biscuits on pretty little plates. I dropped from her arms into a waiting chair. She sighed. 'I haven't seen Mr Sinatra since your birthday party at Romanoff's.'

'That was just the kindest thing anybody ever did for me,' said Natalie wistfully. Muddah was stung by this remark but she cancelled the feeling by saying no to a cheese biscuit while Natalie moved to the fireplace mirror, an actress fixing her lipstick.

'Mr Sinatra is a kind man,' said Mrs Gurdin. 'He gave a lovely speech that night of the birthday. He supports many worthwhile . . . many worthwhile causes.' Natalie turned round and drilled her brown eyes into her mother, the eyes that could magic the doubt behind them into a furious and almost blasphemous certainty.

'I am not a *cause*, mother,' she said. 'I am Frank's friend. That's what I am. Frank's friend.'

'Of course,' said Mrs Gurdin. 'I was thinking of the work he does for the coloured people.' Natalie walked over and put her perfect hands over her mother's, a pose of beseeching and bullying that she had perfected long ago in the first days of her childhood.

'Mud,' she said. 'Please don't mess things up with Frank

and me, okay?' Mrs Gurdin felt that her daughter did not mean this in a romantic way; things weren't good with the Brylcreem Kid back home, she knew that, yes, she understood that it was as much in Natasha's nature as it was in her own to be constantly looking out for signs of betrayal in the people she loved. Her womanly instinct also told her RJ was the sort of man to be driven mad by Natasha's moods. But Mr Sinatra was good news for her daughter and she knew that too. Mrs Gurdin knew that her daughter needed to ally herself with serious adult concerns and politics. Mr Sinatra liked Natalie, and Natalie wanted to reward him by taking seriously the things that mattered to him. Natalie felt that this was how adults behaved. Mud should know. Natalie turned back to the mirror and frowned. 'If Faddah is upstairs with *The Andy Griffith Show* that's the best place for him,' she said in the mirror, meeting her mother's eyes.

'Yes,' said Mrs Gurdin. 'He did not do so very well at Romanoff's.'

'He did worse than that,' said Natalie. 'He was loaded before the soup came and he told Peter Lawford he was a pinko fag from England.'

'Yes, that was naughty of Fahd.'

'Naughty! It was disgusting. He was drunk. Peter is the brother-in-law of the President-Elect of the United States of America.'

'That is correct,' said Mrs Gurdin. 'Nick gets very tired and times have been difficult . . .'

'Oh, please, Mud. *Please*.'

'Well. Since the accident.'

'It wasn't an accident, Muddah. He was drunk and he ran a red light. He drove into the guy and killed him. Right in

31

Beverly Hills.' Muddah looked at the carpet and thought she saw fluff.

'It's unusual to find people walking in Beverly Hills,' she said distractedly.

'Muddah!'

'Don't worry, Natasha,' she said. 'He is in the bedroom and that is where he will stay tonight. He is not . . . as you say, social.'

'It's only a cocktail, mother.'

'Yes.'

'It ain't the Academy Awards. Don't we have to do something with that dog, like give it an injection or something?' I walked over the carpet and disappeared into the hall, at which point I heard Natalie saying, 'I don't think dogs like me.' She popped her head around the door. 'Hey, buster! Everybody likes me! I'm a very liked person! The studio gets five thousand fan letters a week so stick that in your pipe and smoke it.' She followed this remark with the kind of cackle that would have pleased a director very much indeed. Upstairs, I'm sure I heard the theme tune to *Huckleberry Hound*.

Natalie laughed and opened one of the large windows that looked on to the driveway. A cool breeze came round her legs and she pointed up. 'We really are valley girls, Muddah,' she said. 'That's the San Gabriel Mountains up there, isn't it?'

'I wouldn't know such things,' said Mrs Gurdin. 'It's all just the mountains. Give me a beach house in Malibu or give me Beverly Hills. These are mountains I can do business with.'

'Nick Ray told me that when it glows over the hills, it is usually the military doing rocket tests.' Unlike Natalie, who was happily American in all obvious aspects, Mrs Gurdin always experienced a vague flare-up of melancholy at the mention of rockets or bomb shelters, the latter of which Mr Gurdin had long been planning for the bottom of their garden.

'I hope they are not just throwing good money away on those rockets,' said Mrs Gurdin.

'Ha! You sound like me,' said Natalie. 'Your politics are going my way. I thought you were all for us raining death and destruction on the Muddah-land.'

'I don't hate my country,' said Mrs Gurdin quietly. 'I hate what they have done to it.' I stepped onto the patio. In a second I smelled oranges and grapefruits on the breeze that filtered across the valley, I could hear the low snarl of bobcats coming down the chaparral slopes, and wasn't there also a whiff of old Spanish airs and sulphur out in the mountains? All this was broken very suddenly by the sound of a car horn and a glint of teeth.

'Frankie!'

He did have a touch of style, that man. He came out of the car with flowers for Mrs Gurdin, white orchids in a silver pot, and was singing an old song of Bing Crosby's, in that way of his, both transgressing and apologising at the same time. The song said the San Fernando Valley was just the place for him. Frank's neat row of teeth rhymed perfectly with the white line of handkerchief cresting the top pocket of his suit. I ran inside to get away from his charm, but not before I saw him kissing Mrs Gurdin's hand and opening his arms to Natalie, saying, 'Hey, Nosebleed! You gonna make a guy beg?' She kissed him and I witnessed one of those subtle shifts that Natalie was so very good at. It was as if someone had gently turned up the setting on an icebox, her eyes sparkling a wee bit harder as she turned a few degrees cooler.

The style of their speech was off-hand, yet full of manners. Mr Sinatra spat the letter *t* in the New Jersey way while playing the part of the easiest guy on the planet, clicking out words that shimmied over the great topics of the day. It mattered to him that he should seem not to care a great deal. Yet he cared to the point of madness. It was a wonderfully comic kind of curse, the wish to be cool, chiefly because the people who had the curse were generally those whose free-floating anxiety made coolness an impossibility. They were uptight in ways that presented a challenge to molecular physics, but hey, *daddy-o*, what merry battalions of determination they sent out to overcome the needs of your average Joe.* Everything appeared to melt into a shrug, but it was all appearance: Mr Sinatra was actually the least relaxed person I ever met. 'What a blast,' he said, lighting a cigarette for each of them. He was talking about *Ocean's 11*.

'I guess the suits are looking for dollars,' said Natalie, easing into the put-downs of Hollywood she found so congenial.

'Made in the shade,' said Frank. 'Those shmucks will get their money. Say, how's that pom-pom-shaker of a husband of yours?

'Actually,' said Mrs Gurdin, 'RJ is trying out for a serious play in New York.'

'We might have to bend his nose a little,' said Mr Sinatra. 'Give him the Actors Studio look, huh?'

---

* The actors were perfect for the parts they played. They would never grow up. Sinatra was eternally Private Maggio, the weedy and needy antagonist in *From Here to Eternity*. And Natalie would always be the girl who wanted to be cool in *Rebel Without a Cause*.

'Yeah!' said Natalie, laughing. 'Detroit's answer to Karl Malden. Come and see the greatest show in town. Drop dead!' Mrs Gurdin looked at her daughter and said nothing but Natalie felt the full force of admonishment. She had revealed too much in criticising her husband so enthusiastically. 'RJ is just dandy,' she said. 'Handsome as ever and here's to him.'

'Hey, sister. I have an old-fashioned rule,' said Mr Sinatra. 'I refuse to toast anybody until I've got a drink in my hand.'

'Sorry, Frank,' said Mrs Gurdin. They walked to the bar at the back of the room and Mrs Gurdin rang a bell for Okey, Wanika's husband, who was in charge of the drinks. Mr Sinatra dropped a jar of silverskin onions on the bar and spoke directly to the barman, as if the ladies couldn't possibly understand. 'Okay, buddy. Can you do a Gibson – three times?'

'Like guava mouthwash?'

'Come again?'

'His English. It is bad,' said Mrs Gurdin.

'A Gibson martini,' said Sinatra.

'Of course. Three times. Vodka or gin?'

'Gin, buddy boy,' said Mr Sinatra. 'Always gin.' They walked over to the sofa. 'What am I going to do about this guy? Is he messing with me?'

'He has a strange sense of humour,' said Natalie. 'These Hawaiians.'

'I love Hawaiians. We can bring him over to Traders if he wants to see how Hawaiians make drinks. I'll give him guava mouthwash. We have eight decorative tiki gods over there. Somebody carved them. Carved them by hand and we have them in the bar. Is this guy for real?'

'Forget it, Frank,' said Natalie, loving the opportunity to feel mature. 'The guy was just joking.'

'I'll give him joke,' said Frank.

'He and Wanika just bought a house you build yourself,' said Mrs Gurdin. 'They bought it from a catalogue.'

'Sears Roebuck? asked Frank.

'No,' said Mrs Gurdin, 'they haven't done them in years. Some other company does them now. They built it over in Inglewood, near Hollywood Park. The house came in the mail. Okey – you bought the house that came in the mail?'

'Yes, Mrs Gurdin. A house in a box. It is very nice. We make it up with a hammer, that's all.'

I watched from the door as Mr Sinatra scowled and Mrs Gurdin fussed and Natasha sat on the arm of the sofa blowing smoke into the dead centre of the group's confusion. Okey the barman was making the martinis one at a time and he bent down to hand one to Mr Sinatra. 'I make this for you, Mr Frank,' he said. 'I learn to make it in the Porpoise Room.'

'Okey and Wanika worked in the cocktail lounge at Marineland,' said Mrs Gurdin. 'Down in Palos Verdes?'

'I make it good,' said Okey.

'Okay,' said Frank.

'That's his name,' said Mrs Gurdin.

'No, okay,' said Frank. 'The drink is fine.' He looked up at the expectant barman. 'It's okay, Okey. You're not just a pretty face. Now scram.' He turned to Natalie and appeared surprised at his own victory. 'Aren't you having one of these little mothers?'

Four

Like Noël Coward or Holly Golightly, the princess Natalia had what you might call a cocktail-hour mentality. She threw back several of those Gibsons and her breath smelt sweetly of gin and pickled onions, while her mother made dark Russian remarks and the Hawaiian staff stood over by the piano waiting for orders, hands clasped before them and big eyes staring forward. An hour or more passed with laughter, hard looks, industry gossip and little panics, punctuated now and then with bursts of television gunfire from upstairs. All the while Natasha grew more outrageous, more sexy, more Natalie.

Seeking a part for herself in Frank's current preoccupations, she decided to ask him about the Kennedy campaign. Natalie had an instinctive adoration of the high-ranking. 'Well, we got him elected,' Frank said. 'We did the fundraisers. We got him elected. Let's see if TP can't keep his promises.'

'TP?' said Mrs Gurdin.

'The President, Mama.' Natalie swung round with a little too much energy. 'They're the Jack Pack,' she said.

'You're cute,' said Frank. She giggled in the way that girls always giggled around Sinatra, loading every chime with a sonorous appeal for approval. Frank loved it. Frank beamed.

'As the man said, he's the nation's favourite guy.'

'He cares for the underdog,' said Natalie.

'That's right, sister,' said Frank. 'That's my bag, too. I believe in the Bill of Rights. That's why I wanted to hire one of the blacklisted guys to write that war picture. And you know what the Hearst papers did? They murdered me, honey. The bums mugged me. I'm talking about the Hearst papers. John Wayne. General Motors. Cardinal Spellman. It was a high-end lynch mob, honey, and I'll never forgive them. Maybe Kennedy can make a difference in this country. I've been fighting against lynch mobs all my life. But I had to lose the writer.'

'Wayne's a fink,' said Natalie.

'Jesus,' said Frank. 'The guy's been out of line for thirty years. He's a nut.' He made as if to wave the subject out of the way, but he had more to add. 'I tell you, princess. That fella would throw a thousand better fellas in prison, just to show he's the big tough marshal in town. He'd burn a thousand books to avoid reading one. That's a fact, Mrs Gurdin. Well, what can I tell you? John Wayne is a shmuck. He's a loser. And there's no part for losers in the new game.'

'Kennedy!' said Natalie, like a groupie.

'That's right, princess.'

A shadow flickered in the hall and then I heard a thump on the stairs and a door closing. 'That election was in the bag, made in the shade,' said Frank. 'Success guaranteed. It might have been close, but to me it was always a cert. We did a lot of campaigning in Hawaii.' He tilted his glass to the barman, as if re-settling a score. 'But there's a lot to fix in this country. Some Charlies want to hold the world back and I'm talking Democrats, too. You know Sammy got booed by those sons-of-bitches from Mississippi when we were singing

38

"The Star-spangled Banner"? Right there at the Convention when Jack got the nomination.'

'Well,' said Natalie, a flush coming into her cheeks. Pleasure, I thought. She had the clever pupil's delight at finding herself ready with an answer. 'Dr King's father was ready to vote Republican. He said he would be voting for Mr Lincoln's party.'

'Jack was on to that,' said Sinatra. 'When they arrested King and put him up there in Reidsville prison, Jack called his wife. The wife's pregnant. Jack calls her to say he's thinking about her. Is that classy, or what?'

Frank was so jumpy he couldn't really sit down, and he nearly tripped over me several times before we were introduced. Talking about Kennedy seemed to make him worse. 'Maria,' he said to Mrs Gurdin, pacing back from the windows, 'I brought you a little smile-maker. All pretty girls should have presents.' Mrs Gurdin touched her throat and behaved as if her pleasure had caught her by surprise. She stripped the ribbon and the paper from the package he handed her and found inside a blue Fabergé box. I lay on the floor and put my head between my front paws.

'Oh, Mr Sinatra,' she said, tears coming into her eyes, 'this is absolutely beautiful.' She spread her hands over me and lifted me up to his face. 'This little one is your dog,' she said. You got the feeling his blue eyes were able to watch themselves watching you.

'Hey, I was outta line, buddy,' he said, stroking my ear and flicking it. 'I should've said hello when I came in. Hey buddy. You're going to be a present for Marilyn.'

'She's in New York?' asked Natalie.

'Yeah. She's been blue.'

39

'Finished with Miller?'

'Done and done,' said Frank. 'She's at half-mast.'

'So many presents,' said Mrs Gurdin. 'I tell you for nothing, Mr Sinatra, you are a generous man. My husband agrees. Always a generous man. To our Natasha also.'

'Muddah – enough. You are embarrassing Frank.'

'You are,' he said. 'And I love it.'

The noise upstairs got louder. It was as if furniture was being dragged around. You could hear a door handle being pulled and suddenly Mr Gurdin was shouting over the banister. His wife was still weeping with gratitude and a sense of national loss when Nick started shouting, but the sound of his voice instantly mortified her, killing the sentiment, turning off the tears. 'Crackpots!' Nick shouted. 'Goddamn crackpots and communists, I tell you. All Reds. Reds in my own goddamn house.'*

Sinatra smiled and I saw a sting of cruelty moisten his eyes. 'It's Nicky Boy!'

'Oh, pipe down!' said Natalie, giddily, over her shoulder. She mock-shouted back at him. 'Pipe down, Fahd.'

'It makes me sorry,' said Mrs Gurdin. I went out to the hall and could see Nick hanging over the banister, his face all grey and furious, and a bottle dangling.

'We pledge ourselves to fight, with every means at our organised command, any effort of any group or individual, to divert the loyalty of the screen from the free America that gave it birth.'

---

* The combination of cowboy shows and liquor wasn't good for Nick. In that sense he resembled the great film director John Ford, who, every time he had a drop of the Irish, especially when in close proximity to galloping hooves and discharging firearms, would turn into a right-wing lunatic.

'Holy smoke,' said Sinatra. 'He's giving us the "Statement of Principles".'

'Stop it, Nikolai!'

'Don't sweat it, Mud. He's drunk.'

'Straight up,' said Sinatra. 'It's the old ragtime: The Motion Picture Alliance for the Preservation of American Ideals.'

'Oh, heavens. He must stop. It is terrible,' said Mud.

'Shout it out, Nicky Boy!' said Sinatra.

'We dedicate our work . . .' shouted Mr Gurdin.

Natalie rolled her eyes and knocked back her Gibson. 'Work, ha! That's cute,' she said. 'He hasn't worked since he left Vladivostok.'

' . . . in the fullest possible measure . . .'

'That's not fair, Natasha,' said Mrs Gurdin. 'He has tried to work, like any man.'

'Dream on, Muddah. He's a waste of oxygen.'

'Wise guy, huh?' said Sinatra.

'. . . the presentation to the American scene, its standards and its freedoms, its beliefs and its ideals, as we know them *and believe in them.*'

'Shout it out, you two-bit hustler,' yelled Sinatra. 'I have a good mind to come up there and break your legs.'

There were threats and curses. One of the other dogs ran into the kitchen howling. I don't think I had ever witnessed such chaos, whether in Scotland, England, on Pan-Am, or in quarantine, and it ended when Mrs Gurdin threatened to pray to one of her icons or Romanovs or whoever she thought might bring this nightmare to an end. There was a moment of silence when Nicky Boy upstairs ended the hostile fire and slammed the door shut before Natalie started one of her theatrical cackles, looking at Muddah's lips, which were still moving in silence. 'You think my mother's interested in stardom,' she said to Frank. 'But what she really cares about is tsardom.'

Mrs Gurdin wrapped me in a blanket along with a rubber bone.

'Take it easy, funny girl,' Frank said to Natalie. 'Your mother's a widow. I wouldn't give a dime for that lemon popsicle upstairs. Not a dime. He's a total nut.'

'You actually like my mother?'

'Why, sure,' said Frank.

'She was a ballet dancer once,' said Natalie, biting her lip and showing some wish she had to be proud of her mother. Mr Sinatra touched her chin and lifted a pickled onion from his glass, tossing it into the air and catching it in his mouth. 'Now you be careful on that picture. Keep your nose clean. You're still working on it, right? Remember, Kazan is a rat just like that deadbeat upstairs. A snitch. Any flack, you just get on the horn to me, princess.'

'I'm nervous, Frank. They think I'm still the little girl in pigtails.'

'Just do your work, Miss Moscow,' said Frank, 'and remember you owe him nothing. Not Kazan or Jack Warner or him upstairs, neither. You earned the right. Those shitheels are lucky to have you.'

Across the lawn and into the car, I could hear Mud's holy recriminations on the upper floor. I heard a bottle smashing as she shouted in Russian. Mr Sinatra took the blanket off me and placed me down on the furry covers of the back seat. There was a faint whiff of Sicily about Frank, a hint of lemons and jasmine, and I wasn't sure if it was the flowers he

42

gave, the food he liked, Acqua di Parma or just some long-lost scent that lingered about his skin. I detected it when his hand touched my face and when he walked round the car. He blew a kiss at Natalie, who was in her own car and already speeding out of Sherman Oaks with that laugh of hers that seemed to embody the danger of the night and the secret of her own freedom. As I said, Frank and Natalie were the parts they played: I saw this most clearly as their cars swept onto the highway with their headlamps chasing the palm trees into the dark. I wanted to pee. When I looked through the back window I thought of Belka and Strelka, the two Russian dogs sent into space that year, and I wondered what small roles they had taken in the action of the night sky. Yes, they too must have wanted to pee as their capsule travelled through space, and I felt some pride as I looked up and imagined the trouble my comrades had taken for the human race.* The distant sky at night is often a comfort: it lets you believe that we are all alone to the same degree. The car moved with pent-up fury towards Bel Air, and only then did I let the long day pass into the lower regions. I relaxed into my adventure, counted my blessings, and did a long, warm wee-wee in the back of Frank's car.

It must have been catching because he stopped the car somewhere near the top of Beverly Glen, and went outside, muttering, cursing, to find a spot at the edge of the scrub where he could take a leak. I stared out at the silver stars. A cat came along and stopped by the road. It licked around its

---

* Belka and Strelka were now back on earth, doing other stuff for the human race. I mean, they were having *pupniks*, which were proving to be top-of-the-range diplomatic presents. Khrushchev gave one to Kennedy's daughter, Caroline.

mouth when it saw me and spoke the beginning of a languid, narcissistic sonnet, made in the Italian style as a compliment to Frank. The window was down and I could feel the breeze coming up the canyon.

> Life is excessive but not enough,
> The trees are my witness, passing cur.
> Around Tulip Lane I stopped for love,
> And breathed the heaven of a single her.
> She was perfect, knowing, wishful, dark,
> The living shadow of impervious night.
> Her love was mine for one remark,
> And yet I stole away in fright.

In the middle of the morning two days later, the men in Frank's entourage were having a stupidity contest. I'm not saying they were all mutton-heads, but they took the menace of B-movie gangsters and mixed it with the gutsy malice you might find in a sorority circle, surrounding Frank in a bubble of free-floating aggression and mild bitchiness, a state of affairs which appeared to make him feel good about himself. Frank liked people to be frightened of him but also dependent; it was his favourite combination in someone he considered a friend. So these lugs from Chicago or New Jersey or, heaven knows, Palm Springs, they wouldn't have jobs or proper roles, they would run errands, answer phones, pick up cars, make drinks, find girls, and act the wise guy whenever possible. But mainly they talked a steady, constant stream of pure nonsense to one another, very proudly plumbing the depths of their own ignorance beside a swimming pool of stultifying blue. 'Ah dunno, Tony. If you eat morels you get sick.'

'No, shitstick. You get fat. It's a well-known fact that

mushrooms make you fat.'

'Ask Legs over there.'

'Ask him what?'

'Ask him about being fat. He ain't seen his cock in twenty years, the bitch got so fat.'

'Hey, Legs. You been at the mushrooms again?'

'Bite it, Marino. Your mother ain't seen her pussy neither but everybody else has.'

'Oh, Legs. My friend. That is cold.'

'He ain't been eating no mushrooms,' said a little pasty-faced one with a mule laugh. 'Legs been stuffing his face with fried chicken since Ernie Lombardi first came out for the Brooklyn Robins.'

'I'm goin' eat me this little pig,' said a guy with gold in his teeth, a guy putting on his shirt. He'd just been inside with Frank at the massage tables. He walked towards me beside the pool and I yapped at him. 'Fry me up some of them morels, Tony. Fry them nice in butter. I got me a little dog no bigger than a drumstick. He finger food.'

Grrrrrrrrrrazzle.

'Woah, baby. I'm just jazzin'.'

'There's your finger food,' said Legs, chortling into his chest and presenting his middle finger.

When I went inside the villa I saw Frank was now in the living room, suitcases open on the floor, sorting things out with his valet, Mr George Jacobs. He always took too much stuff everywhere he went. A few days in New York could be fifteen pieces of luggage. There was a fair amount of broken glass from the night before. Some news about Kennedy had riled him, and he had lifted a piece of Lalique crystal and thrown it at the fireplace. 'Don't sweat it, Pops,' he had said in his bathrobe while chuckling to Mr Jacobs. 'The world's our ashtray, right?' Mr Jacobs had seen many disruptions not only from Frank but from everybody around him. First time Frank's mother met George she looked him up and down, saw he was wearing a white jacket, saw he was black and ready to serve her, and she turned to Frank and said, 'Who do you think you are, Ashley Wilkes? Well, I ain't no Scarlett O'Hara.'

Nimes Road. What a place. I had managed to escape the house that morning and had enjoyed ten minutes alone in Nimes Road before Mr Jacobs came to find me. Frank lived in a Tuscan villa at the top of the lane, next door to a French chateau. On the other side of Nimes Road there was a mini-White House with Greek colonnades, and further down, in the direction I wandered, was the perfect example of an English country cottage, covered in ivy and roses. The real difference between humans is that some care about authenticity and some don't care at all. The people in Bel Air don't care. To them, Frank's villa was nicer than any genuine villa ten miles from Lucca. If one were to speak of the Californian vernacular, I wouldn't, personally, be speaking about adobe *fincas* in a beanfield: I would be talking about that wee English cottage with its perfect symmetry and its apple trees. There was something beautifully real, something essential and human at the core of its inauthenticity. Dogs have always lived comfortably with that kind of reality. There it is. There it was, Frank's Tuscan villa on Nimes Road, an importation of rosemary bushes and terracotta, the fountains chucking jets of water into the air of this beautiful desert.

Frank's best friends had long since forgotten there were limits to their superiority over the world. They had Italy's

46

might without its sense of ruin, so plenty of Augustus but no Epictetus, plenty of Machiavelli but nothing of *The Leopard*, and they obviously believed man was in the business of getting better all the time. The mutton-heads assumed they were the summit of what the universe had to offer, which was immodest of them indeed, not to say cute, but I admit that sometimes their assumption of my subservience got to me. While they scoffed and burped, I wanted to present them with Swift's talking horses.

I don't actually blame the Italians. I blame the French. I blame the Enlightenment. I blame Descartes in particular. He think therefore he Am – well, good for He. Good for Am. And then this devoted father of modern science wishes to argue with Montaigne, my personal friend, and that nice Pythagoras, saying animals cannot be thinking beings because they have the apparatus for speech but don't use it, therefore no thoughts, no speech, no Am. To think – ah, to *think!* – the little brown mice housed all those years in the Collège Royal Henri-Le-Grand at La Flèche, who whispered mathematics in Descartes's dishcloth ears while he slept, and the crows who spoke law as they flew over his head at the University of Poitiers, to think that none of them is recognised in his modish reasoning. Oh, there you have it, the abundant arrogance and certainty of man. I don't know where I picked it up, Mr Connolly probably, but I have in my memory parts of a letter Descartes wrote to the Marquess of Newcastle in 1646. I'm afraid to say it vexed me to remember it when I looked on the mutton-heads by that nicely invented house in Nimes Road. 'I am not worried that people say that men have an absolute empire over all the other animals; because I agree that some of them are stronger than us, and

47

believe that there may also be some who have an instinctive cunning capable of deceiving the shrewdest human beings. But I observe that they only imitate or surpass us in those of our actions which are not guided by our thoughts. All the things which dogs, horses, and monkeys are taught to perform are only expressions of their fear, their hope, or their joy; and consequently they can be performed without any thought. Doubtless when the swallows come in spring, they operate like clocks.'

Mmmwwwwince. Thank you for that, Mr Descartes. It wasn't a dog that wrote the *First Meditations* but it wasn't a dog that invented the atom bomb either. 'Who taught the tortoise to heal a bite with hemlock?' (The question was present at my birth: spoken by Simplicius Simplicissimus in a novel my owner adored.) 'Who teaches the snake to eat fennel when it wants to slough its skin?' The memory of mouse-avoider got me bristling and yappy, as did the man with the gold in his teeth, but I felt better once I'd followed Frank's valet into a closet off the main bedroom that housed only neckties. 'Too damn many,' said Mr Jacobs. 'I tell you, Rinty. Mr Sinatra has had girlfriends younger than some of these ties.'

The room was a study in pastel baroque, a place of menacing contentment, like those sets in the films of Douglas Sirk.* Most dogs have a big heart when it comes to interior decoration, especially Maltese dogs. During my

---

* Born Hans Detlef Sierck, the director is known for a certain goodness of bad taste. At the time of their release, his films were hated by the critics for seeming too unreal; later, they were loved for being so ironic. Despite my difficulty with some of his colours, I always felt he was a master of artistic charm.

48

travels I often thought of my brothers and sisters: would they, like me, be at carpet-level somewhere nice, perhaps inspecting a grand sitting room in Kensington or dappling among the yellow chinoiserie in a European boudoir? My hero Trotsky would have made a great interior decorator: after all, decoration is all about personality and history, the precise business of making, discovering, choosing the conditions of life and placing them *just so*. The best decorators finding it quite natural to inject a splash of the dialectical into their materialism. Papa Hemingway once said that prose is architecture not interior decoration, but he was only half right: good prose is both, as he must have known in the velvet chambers of his crimson heart. Papa was another one of those geniuses who spent his entire life making a hysterical effort to appear effort-free, sitting down there in his all-day pyjamas with those overflowing tumblers of Dubonnet, shaping his grievances into the mannered simplicities of *The Old Man and the Sea*. In fact, Papa at his best was like Wallace Stevens, the great, inspired Interior Decorator of American Literature, the tycoon of poetry, whose idea of order at Key West was one where nothing was given and everything was made. 'For she was the maker of the song she sang . . . repeated in a summer without end.'

I mused on this while Mr Jacobs laid several ties on a stool of dark yellow. This floor of Frank's house had been done by Alexander Golitzen, an art director who had worked at Universal, an expert in marrying the arts of sedation to the blaze of Technicolor. That's what Frank wanted more than anything, a house built of certainty, a style that knew itself, a yellow chair in a very blue room, a dark suit and a perfect cream tie. Mr Jacobs looked down at me as I scratched

49

the fibres of the carpet and licked my paws. Cars were being revved outside: the mutton-heads were arriving and leaving with gratuitous despatch. I was licking a bone and remembering the words from Mrs Higgens's box of cookery cuttings in the kitchen at Charleston, all those yellowed papers talking about meats and bones being succulent and braised.

Mr Jacobs was considerate and he would often switch on the television if he saw I was in a room alone. When we ambled back into the living room I saw Mr Sinatra was getting heavy with some guy who had his back to me. It was Mr Lawford and my friend turned on the TV as a way to avoid embarrassment. The TV was way over in the corner of a giant room and I sat down in front of a bunch of *Tom and Jerry* cartoons. Now, not all cats are poetic just as not all poems are cat-like, but this kid Tom was wild and he ran around like a thing on fire, dodging the musical soundtrack, lurching – I'd say scrabbling, *scatterising* – like everybody you ever saw in those years, between brutality and sentiment. But boy those cartoons were a great venue for politics. That day at Mr Sinatra's was maybe the first time it occurred to me that a lot of those Democrats would get ahead quicker if they watched more cartoons. That's where you saw the world growing up. Frank was mostly oblivious to the call of reality, however, and was arguing with Lawford about some aspect of the Kennedy plans.

'The hell with that, Peter,' he said. 'Okay? The hell with it. I'm knocking myself out over here. Do you get that?'

'Of course, Frank.'

'Do you see that? I'm taking pills to sleep. I'm sick in my fucking stomach over this – this bullshit. Who's feeding this shit to the newspapers – Mr Sinatra's "connections", Mr Sinatra's "associations"? I'll feed their fucking children to the piranhas at Oceanworld, d'you hear me? I've had bad ink before.'

'Of course.'

'Oceanworld, I'm saying.'

'Frank.'

'I'm organising a fucking inauguration, Peter. Do you see what I'm doing? I'm getting every motherfucking star on the planet to come and adorn the Kennedys' motherfucking party. I'm knocking myself out. I'm making myself crazy over here.'

'I know, Frank . . .'

'Don't give me "I know", okay? I'll cut your fingers off.'

'The family appreciates it . . .'

'Don't give me "the family", you smooth-assed English creep. Don't give me that.'

'Frank.'

'I'll fucking destroy you. Do you hear me? I'll put my fucking hand through your fucking chest and pull out your fucking liver, you fucking limey shmuck. I'm knocking myself out for these people. I'm putting myself on the line for these boys. Do you hear me? These invitations are to personal friends of mine. Personal friends! You tell Jack or Ted Sorensen or Jesus H. Christ that these gentleman are coming to the capital as my guests. You dig? Otherwise they can forget the show. I'll do a Farewell Gala for Adlai Stevenson. I'll do a fucking roast for Richard Nixon. You tell them. You tell Ted Sorensen I'm out. I'm done.'

'Please Frank. Jack knows . . .'

'Don't give me what Jack knows! I'm about to leave for

New York to do more work for Jack Knows.'

Tom and Jerry used to be called Jasper and Jinx. The cat had the mouse by the tail and was trying to make him run over the Welcome mat into his mouth.

'I will sort it out, Frank. Honest.'

'Today, Peter. I want it fixed today.'

The black housekeeper came in with a broom and a big ol' Southern voice, a big fat lady with orange stockings and blue slippers. She shouted, 'Jasper! Jasper!'

'There are big things to be done, Frank. I'm sorry about any confusion. Dr King's lobby is on their tail and Jack's special assistant Woodruff is kicking up. Jack's just trying to keep everything on the down-low, with the segregation issue pressing in and the right-wing columnists . . .'

You never saw the black lady's face. Never. The respect for social realism at MGM meant you never saw the face of a domestic servant in a cartoon presentation. Yes, ma'am. And here was the faceless lady coming down the stairs shouting at poor Jasper for breaking up the house. 'Wait just a minute you good-for-nothing cheap fur coat. One more breakings and you is out. O-W-T out!'

'Well, Slim. Just you remember that some of us have been pushing for change just as long as brother-in-law over there has been pushing for office.'

'Yes, Frank.'

'And we've paid a price for it. The world has changed but we've paid a price.'

'Indeed. I know that.'

'You get that?'

'I got it, Frank.'

'You get it?'

'Certainly I do.'

And the clever mouse tricks the cat and makes him break up the house all over again. The housekeeper comes down the stairs and she's still got no face, no history, and that big Southern voice coming at you with her broom and her good sense about the house. 'When I says out I means out!' The door is flung open and out goes the cat. The mouse is happy with the world.

Mr Jacobs tied up the last of the suitcases and gave me some lunch in the kitchen before we all met at the limousine next to the fountain. I had to go into a little carrying case but I didn't mind; somehow, Frank's exhaustion had filtered through to me, and I just lay watching the palms disappear through a scrap of window as Frank's voice grew silent. Winter sunshine was falling into the car, and I remember feeling the engines of puphood were beginning to push me in a whole new direction. Thomas Mann understood how strange it is for a dog to watch everything and say nothing and to live a life of wan good nature, worn out with resting. The German pointer Bashan used to lie beside Mann, the blood-heat of his body pleasing the master and making him feel less lonely. 'A pervasive feeling of sympathy and good cheer invariably comes over me when I'm in his company and looking at things from the dog's angle,' Mann wrote in the middle of his life. As we drove onto the freeway I recalled the story of Theodor Adorno, who pondered the liquidation of the individual from a house in the glades of paradise, a house in Malibu that looked into the blue water of the Pacific Ocean. He may have been a creature of the war years, but his moment came with the 1960s, a decade that really began for all of us with the fading brightness of Marilyn.

Five

The skies were friendly, or so they said. The sky was a place of rest for the tired businessman with his flagging handshake and his Friday face, and who would deny him a bourbon on the rocks and a pretty girl in her TWA cap to smooth his cares away? If you believed the adverts, and we all did, the period in and around Christmas 1960 was a regular party above the clouds, a world apart from the hassles below.

Frank had his own jet, but it was grounded that month. The early days of jet travel were made for Frank. He was an absolute natural for the roped-off areas and beaming girls of the early airlines. 'Welcome back, sir,' said the girl. 'It's been a long time.' Her white shirt stood outside her collar, and she leaned on the bulkhead ready for something new. The arched eyebrows, the amused eyes, the crimson lips: everything about her said 'yes' to an indecent proposal. 'What a cute dog,' she said.

'You like him, huh?'

'Why, Barbra. Look at Mr Sinatra's dog. Isn't he just adorable?'

'Uh-huh,' said Barbra. 'And the puppy's not bad either.'

'You girls,' said Frank, smiling. 'Trouble. A whole heap of

trouble. We having a clam-bake in here tonight, pussycat?'

'Afraid not, Mr Sinatra,' said the girl. 'Barbra has church in the morning.' They chuckled. She drew her tongue over her teeth, real sassy. 'She done been bad before now. She got prayers.'

'You girls are trouble. Well, tell her to bring me some communion wafers over here.'

'Coming right up. Barbra, could you bring Mr Sinatra a double Jack with ice on the side?'

Frank was always making sure his rights were protected. He winked at the chief hostess and she leaned over the seat. He hit her with a fifty-dollar bill right there in her palm. 'Make sure there ain't gonna be no Harveys near this spot,' he said. No virtue, no fellow-feeling, no country or pleading voice, could stand in the way of Frank's pursuit of his own way of life.* He did what he wanted, good or bad. And yet, he appeared in our time to exude the kind of goodness that made people healthy.

I was supposed to stay in my box on the plane, but I was with the Chairman, so he lifted me out and I had a seat to myself. I was an old-fashioned traveller, though – that's to say, I was scared. By that point, the airlines didn't worry about people being scared any more, they worried about people being bored. Frank made my fear worse by immediately unfolding a copy of the *New York Times* and falling silent over a story about two planes colliding the day before over

* It was evidence of something special in Frank that he appeared so good to so many, because, in actual fact, he was as Locke described man after the absence of God, with 'no law but his own will, no end but himself. He would be a god to himself, and the satisfaction of his own will the sole measure and end of all his actions.'

55

Staten Island. I turned towards the window but I could hear every word as it passed through his tough little mind. Frank read the story four times. That was the kind of person he was, and by the last time, we were deep in the bright clouds above Nevada. Frank read the paper and signalled for another drink, then another one, the story in the paper enveloping the cabin in dread but not Frank, who found the experience beautifully comforting. (Bad things happened to other people.) The wreckage from one of the planes had fallen on Park Slope in Brooklyn, setting fire to several brownstones, killing a sanitation worker shovelling snow and a man selling Christmas trees. A boy on the United 826 coming from Chicago had survived for a while in New York Methodist Hospital. He remembered in the seconds before the collision looking down at the snow falling on the city. 'It looked like a picture out of a fairy book,' the boy said.

There was a night at the Waldorf Astoria. I remember Frank shouting at a half-dozen bellhops under a massive chandelier. He wanted a shoeshine. He wanted two dozen white roses. He needed a drink. He needed a town car and a goddamn private line. Frank's needs always came out like urgent threats, but the boys seemed glad to have them and happy to oblige, their handsome young faces readily opening up to Frank's abuse and the heavy tips that were sure to follow. My legs were stiff and I felt sore after all these hours in cramped surroundings, a feeling which I tried to show by the usual means, whining a little aria and hopping on the sidewalk. I think Frank got the message the next day because he sent the car away and we walked from the Waldorf to 444 East 57th Street. Frank never walked anywhere. It was a lovely, snow-filled day, and my paws were enjoying the skiddy ice on the streets. Frank was busy cursing as he pulled down his hat and exhaled wildly, the king of Sicily pulling at the leash, saying, 'Heel, goddamnit, heel,' and me feeling pleased with this nice levelling moment, the Chairman being dragged up Park Avenue. 'Take it easy, baby! Slow the *fuck* down.'

As we approached Sutton Place, Frank took a deep breath of the East River and felt nostalgic. Humans feel such compassion for themselves, it's one of their charms, and Frank, who loved to think he was above all that, was travelling that day into a sepia picture of his old mother and how the rough persistence of her love once mingled with the river noises. He looked up at the Queensboro Bridge. The other side is paprika shops and sausage houses, he thought, and over here it's one perfume counter after another. With Frank no feeling ever survived long enough to challenge his basic sense that life was a load of baloney. He caught himself thinking of the paprika shops as we walked down the street and he sniffed into the breeze and put his hand in his pocket. 'What a shmuck,' he said.

Vince was the doorman of the building at 444. A pigeon was pecking a low brass grille beside the door as we walked up. 'Hey buddy,' said the pigeon. 'Listen up. This guy's the nuts. Are you gonna be hanging around here? This guy's the business.' Vince came out of the lobby smiling like a benighted failure. Vince had qualities few of us have: I admired the guy. The great comedy about most people is they think this life is the only one they're going to live: they stock it up with panic, pain, worth, and glory; they fly a metal bird from Los Angeles to New York, but they haven't yet grasped the basic facts. God is not in his place of work and is not answering his phone – get it? You don't get saved, brothers and sisters, you get *reassigned*. The only person I ever met who acted like they knew this was Vince, who must have lived some other life as a pig in shit. None of us really remembers where we've been. We don't know. He laughed easily at events and slapped his big fat thigh, eating donuts and laughing like every day was a holiday, which it is – it's a holiday from being somebody else. Vince was the first man I met who didn't think he owned himself.

'Well, looky here at this nice English lord,' says he, stroking me in Frank's arms.

'I'm Scottish, actually.'

'And look at how he yaps so nice. I could swear he is singing a song to you and me, Mr Sinatra.'

'Watch him. He's a playboy. Is she ready?'

Frank nodded upwards and Vince got his meaning. 'She ready for you,' he said. 'Go right up to 13E. I'll give this little duke his lunch.'

What a guy. We must have been down there for a good half-hour together. He opened a tin of Dash and mixed it in a bowl. What can I tell you: Liver Treat with a side order of National Biscuits, ready to eat in the mirrored lobby, under the electric candles, Vince at his little desk listening to a football game from Yankee Stadium, the Giants playing the Cleveland Browns. Dash was probably the best of all the tins they had in America. It wasn't up there with Mrs Higgens's own small casseroles, but after prison slops, you know, and after Mrs Gurdin's cakes – she fed her dogs mille-feuille pastries, which she called *Napoleons* – it was just heaven to fall in with Mr Vince of Jackson Heights, Queens.

Plutarch thought creatures could live on goodness alone.

That was sweet. A philosopher can't have everything. I am happy he recognised the speech of animals, but he failed to admit our bad character, when we so obviously love to rend a piece of ox with our teeth and worry a hog with our mouths and feel good about it afterwards. Yet our learning is there to bridle our conscience, is it not? Do we not educate ourselves in order to be moral? So it was with livery breath that I passed my first snooze on those cold floor-tiles, digesting my carrion and worrying it might mean I was not personable.

Frank was whistling in the dark hallway, spinning his hat on his finger, when the lift opened on the thirteenth floor and Vince handed me over. Frank's great joke was to place me inside the apartment and let me find my way to Marilyn. The door was open. I stepped over a pair of stiletto shoes covered in bright grey rhinestones – *Ferragamo*, it said inside them – and stopped to nibble the strap of a Pucci handbag that leaned against a drinks trolley. She was nowhere to be seen so I sat on a copy of *Paris Match*. 'Go on, shoo. Keep walking, shitstick,' stage-whispered Frank from the front door, bending down and urging me on. The carpet was white and fluffy and smelled of carbolic soap, an English smell of rotting flowers. When I got to the living room I could hear her voice, then I saw she was sitting on a Louis XV provincial-style ivory and yellow painted chair, her nice legs folded under her. She wore a lace dress. The chair was right next to a small white piano and she was speaking on the telephone, her head tilted back, her eyes absorbing the light coming from a cut-glass clock that hung above the television. 'It isn't a story for Marilyn Monroe,' she was saying. 'I guess he's a good writer but the girl is some kind of tramp, right? Well, Lew. I happen to know she wouldn't

say those lines. She couldn't. There's no Sugar in them and
there's no Cherie in them, and gee, Lew, there's no *me* in
them. Don't you think that's important? If I'm going to play
a tramp I'd sooner do *Rain* for NBC. Lee says I'm ready. Mr
Maugham wants me, right?'

She didn't see me coming in. She listened like an old-
fashioned listener, ready to learn, ready to change, alert to
the sudden wisdom that makes all the difference. She bit
her nails one minute and twisted the phone wire the next.
It was a feast to my hungry ears. 'Well, that is possible too.
Yes, I know all that . . . Not where I come from . . . But don't
you ever just want to surprise yourself, Lew? I mean get up
and not have to . . . gee, it's humiliating. I don't want to do
an imitation of myself, okay? . . . Well, it's nice of you to say
it, Lew . . . I'm always running into people's unconscious.
Maybe. I hope so. Which part? This part? I don't think so.
Maybe this time round I could just start myself over again.
Hey, is that possible? I know what she is and she's not that
way. I'm on a freedom ride, Lew.'

She laughed and poured some champagne from a bottle
next to the telephone. 'Are you listening to me? . . . I'm a
monster, Lew, okay? I accept that. Now listen here . . . But
. . . Yes, I was born nervous . . . Listen here. Lew.'

I had never seen anyone so enraptured on the phone
before; she seemed to have forgotten about Frank and she
only noticed me when she put back the receiver. 'Wow,' she
said. 'O Lord. Wow. Hattie! Lena! Frankie!' She was the
only girl I ever knew who could whisper an exclamation. She
lifted me into her arms and kissed me as if I was the returning
hero, and I did feel special, you know, for a moment, held up
high by Marilyn like the dog who finally worked things out

and made it home.

Well met, Comrades. Marilyn's helpers came rushing into the room with Frankie laughing. 'Oh, my!'

'How darling!'

'Oh, my Lord.'

'The baby. Oh, the baby.'

'Little thing.'

'Just a pooch I picked up on the West Coast. He's from England.'

'Oh, a proper gentleman.'

'I guess . . . I love him, Frankie.'

'Good, honey. He's for you.'

'I love him.'

'Natalie Wood's mother deals in dogs,' he said. 'She finds them and she . . . well, she collects them. That's how I found the ankle-biter.' Hattie the cook and Lena the housekeeper disappeared out of the room in a flurry of warm and tender mouthings. It seemed like they were happy. 'Every girl needs a man around the house,' said Frank.

Her eyes had filled up. 'Gee.'

'What's his name going to be?' asked Frank. She rubbed my nose with hers and I felt it was stone cold.

'This little tough guy? Gee.'

'How about Britt?' said Frank. Cradling me in her arms she looked very tender, a long lock of blonde hair falling over one eye. She caught her breath and smiled a perfect smile.

'You mean like English?'

'Naaa,' he said. 'I think you should name him after Sammy's new wife. She's Swedish. Britt's a good enough name for a blonde.'

'No,' she said. 'He's a tough guy, isn't he? I'm calling him Mafia – Mafia Honey.'

'Oh, that's cute, kiddo.'

She kissed me again and let out a cascade of giggles. 'You like it?'

'That's fresh. You read too many newspapers.'

'Oh, I don't read any. If I wanna see myself I can look in the bathroom mirror.'

'I'll give you Mafia, wise guy.' He smiled and wandered out of the room to find his coat.

Sizzle, Maltese, *Mafia Honey*. Is there any chance of sticking to a name around here? Scott Fitzgerald once said that there could never be a good biography of a writer, because a writer is too many people if he is any good. I buy that. I believe it. Writers mattered to Marilyn. She was reading a fat Russian novel that whole period in New York, carrying it everywhere in her bag. She read it very slowly and perhaps she gave it more respect than it deserved. It made her feel accompanied.

So I was Mafia Honey – Maf for short. The days just drifted into one another on the East Side. For the first time since leaving England, I felt I might be on solid ground, in safe company every day with the same maid and the same housekeeper. It seems I was destined always to enjoy the briefest of stays wherever I landed, but in many ways I will always consider the apartment at 444 to have been my home. Marilyn was a strange and unhappy creature, but at the same time she had more natural comedy to her than anybody I would ever know. More comedy and more art. Not for her the stern refusal of life's absurdities: Marilyn had a sensitivity to jokes and moral drama that would have delighted the chiefs of psychoanalytic Vienna. It didn't take long for her to become my best friend.

'Maf. Today I give you meatballs.' This was Lena Pepitone, who looked after the clothes and sometimes the kitchen. She could mostly be found in the utility room, darning the edge of some Jean Louis sheath dress, re-attaching spangles, biting off threads, but regularly she came out and offered to make big Italian dinners for us. She worked under a Renoir etching, *Sur La Plage, à Berneval*. I always thought Renoir was so overdone: I mean, all those wispy strokes, they gave me a headache with their infinite prettiness. A body needs a little ugliness to keep it going. Like Frank, he always knew the benefit of some grossness; he gave Marilyn a set of gold lighters that said Cal Neva Lodge on them. They sat on the bookshelf beside a tray of toothpicks and a copy of *Madame Bovary*.

There was a strong sense of third-personhood about the apartment on 57th Street, right down to the mementoes of a largely invented past and the many pictures of Marilyn herself that hung on the walls, most of them painted by fans. All too soon, I felt like her protector, a common feeling and maybe a bogus one, but I believe it meant something to each of us. It seemed I had been sent to look after her. Now that she was back living on her own, Marilyn's state of mind was, at the same time, fresh and depleted: she wanted to learn to take herself seriously,* to value her experience. And yet she was hitched to the person she had always been: the girl

* There was always a story in Marilyn's bid for seriousness. Arthur sought to capture it a number of times, but probably he got the male attitude towards it most accurately in his play *After the Fall*. His version of himself, Quentin, says of Maggie: 'I should have agreed she *was* a joke, a beautiful piece trying to take herself seriously.'

who was sweet and available, who now took pills and drank. She found it hard. Many of the old bids for independence had fallen short. She was tired. When she hugged me, her comforter, her guardian, I felt a weight of disappointment about her, as if the stands she had taken in life, and in love, had only revealed her personal shortcomings and the impossibility of respect. But she was glad that winter to be free of Arthur and his inky old blameless honour.

The apartment had a powerful feeling of departed resentment, as if Marilyn had finally freed herself from a person whose energy had been destructive, the kind of person who had no interest in sustaining what was good in her nature or necessary to her survival. Spouses are sometimes competitive, aren't they? And the bad ones want not only to destroy the thing they love, but to crush that thing's ability to offer love, too. Such spouses imagine that no one will ever remember their lies, their aggressions, their capriciousness, and yet, in the end, that is all their former loved ones will remember about them, their terrible behaviour. Poor married people: perhaps they could learn something from dogs about how to settle the business of oneself before setting up shop with another.

All that was gone from the rooms. All the blame had gone and all the typewriters. But in my universe, which, let's face it, is the universe of the floor, I found myself constantly stepping over evidence that Mr Miller had tried to be Marilyn's educator. All the books were recent, from the last few years, and none of them spoke of the attachments that had tethered Marilyn's mind in her twenties, or, further back, in her youth. Outside the bathroom, on another Ferragamo box, stood *The Roots of American Communism* by Theodore

Draper, *The Works of Rabelais*, De Tocqueville's *Democracy in America*, *A Piece of My Mind* by Edmund Wilson, and an expertly illustrated edition of *The Little Engine That Could*. Apart from the last one, you never saw Marilyn reading them unless a photographer came to the apartment to take pictures. She was always appearing in *Life* magazine with a copy of *Ulysses* or *The Poems of Heinrich Heine* balanced on her palpitating breast. I wished I could tell her to leave all that to the mutts: anybody can read a book, but Marilyn could make people dream, just as Lena could with her wonderful tagliatelle in meat sauce. After a while I began to feel Lena was treating me as Dr Johnson treated his favourite cat, Hodge. The moggy spoke in alexandrines which the great moralist couldn't hear, but he fed him oysters all the same and the cat was very happy.

Marilyn took me everywhere. We had a lot of fun going up and down the avenues, Marilyn sometimes in a headscarf and sunglasses, completely unknown, running into the wind with our mouths open, and hungry for experience. I think we shared a feeling for the tribulations of the period, an instinct for killing the distance between the high and the low, something that would come in time to explain the depth of our friendship. If she brought out the actor in me then it might be said that I brought out the philosopher in her. The Marilyn I knew was smelly and fun and an artist to the very end of her fingertips.

I loved to sit on the white piano and watch her get ready for a night out. There was something perfectly shameless in the way she admired her reflection. It was like the central panel of Hans Memling's remarkable triptych, *Earthly Vanity and Divine Salvation*, in which Vanity is pictured with her little white lapdog, a model of companionship, standing beside her on a carpet of fresh flowers. I used to watch her – the Leichner, the eyelashes, the Autumn Smoke, the Cherries à la Mode, the Day Dew, the tissues, the pins, the small brushes and the lipsticks scattered on the tray like gold bullets – and I would wonder how much of our love is inspired by our need for a secret. Wasn't Emily Brontë's great dog Keeper the love of her life? Did she not love him above all creatures for his strength and silence, and punish him for knowing her so well?*

Some women need a fully accompanying silence to help them speak, and that was how it seemed sometimes to be with my owner, the pupils of her eyes engorged in front of the mirror as she completed her rituals of becoming. Next to me on the piano was a framed photograph of Marilyn with a letter by Cecil Beaton. 'Somehow we know that this extraordinary performance is pure charade,' he wrote. I nuzzled up to it. 'The puzzling truth is that Miss Monroe is a make-believe siren, unsophisticated as a Rhine maiden, innocent as a sleep walker. Like Giraudoux's Ondine, she is only fifteen years old and she will never die.'

One night she really got into her stride and by the end of doing her make-up she was promising me a perfect night on the town. She put on a black cocktail dress and a white ermine coat and lifted me off the chair with a great whirl

---

* Love is strange. Emily said her dog seemed to understand her like a human being. And she punished him the way people punish those who know them too well. In *Wuthering Heights*, the dogs have a worse time of it than the humans.

of laughter. 'Say,' she said, stroking me with her kid gloves. 'You are one little dressed-up Maf, aren't you, honey?'

'Well, actually. I'm dead beat . . .'

'You're coming with me tonight.'

'But . . .'

It wasn't her fault she couldn't hear me and only saw me as she figured. That's just how it is. She called the car service company and checked when the car was coming. I could hear the man speaking through the receiver in the muffled chipmunk-speak that works so well in the movies. 'Miss Monroe, the car has been waiting for an hour.'

'That's his job, buster,' she said.

She put on a Dean Martin record and swayed to the music while drinking a glass of champagne. I bounced down the cushions onto the carpet and walked over to the window and licked her toes. They tasted fizzy. She was oblivious for a minute or two as she looked at a book called *Baby and Child Care* by Dr Benjamin Spock. The hesitation became operatic. Marilyn could turn waiting into a kind of surreal, existential caesura, as if her spirit had stopped for a spell. Then, she chucked the book onto the dining table and her face broke into the most beautifully lascivious smile. 'Come on, Snowball,' she said, scooping me up. Her eyes sparkled. 'Our heart belongs to the Copacabana.'

Six

There was a neon halo over Times Square. The puddles were lighted pink and the bulbs made a cartoon beauty of Midtown, pulling shadows and poor men out of the alleys. The snow was falling and bright commerce took advantage of the dark, the changes in colour feeling like events, the battle of noises seeming like news. In the middle of all those twinkles, you might wonder if people even had a chance of spending their lives wisely.

She wanted out at the corner of 44th and Broadway. The pharmacy was open all hours and we skipped into its methylated environs, the car going on a block to wait for us. We were way off course, but that was always part of the excitement. In the pharmacy, Marilyn caused looks you wouldn't believe: she thought it would help to wear sunglasses but they only picked her out and made a show of her. I walked past the toothpaste and the mouthwash, sniffing out the perfumes. But after a minute I took my chance and ran out the door again. There was lots going on, especially at the theatres. The St James: *Becket* starring Laurence Olivier and Anthony Quinn. The Hudson: *Toys in the Attic*, a new play by Lillian Hellman, with Maureen Stapleton, Robert Loggia, and the long-serving Irene Worth. The Majestic: *Camelot* with Richard Burton and Julie Andrews, 'the hit musical of the season', an explosion down there of bright lamps and what I imagined were deep Arthurian greens. It must have been after 11 p.m. because the theatres were closed and the people who passed were sealed in their overcoats and a little high on cocktails.

'Maf!'

As she called my name, I saw a rat emerge from a spout on the building next to Twain's Diner. The rat had a jittery, downturned little mouth, smirky with self-esteem, and it spoke in a broad Brooklyn accent that instantly drowned Marilyn out. 'Mind your goddamn business,' he said as I stared at him and yapped my loudest. 'Summa us got woik to do.' The horns hooted and my blonde companion shrieked at top volume as I bounded across the road to catch the wee bugger. The rat was a ringer for J. Edgar Hoover. He ran straight up Broadway and shouted over his oily shoulder while he shot away as fast as his pink feet could carry him. 'Hey, fella. Pick on somebody your own size.'

The rat disappeared through a crack in the wall of a pizza joint and was gone from my story. Damn. I was disappointed in myself: I wanted to show my companion I could be as good as Lailaps, the magical dog destined on every occasion to catch his prey. Marilyn quickly had me by the collar. 'I am Lailaps,' I said. 'It was his job to guard the infant Zeus!'

'You are a bad boy,' she said. 'Running off like that. Oh. Don't you know something bad could happen?'

'My master was Kephalos of Athens,' I said. 'He used me to hunt down the Teumessian Fox, the scourge of Thebes.'

'Quiet, Maf! No point crying,' she said. 'I was just so frightened when I saw you run into the road like that.'

There are good animals and bad ones, that's for sure. Adonis was killed by a wild boar. Bad animal. Actaeon was turned into a stag and torn to pieces by his own dogs. Bad animals. Tom was hit on the head with a frying pan by Jerry and then pushed off a roof. *Bad animal.* And here I was with this nice, smart lady, being made to feel like Virgil's Aethon, the war horse stripped of its insignia who comes weeping and drenching its face in mighty tears, all because I had tried to show some fierce and righteous opposition to Ugly.

'I'm one of the good ones,' I said rather pathetically, laying my head against her arm as we stepped back into the waiting car.

We were going to see Sammy. Marilyn wasn't talking to me in the car and I wasn't particularly bothered. When it came to human sulkiness I always kept the same policy: forgive them, for they know not what they do. I borrowed this idea from accounts of the big man, the *Deus absconditus*, whose son Jesus says it in a film about somebody putting nails into his hands and feet. I think it was a Cecil B. DeMille film called *The King of Kings*, a bit lush, if you ask me. Anyway, they crucify Him, lots of people wail, then he jumps up like Sylvester the Cat or Wile E. Coyote after an accident involving heights. Marilyn told the driver to head for the Copacabana on East 60th Street and then she turned to the window and looked out at the passing shops, as I sat nuzzling her hand and the car moved slowly uptown. Eventually, she softened and touched my nose.

'Hello there, Snowball,' she said. I pressed my head into her coat and she lifted me up and kissed me. 'There's an Irish linen dress at Saks,' she said. 'They have it in palm green. Don't let me forget to pick it up, okay Slugger?'

70

The Copacabana was a nightclub with good food. They didn't welcome dogs, but Marilyn was Marilyn, or, more to the point, Frank was Frank, and the driver brought the car round to the service entrance. 'Oh boy,' she said as the car pulled up in the rear car park. 'Hold tight, Maf. I see some shutterbugs.' In a second we were out of the car and I was inside her coat, my head poking out as we headed for the door. Three cameras popped and I could feel her body stiffen as she smiled and turned for them.

'Will you and Mr Miller be divorcing soon?' shouted one.

'Not tonight, boys,' she said. 'I mean, no comment.'

In Frank Sinatra's world, the bigger the shot the closer you got, so his table at the Copa wasn't just a table, it was an epicentre, the middle of a golden pond with lesser tables rippling away. The tables at the back had patrons who craned their necks as they blew their annual bonuses, happy to be in the room, enjoying the Christmas atmosphere. Marilyn sat down at Frank's table, took a cigarette and accepted a light, half-closed her eyes and said 'I don't mind if I do' when a champagne glass was offered. There was a small patter of applause from the dark corners of the room, and Frank, standing in an impeccable blue suit, scowled slightly and bent a busy ear first to Roddy McDowall, who was sitting next to Marilyn and me, and then, with a smirk on his face, to his friend Frank Todaro, who was sitting on his right. The applause was intriguing: it could lead you to believe that Marilyn was the discourse of the whole city. Sinatra pointed at me as he gave an account of my existence, so far as Sinatra understood it, going on to describe his part in the journey that led to my being with Marilyn. 'Hey, sweetheart. How's your dream dog?' he said.

'He's swell,' said Marilyn being Marilyn. 'I guess he's a naughty boy, just like you, daddy.'

For Mr Todaro, that summed up the decade just past. He had no idea about the fun that was brewing, still believing America had reached its peak in the days of Al Capone. But it gave him a regular buzz to be sitting across from such a famous girl. Looking at Marilyn over there with a finger propped on her pretty cheek, he thought her health was the sort that could make everybody else feel better, and that was really something when it came to old heart-attacks like himself. She looked back with a look she'd been practising for years, a look that said, I would like to be nice to you but nothing more. I remember he tapped his fingers on his champagne glass as if he was playing an instrument, tipping it up to his face with expertise. He winked at us. From a decorating point of view, I wondered if his gloss wasn't just a little too even. 'There are two things you'll never get a guy to admit he's no good at,' he said. 'I'm talking about driving and I'm talking about making love.'

'I know,' said my owner. 'And he's often too fast at one and too slow at the other.'

The dancing girls weren't great dancers, but they whipped and pony'd their way around the floor in their Latin blouses. I've always found the maracas to be a strangely obnoxious instrument, but these girls shook them like they've never been shaken in the long annals of merriment. By the time Sammy Davis Jr came bojangling his way downstage the joint was delirious. I got under the table to drink from a bowl of water they put down, and then I went further under the table to enjoy the shoes, Mr Todaro's brogues jumping to the music, Marilyn's stilettos tapping a nervous beat on the floor. The smell of shoe polish and floor resin was strong, and so was the sense of a powerful connection, right here, right now, between coolness in public performance and mystique in political life. Looking at a small hole on the sole of Sinatra's shoe, I felt at home with the perfect Democrats, attached to a new dictatorship of good intentions.

I leapt back onto the chair. 'Play regular and no messages,' said Sammy to the black drummer, and wasn't Sammy loose-limbed in his shiny suit? And wasn't he drilling the whole history of human charisma into that song? If being cool was a slim-tie version of Hemingway's thing about grace under pressure, then Sammy had it more than Frank: the inhabiting of a great and attractive personal calm in the face of overwhelming stress. 'I'm coloured, Jewish, and Puerto Rican,' he said. 'When I move into an area I wipe the whole place out.' Not only did everybody laugh, everybody felt privileged to laugh: they felt their laughter was an aspect of liberal confidence and authentic change. 'Send Me the Pillow that You Dream On,' he sang, and Marilyn brought her eyes to mine. She blew me a kiss. 'Send me the pillow that you dream on.'

'We've just seen the election of a new Chief Executive,' said Sammy. 'President Kennedy.' A round of applause. He held a cigarette in his hand and he rotated the hand as he spoke, watching the smoke wreath through his fingers.* 'A great new President.' He waited. 'I also have a great new

---

* This was the era of valiant smoking. People smoked: that's what they did. Like Sammy, many of them used a Lucky Strike as if it were a baton, conducting the symphony of their own coolness. I have a few small talents, but I always regretted not being able to smoke or stick out my tongue at passing enemies.

wife. Her name is May Britt and the next song is dedicated to her.'

'Good for him,' whispered Roddy McDowall into Marilyn's ear. 'The great new President wouldn't let him and his wife – his *white* wife – into a reception because it was sure to upset the South.'

'Gee,' said Marilyn. 'No kidding.'

'Sammy held off on the wedding until after the election. She had to hold the breath, ya? He didn't want to throw any schmeer at the Prez.'

'Have you met the lady?'

'You kidding? She's been in hiding. The last time he wanted to marry a blonde the whole country decided to lynch him.'

'She's Swedish, you know.'

'I know.' He smiled. 'A natural blonde.'

'Whatever that means,' she said. 'And incidentally: fuck you.'

Martinis were arriving. Hi-balls. Girls were passing with trays and the smell of sweat began to corrupt the fruity tang of expensive perfumes. People fanned themselves and now and then our party froze as an invited photographer got his moment. Mr Todaro was never in the pictures. It was nice to have my own chair beside Marilyn's. I wasn't interested in the soup, cool bowls of stringy asparagus, which none of them touched, apart from Todaro, whose mother told him never to waste food. A fly was floating in Marilyn's soup and I bent down to hear him. He was some kind of Aesop guy, all messages, all wisdom, but I told him to relax and eat the cream because nobody was paying attention tonight. They were all drunk and the music was too loud for morality. 'I know, I know,' I said. 'You want to give me some big story about how you have soaked your wings and destroyed all chance of flight. For the sake of a little pleasure you have put yourself in danger. Ho hum.'

'Wrong again, buster,' said the fly, sounding of the Bronx. 'Fact is, I've had my thirty days. This is a neat way to go. You oughta be careful who you're supping with – they ain't stable.'

'Who's stable?' I said. 'Not you. Not me.'

'That's true,' he said. 'But we have no side. We take the world as it is and find comfort in its illusions. These people are nihilists, my friend. They say of the world as it is, that it ought not to exist, and of the world as it ought to be, that it will never exist.'

'Dry your wings, Harvey,' I said. 'I'm not doing Nietzsche tonight. There's too much fun to be had.'

'Schopenhauer, actually,' he said. Then a spoon came down on top of him and that was the end of that.

Ella Fitzgerald sat at the table during Sammy's break. 'Hello baby,' she said to Marilyn and she stroked my ear.

'You look beautiful,' said Marilyn.

'That's right, honey. I open my eyes and I step outside and I stop traffic. Look at this cute thing. He's as cool as they come.'

'He's a customer all right,' said Marilyn.

'I'm not actually,' I said. 'It's boiling in here. And this English actor keeps giving me licks from his champagne glass. See. Look at him!'

'Cool as Christmas Day,' said Ella. 'Do you like dogs, Mr McDowall?'

'Well,' he said. 'You know the thing about children and

dogs. And I was a child working with a dog – can you imagine what a trial that was?'

'That's right,' she said. '*Lassie.*'

'A pretty smart dog,' said Marilyn.

'You're telling me,' he said. 'That dog made Albert Einstein look like Jerry Lewis.'

One of the waiters brought a note to my friend. She looked at it and showed it to Ella. 'For Marilyn Monroe, a credit to the human race, mankind in general + womankind in particular. Brendan Behan.' The women looked up and saw a bright-faced, tousled person raising a glass three tables over. Marilyn blew him a kiss and pressed the card into her purse. 'A writer?' said Ella. 'An Irish writer. Playwright, no?'

'Sure,' said Marilyn. 'They're blind but they see everything.'

'Writers in general?'

'Playwrights in particular, I guess.'

The two women laughed. I gathered Mr McDowall was a great friend to women. They all adored him because he cared in an off-hand way about the things that mattered to them. He once said that the French must truly love women because they invented the bidet, and that was the kind of thing women loved him for observing. 'This one's friendlier,' he said, not quite looking at me. 'I have to tell you, Lassie was something of a diva.'

'No!' said both women.

'A diva,' he said, eating an olive. 'Much like you two. A proper diva, no doubt about it.'

Frank looked over to see what all the hilarity was about. He didn't mind fags. He was used to them. But he sometimes worried they were laughing at him. 'What's the big idea?' he said.

'Roddy's just been telling us about some of the geniuses he's worked with,' said Marilyn.

Sammy was back. There had been a rather extended maracas interlude while he changed his tuxedo. 'Speaking of which,' said Roddy. 'I'm working with Richard Burton just now. *Camelot*.'

'I saw the theatre on 44th Street.'

'You must lay off the Ibsen,' Marilyn said.

'Fuck you.'

'We're both making a movie with Elizabeth next year. Fox are doing *Cleopatra*.'

'Hiss,' said Marilyn.

'O, don't be like that, *swinehunt*,' he said. 'You love each other really. You and Liz are the only stars left in this bloody industry. Now shut your trap.'

'Kiss my ass.'

'Kiss my asp,' said he.

The music was going crazy and I was still thinking about Lassie. I must say Lassie was always the doll of dolls to me, so sleek and elegant for the cameras. 'Listen,' I was saying. 'That Elizabeth person was in the dog picture, too. The first of those Lassie movies? Him there and Elizabeth and Lassie all young kids together, right?'

But Sammy was already mid-flow, chewing the air and tasting the sweet triumph of his talent. Roddy looked at me once more. 'What's the dog's name?' he whispered to Marilyn. She glanced up and saw Frank looking over.

'Tell you later, honey,' she said.

There wasn't a part of Sammy that wasn't responding to the occasion, hearing the music, absorbing the lights. There wasn't a cell in his body that wasn't meeting the thrill of

77

the audience. I'm sure his stomach muscles pulsed to the rhythm, an eye rolling to the ceiling here, a finger stabbing to the floor there, a foot tapped and pointed to the side just so, on the beat, on the moment, while the follicles of his hair itched in sequence. He was a showbusiness entity to the ends of his nerves, projecting hope and capability, all wrapped inside this strange little man from the worst slum in Harlem. He was singing, dancing, impersonating people, the most canine person I ever met. 'I ain't got nothing to be bitter about,' he said between songs. 'I ain't had it this good in my life, you dig? I got a pool and I can't even swim.'

In the ladies' room, a bottle of L'Heure Bleue was sitting on the ledge beneath a misted mirror. Marilyn sat me in the sink as she fixed her face. The nice attendant was amazed to see us coming in. She said hello as if she were accepting a prize and then went on wiping the mirror and looking at Marilyn working with an open compact case. You must have noticed: people talk to dogs as if they are people, speaking the words they wish the dog would say. 'You are a tired little dog and a brave man, aren't you?' Marilyn said. 'Yes. You are. All these noisy people. Yes, you are a tired little thing. You want to go home, don't you? Want to go home and see what Hattie's left for you.'

'He's a fine animal,' said the attendant.

'Why, thank you,' said Marilyn. 'Only had him a few weeks. He's a tiddy biddy little thing who just wants his bed. Good dog.'

That's what humans do. They talk to you. They talk nonsense. They talk to you and they talk *for* you. And so they create a personality for you which is defined by the way they act you out. Every minute they are with you they are constructing you out of what they want, a companion, a little man, a furry friend who can only love their owners for their mothering tongue. 'What do you say to the nice lady?' asked Marilyn.

Come on. You know damn well you can't hear me. You're doing to me what you say those studio bosses do to you. Stop assuming I'm only really here to accord with your goddamn version of me.

'I'm afraid we don't like too much noise, do we now, Toot-Toot? Too many people. We like to walk in Central Park.'

I suppose it's all acting. And I'm not going to pretend I don't love that aspect of people, the part to do with acting. Other animals don't have that capacity and are all the poorer. And maybe Marilyn was right: maybe I *was* tired and maybe we did like to walk in Central Park. In any event my subservience was always the greater part of my charm.

An elderly lady came into the restroom. She looked at Marilyn and immediately came over to her. 'I am Lillian Gish,' she said. Her voice was lovely and her manner was direct. Marilyn immediately arranged for her to have a chair and she behaved so beautifully with the older actress, whispering such endearments and compliments, and soon there was a little conversation over two glasses of iced water. Ms Gish spoke of Springfield, Ohio, and also said things about Mr Griffith, the director. The whole encounter seemed to make Marilyn calm; she was now away from the tension of messy, judging people, and safe with a pure actress like Sarah Bernhardt. It was a fact about my fated companion: she always felt calm with grand old ladies who flushed with self-pleasure, as if her own radiance could be no threat to them. Sybil Thorndike had been like that on the English

79

picture, so had Isak Dinesen when Marilyn and her friend Carson met her for dinner, and Edith Sitwell, who was so much herself that she only felt charmed by Marilyn's face and mind. Old age was a badge of honour on those women, not a guarantee of envy and unrest as some other people found it to be. These women had suffered losses and they faced the fact with a humorous defiance. Of course, they each had the air of an antiquated beauty, which is an evergreenness in itself, quite different from the disposition of persons who were never blessed in that way. Marilyn liked them: she liked to feel survival was a trick women could pull off, in spite of everything. (There were few signs that her mother had ever managed such a trick.) Ms Gish had a very relaxing air of artistic fastidiousness, and Marilyn took it in naturally. They spoke of acting classes and Ms Gish said she was delighted to be back on stage, at the Belasco.

'Your dog has a very kind face,' she added.

'I guess he's not a bad little soldier,' said Marilyn. 'I would say he's feeling a little overawed by tonight.'

'It's nice to have a friend,' said Ms Gish. Then she pressed her lips over a piece of tissue and turned to Marilyn. 'When you were very young, Miss Monroe, did you have a best friend?' Marilyn paused only for a second to register both her surprise at the question and her general satisfaction that such a question could be asked in a place like this. Marilyn had a gift for immediate intimacy.

'Yes I did,' she said. 'Her name was Alice Tuttle.'

'That's what I find as I get older: the little girls of one's past step forward to keep you company. In my dressing room at the theatre I often find I'm thinking about them. Isn't that strange? Only the other day I found a picture of a girl

80

like that – haven't seen her in fifty years – and I put it on the mirror in the dressing room.'

'I bet you are a swell friend,' said Marilyn.

We allow the human story always to take centre stage: that is what makes a dog the perfect friend. And yet I was thinking of the wild dogs that wandered the streets of ancient Rome, the ones remembered by the philosophers for haunting the city in the dead of night. They were Celtic hounds who came from the mountains, keeping to their own kind, threading through the pillars, licking dust from the mosaics and circling the Forum to bark at the mysteries of civilisation.

Friendship. It depends on a suspension of the instinct merely to propagate oneself. One must leave parts of oneself dormant in order to succeed as a good friend. I never wanted to be the sort of animal who inveigles others and nuzzles his way to a summit of affection. Being a good friend requires a willingness, on occasion, to appear to subvert the cause, being critical when clarity and progress demand it. My career as Marilyn's pet was pursued with a degree of moral vigour: in that universe of flattery I tried to sing my own notes, not very successfully, but I think she got my meaning through a long concatenation of looks and yaps.

Before we took off, a fan called Charlie, whom she knew very well, asked the doorman to take a quick picture of him and Marilyn, and she was happy to do it, taking his arm. 'Gee. Your hands are cold this evening, Charlie. How long you been standing out here?'

'Two hours.' He shrugged. 'Less than that. I went to see *Exodus* at Warner's on 47th Street.'

'Preminger,' said Marilyn.

'And Dalton Trumbo.' Together they walked the few steps to her waiting car. 'Can you believe it, Trumbo writing again?'

'They blacklisted him, right?'

'Oh, yeah. Big time. Maybe things are easing off.'

'Mmmm, I doubt it,' said Marilyn. 'Not while Khrushchev is still banging the table with his shoe. What did you think of the picture?'

'A bit talky,' he said. 'Cobb's good.'

'Lee Cobb?'

'Yeah.'

'Arthur knew him.'

'I know,' said Charlie. 'He was in his play.'

'He named names. They always get forgiven in the end.'

'Who does?'

'Men.'

'Oh get lost,' said Charlie, wrinkling his nose. Charlie was one of those smart kids it makes you feel nice to like. 'The picture tries to be fair to everybody, which is always a mistake in drama, wouldn't you say?'

'I guess so,' she said.

Charlie was one of the Monroe Six. This was a group of kids who hung around in front of Marilyn's apartment building and who used to wait in the lobby in the days when she lived at the Waldorf. She often saw them as she made her way to appointments and she would always smile for them and sign autographs. They looked after her if she was out walking by herself, following her at a distance, and I got to know Charlie. Sometimes she would let him ride with her in the limousine across town.

'Not tonight, Charlie.' She meant about the car. But she

looked at him as if he was the right kind of friend, and my earlier ruminations on the subject began to fade into the cold night air. 'Some other time, huh? I mean, some time soon.'

'Sure,' he said. 'I got work tomorrow.' He was already walking backwards and stuffing his camera into his pocket and winking goodbye. Marilyn thought he was the future. I heard her thinking it as he walked away. The boy was able to take something for granted about fame and politics, about their joint power, and Marilyn took it for granted the same way. The difference was that it gave her a strange feeling in the pit of her stomach. I was just getting to know my fated companion but already I loved the quality identified by Carl Sandburg. 'There was something democratic about her,' he said. But the question of fame and intellect often haunted her reveries. Driving away from the Copacabana, she waved to Charlie from the car and said to herself that if anybody had made her a star it was the people. That's all. But popularity has many snares. As we crossed onto Lexington she recalled that a picture of Rita Hayworth in a pink negligée was pasted on the bomb they dropped on Hiroshima.

The park on Sutton Place faces the East River. We often went there in the daytime and watched children playing in a sandbox. Other dogs would come and Marilyn would sit on the bench and stare at the water, imagining the lives of the people on the passing boats. The night of the Copacabana we went down to the park and she sat there smoking a cigarette. People can be alone with their dogs, perfectly alone, so long as the dog knows how to pipe down and simply be vigilant over their owner's privacy. On such occasions, Marilyn would often just stare into space and mention names. Men's names. She felt alienated by the thought of how indebted to men she was, all those men who had given her something large while meaning to take something away. It always bothered her that she had been so dependent on the men she admired. She looked into the water and said, 'Tommy Zahn.' Turns out he was a lifeguard at the beach in Santa Monica when she was a mousy-haired teenager desperate to be noticed.

The Queensboro Bridge was covered in lights that looped to Welfare Island, and staring at them I saw in my mind the image of Emma Bovary and her little Italian greyhound, Djali.* I believe it is well known that Emma would walk her as far as the wood of beech trees at Banneville, where our attentive and happy mutt would busy herself yapping at the yellow butterflies while Emma opened her mind to her. She opened her mind without reservation. The dog was the only one to hear her secret. 'Oh, why, dear God, did I marry him?' The essence of dogs often lies in pictures. I thought of Fragonard's painting called *The Souvenir*. Ah, the lonely spot, the darkling wood, the young lady lost in reverie, and the small dog looking up at her, eager to understand. Art makes relatives of us all. Sitting on the bench, Marilyn put a finger down and stroked my chin. 'My mother told me life happened in fifteen phases,' she said. 'Isn't that a strange number, Snowball? She picked it up from a door-to-door salesman. Fifteen strides, he said. Fifteen *tracos*. But maybe there's just two phases: before and after.'

In the apartment, she dropped her clothes all the way down the hall, except the coat, which she dragged to the

* A dog is bound to like footnotes. We spend our lives down here. And in a sense, all literature is a footnote. Djali, for instance, Emma Bovary's dog, was a footnote to Esmeralda's little goat in Hugo's *Notre-Dame de Paris*, also called Djali.

living room and laid by the white piano. 'Here's yours, Snowball,' she said, kissing my nose. I snuggled down into the ermine and sniffed her essence of roses. Marilyn took a bottle of Dom Pérignon from the fridge and went back along the hall, and soon the voice of Mr Sinatra was coming from her turntable, the sound escaping with a bar of light at the foot of her bedroom door.

Seven

One Easter Sunday they brought out the dogs in Alabama. I'm talking about a couple of years after the time I was in New York with Marilyn. It's not part of our adventures, but I want to mention it here. They brought out the dogs and they brought out the fire-hoses and they turned them on the people who asked for freedom. The dogs were barking and the people were scared of being bitten but just as scared of their own anger. I'm talking about the kind of anger that can wreck a person's life. The thing in Alabama was a terrible mix-up because, Holy Lord, I saw the dogs on TV pulling on their leashes and weeping for shame as Bull Connor's men dragged them in to oppose the black people. Trotsky said insurrection is an art with its own laws, but at Birmingham the laws were horribly corrupted: the dogs found themselves acting the part of slaves set on slaves. Only humans could fashion something so profoundly inhuman. The dogs were adding their sound to the voice of democracy, singing *Freedom Land* with the freshness of Betty Mae Fikes. 'Walk,' they barked, 'Walk, Walk, Walk out of Slavery.'

Anyone with experience knows how life can turn our instincts against us. I saw that back when I was young, a while before Alabama, when I was still with Marilyn. I often think of civil rights when I think of New York that spring, because there was a pulsation on the streets and at the lunch counters, in the parks and in the bus stations, a sense that the times were equal to a change of some kind. One morning, we walked twenty blocks in the sunshine. A black man with a harmonica was sitting on a fire hydrant at the corner of 77th and Madison. At the other end of my leash, Marilyn was wearing a black wig and dark glasses; a Hermès scarf encased her head in clouds of blue and gold. We stopped and she made to open her purse, but the man dismissed her. 'Save yo' money while you can,' he said. Then he sang a snatch of song. 'Your Dog Loves My Dog'.*

The Castelli Gallery was situated in a dark townhouse. Marilyn wanted to spend an hour looking at some new pictures: we'd heard a lot about the artist, this thirty-seven-year-old jazz fan called Roy Lichtenstein. As soon as we entered, Mr Castelli came over and kissed Marilyn's hand. He had a very Italian willingness to be charming and I could see, from my

---

* Marilyn pulled me away too quickly. I wanted to say something to the man about Lincoln's dog, Fido. He was a freedom-loving animal, a golden retriever. He lived in Springfield, Illinois, and stayed there after the great man got the call to Washington. It was Fido who gave the future president his love of the untethered, but the dog was later killed by a drunk man only months after his master got the bullet in Ford's Theatre. Incidentally, Lincoln played an important part in my moral education. Marilyn was friends with Lincoln's biographer Carl Sandburg. He came to the apartment once and I picked up a whiff of knowledge about young Lincoln walking all the way from Pigeon Creek to Rockport to borrow books. According to the story I absorbed from Sandburg, the future president's favourite books were Aesop's *Fables* and one other, *The Life of George Washington, with Curious Anecdotes, Equally Honorable to Himself and Exemplary to His Young Countrymen.*

level, that he had put a lot of thought into his shoes, a pair of velvet slippers that still blushed with the cobbler's pride. Curious: there was black and white tiling on the floor and Mr Castelli only walked on the white tiles. I wondered if that was Masonic or something. In any event I took up residence on one of the black ones and watched with pleasure as the impresario talked to his famous guest about the wonderful new work. Not since Duncan Grant had I heard anyone be so eloquent about the transitoriness of beauty. Unlike Duncan, though, and unlike Vanessa Bell or the critics, who always talked about meanings, Mr Castelli mainly enjoyed pointing out that the paintings in his gallery had no meaning at all. They were meaningless. 'It is an optical experience. Humour is the only acknowledgement possible.'

He was epigrammatically inclined. Everything he said was a fast brutal truth, a clean stab of insight. He took a breath between each word. For those who live in the grey areas of life, it could prove a very exciting but strangely emptying kind of talk. Castelli dispensed his great utterances as a child might sprinkle sugar on their Frosties. 'These are post-historical history paintings,' he said. 'No ideas but in things.' 'Visual genius is simple-minded,' he said. 'Laughter and colour are the only answers to modern life.' We walked further into the room where the canvases he was talking about had been stood against the walls rather than hung up.

'These are the Lichtensteins?' asked Marilyn.

'Yes,' he said. 'Cartoon objects. Cartoon characters. Cartoon meanings. Lightness is the new profundity.'

'Wow,' she said.

'That's right. Wow is right. Wow is the new Why.'

I sniffed the base of a canvas called *Washing Machine*, 1961.

'Back, Maf Honey,' she said. 'Stand back.' The one hanging up was very yellow and blue and it showed a chatty Mickey Mouse fishing with Donald Duck. 'But it's all so different . . . so different from what you used to do, Leo?' she said. She bit her lip and laughed to make clear it wasn't a criticism. Her breathiness was a cartoon, too.

'We are like sharks: we must keep swimming or else we die. Immediacy is everything, darling. Everything. Roy started by doing bubblegum wrappers. He's so sweet. I mean, *sweet*. They are more real than the real thing. I mean, they have a better reality. I love them.'

'Are they hand-drawn?'

'Yes,' said Mr Castelli. 'But Roy would be happier if they were done by a machine. The thing is, with these new boys, they don't really believe in death or they don't understand it. It's not like Picasso, who *exuded* death, no? Who was like Goya – emitting death, no? These boys don't understand that. They only know life. All the pop artists want to burn, burn, burn, you know, and repeat everything. They're so caught up in life they just don't have time for death. Poor Pablo. Poor *Pablissimo*.'

'Mmmm,' I said. 'Maybe it's time to start looking into death. We're all pop artists while the lights are on.'

The gallery room had deep brown panelling and Marilyn wondered what it would have been like to come to a salon here, maybe at a showing of Whistler or somebody, when the visiting ladies wore puffed sleeves and large, beautiful hats. 'Some people say it is anti-art,' continued Mr Castelli. 'They say the material is not transformed and the pictures are not composed, but I say to hell with that. I say drop dead.'

'I think it's cute,' she said. 'But isn't it kinda cold?'

'Oh, Marilyn, baby – don't sound like *them*. Some curators say it's fascistic and militaristic. They think it's despicable. What else are they going to say, these men from Mars or Harvard Square? I think they ought to see a lot more, do more seeing.'

'Do you think the pictures are very American?' She twisted the waistband of her skirt and bit the stem of her sunglasses, tilting her head. Mr Castelli looked at her blue scarf and thought it very Klein.

'They're the acme of industrial. Cartoons are the only politics we recognise. They are anti-contemplative, anti-nuance, anti-getting-away-from-the-tyranny-of-the-triangle. They are anti-movement-and-light, anti-mystery, anti-paint-quality, anti-Zen, and anti all those brilliant old ideas that everybody understands and depends on so thoroughly.'

Marilyn's cherry-coloured smirk bloomed into a laugh. 'That's a helluva lot of anti to put into one washing machine.'

'It'll take,' he said. 'Disposability is the new permanence.' A column of ants was marching round the frame edge of a lovely sash window, talking like the critic Clement Greenberg. They just went round and round the window casing, failing to get away from the tyranny of the rectangle, the window framing the bustle of New York. The ants were speaking the name Jasper Johns and they said something about the influence of old Willem De Kooning. They marched together and talked over each other, trying to get a word in, blinded by light, eager to hit on a theory about the prodigiousness of American invention.

When Mr Castelli and Marilyn came from the back room he had his arm around her and they were still talking. I snoozed for a time on one of the black tiles while he showed her some drawings. My dream was grey and I woke up startled. 'Gee, you've been so kind to us, Leo. Hasn't Mr Castelli been kind, Maf?' She looked down at me and I tilted my head. 'I have an appointment with my analyst,' she said. 'Better not be late or that will figure.' Mr Castelli smiled and kissed her in a very European way as she reconstructed her disguise. The sunshine popped with whiteness outside, and, as we touched the sidewalk, I saw a young, pasty-faced blond man come past us onto the stoop. He was carrying a folder marked 'More Popeye'. 'Everything is so glamorous,' he said to the person walking at his side. 'Gee. I think we should go to Bergdorf Goodman after this.' The man who spoke was wearing a bow tie. He didn't notice Marilyn. His skin was poor and his eyes were pink and filled with wonder.

The black man with the harmonica was reading a copy of *The Negro Motorist Green Book*.* 'They say I should feel liberated,' he said. 'How'm I meant to feel liberated if I ain't got no car?' This seemed to me a very low-grade comment.

'That's one noisy dog you got there, lady.'

'I'm shocked,' I said. 'Haven't you got better things to think about?'

'Come on, Maf,' said my owner.

I barked at the man. 'Don't you know there's a revolution coming down, brother?' I sniffed his shoes and growled, turning to Marilyn. 'As I thought. When he's not reading

* A not entirely un-obnoxious publication, first published in 1936. It was invented by an enterprising New York travel agent named Victor Green, who saw what we were learning, in the early 60s, to call 'a gap in the market'. It listed the restaurants, barber shops, nightclubs, and so on, that catered to black customers. It was said to be very helpful, in the years before better help came along.

the racist driving book, he's reading Uncle Remus. I mean that is some goddamn stupid nonsense made up by some human to prove the baseness of animals, is it not? All that "Brer Rabbit he tuck de chilluns by der years en make um set down". The wise old bespectacled darky telling tales to the kid of Miss Sally.'

'Yo' is buzzing, little dog. Quit molestin' me. Come here and I'll kiss yo' nice white face. I ain't no bone.'

'Maf!'

'The dog he likes to say his piece, Miss.'

Marilyn was quite puzzled by the man's words. She reckoned he was one of those refugees out of Bellevue, mad or half-mad. She put me up on her shoulder and I yapped at the man as we walked away. Certain human things are beyond me, like sticking out my tongue.

Marilyn loosened Pinker's collar and placed me back on the ground. 'You are a bad dog.'

'Trotsky said there is no place for self-satisfaction at the point of revolution.'

'Stop yapping, Maf,' she said. 'Be quiet now. Quiet. Gee. What's got into you today?'

Every human has his day. Yet they forget we are all animals. Let me tell you, speciesism is no better than racism; it comes from the same dense briar of unimagination. Non-human animals outnumber man by trillions, yet we are assigned successively lower places in Aristotle's great *scala naturae*, the great chain of being. But I say – at least, I said as we walked towards Central Park – let us not assume that the great outnumbering beasts must always bow down before the opinions of man, which are often dumber than anything we could manage. We entered through the gate at 79th Street and my mind reached out to the kinds of human who were better at animal reason. Those, indeed, who had a stomach for the greatest good for the greatest number. 'The day may come,' Jeremy Bentham wrote in his *Principles of Morals and Legislation*, a book I knew via the old lady Stodge, 'when the rest of the animal creation may acquire those rights which never could have been withholden from them but by the hand of tyranny. The French have already discovered that the blackness of the skin is no reason why a human being should be abandoned without redress to the caprice of a tormentor. It may come one day to be recognised that the number of the legs, the villosity of the skin, or the termination of the *os sacrum*, are reasons equally insufficient for abandoning a sensitive being to the same fate. A full-grown horse or dog is beyond comparison a more rational, as well as a more conversable animal, than an infant of a day old.'

The baseball players were shouty in Central Park. Marilyn got nervous about snoops and shutterbugs, so we walked more quickly than usual and I had no time to sniff around the trash cans or worry the ducks at the edge of Belvedere Lake. My friend moved her lips. 'I love to watch the ships passing.' It was clearly a day for walking and for being incognito. She seemed to be addressing an audience that wasn't there. 'I'm going to tell you a story . . . no, I'm going to tell you a *funny* story. A funny story. I've been meaning to turn it loose on him every time he gets my goat with his bull about keeping me safe inland.'

She was trying to learn some lines as she walked, getting anxious about forgetting them, feeling turned inside out by them too and wondering why. She was due to do a scene at the Actors Studio that afternoon, Act III of *Anna Christie*, and her lips were moving and her eyes were filling up as we walked in the park. 'I want to tell you two guys something. You was going on's if one of you had got to own me. But nobody owns me, see?'

I looked over into the trees, where a small girl in red mittens was hitting a spruce. Her father seemed so perfectly made when he walked over to her, so constructed, so complete, with his Brooks Brothers suit, a brushed hat and a raincoat over his arm, and that morning's aftershave still scenting his hands and face. Under all this a naked soul was present, a person nobody ever saw or spoke about, a ghost in his early fifties who wondered if the little girl was the only good thing he ever did.

In a single moment, the park began to speak of its own past, the long-ago past of New York before it was called anything like that and before there was Central Park or us, the noise of car horns or the snowdrops surrounding the trees. We sat on a bench and the day faded out, replaced with a vision of a forest after the Ice Age and swamps filled with boulders that nature had carried here from Maine. In the gloaming I could see elks and moose, mammoths, mastodons, the giant beaver and the musk ox, the great brown bear standing up in a clearing and looking down the hill to the mouth of the Hudson. In the soil beneath where the bench now stood there were layers of sand in which stone scrapers could be found buried, the tools of the first Americans, people who had crossed the Bering Strait from Siberia to Alaska. 'I think you are all Russians,' I said to Marilyn in the midst of my dream. The coloured feathers once worn by the Munsees and the Algonquin were lodged deep down in the sand along with their wampum beads and their charred bones. I could see it all from the bench as we sat there: the tall buildings disappeared and I saw only scattered trees and small fires reaching down to the tip of Manhattan. As I watched I saw it grow and change with time, a ship rounding the hillock at Tubby Hook and sailing into the harbour. The oyster shells and the old canoes were covered over now, the ancient elephants were long dead and the moose had departed. Sand and silt, landfill and leaves, tons of asphalt – in their turn they had covered everything I was thinking of. At a corner near the West Side Highway and Liberty Street, they found underground the wooden beams of a house, and lying on a broken table were tobacco pipes and Dutch coins. When they wiped the coins they shone in the sun. My thoughts cleared with that glint of silver and I saw the openness of Central Park in front of us. The girl in the red mittens had gone and her father too was gone. I think it was the only time in my whole life when I saw the colour red as it was.

Dogs love public parks. We spend half our lives in them, being 'walked', though I have found that the creatures being walked are more often our owners, who use the occasion to inhabit their secrets. Owners like to imagine a dog enjoys nothing more than leaping after a stick or chasing a tennis ball; in actual fact, we like nothing more than lying by a roaring fire chewing a bone, listening to conversations and imbibing opinions. But, given the paucity of stimulating conversation in most English and American households, we are happy enough to be taken off to some large expanse of yellowish grass, where we can meet and debate with other flatulent slaves of enchantment. The perfect park must have grass to prowl in as well as a pond where one can worry the supercilious geese. It should have a water fountain and a decent variety of ancient trees to piss against. Benches are a complete must and so are little cafes, where a sausage may be *gruntled* or a cake procured for the price of a yearning look.

My top five:

1. Central Park, New York
2. Regent's Park, London
3. Botanic Gardens, Glasgow
4. The Royal Pavilion Gardens, Brighton
5. Luxembourg Gardens, Paris

I admit to a certain degree of sentimentality in my choices. These are the places where I have been happiest. Not Paris: I have never been to Paris, but Duncan Grant was never away from it, and his love rubbed off on me despite my ignorance. In any case, is it not a fact among creatures, each and every one of us, that we are often happiest where we have never been?* I might have chosen Prospect Park in Brooklyn, but I was kicked there once while walking with Marilyn and her friends the Rostens. I would have said the Plaza Hidalgo in Mexico City but thinking about it makes me feel too sad, on account of the Old Man. I might have chosen Hyde Park in London, but Vanessa Bell got into a state of nervous exhaustion the one time we went there together, leaving me panting with thirst. I think it was something to

---

* And perhaps that is the most sentimental position of all. Proust, for example, conjured a whole life and an excellent novel out of such nonsense. Those of us who tell stories are committed slaves to the past's dominion, to the fresh echo of the little bell which announced M. Swann's arrival. We hear it now, though its peal rings out in the far distant past. It is never quite a place we have been and is always a place we imagined.

do with the drama of forgetting, the resurgence of the past, the remaining reminders, or some such thing. At least that's what Cyril Connolly said with a mandarin grin. Vanessa spent the evening warbling about the last issue of *Hyde Park Gate News* and the park as viewed in her childhood, past a windowpane and a ledge of chimneypots.

Marilyn was reading her Russian novel, then suddenly she shifted on the bench and looked at me. 'What's the story, Snowball?'

'The novel is our daily bread,' I said. 'That's Trotsky's opinion, not mine. He loved the old *spiritus papyri*. I have it on good authority, too, that his favourite novel was from the German, the book they call *The Adventures of a Simpleton*. The thing was written by a certain Hans Jacob Christoffel von Grimmelshausen. Very lively. Very tart. My breeder was reading it the day I was born.'

'I could swear you hear me half the time. Okay, little guy. I guess it's time to face the music.'

We walked round the path and she laughed when I began dancing with a nearby shadow, this dark event on the ground, a real character with a life of its own and absolutely determined not to leave my side so long as we walked. It changed sides and I wondered if it had a story, the four-legged friend that liked to keep in step and never speak. Plato has a lot to answer for in this world of dogs, men, and other ruins. Your average person ignores his shadow, but it might be the best thing about him. It might be his ideal self: there but not quite there, and dense with reality. The asphalt path at the top of West Drive held a very recent memory of snow. I could feel the lingering cold and the grit under my paws. A grey squirrel appeared at the bottom of a tree with half a sandwich in its little claws. 'Peanut butter,' it shouted over with a toothy grin. 'Life is sweet.'

We made our way to 135 Central Park West. From the analyst's apartment, the world below seemed uncomplicatedly yellow, a busy jungle where plants spluttered carbon dioxide and billions of creatures had their say. The people were out-numbered and I guess they came to apartments like this one, high above the insects and the traffic, to find a place where they might be heard. Dr Marianne Kris was already standing by her desk. She was wearing those small-heeled satin shoes once popular with senior ballet mistresses, and, as we came in, she was in the act of dropping something into the wastepaper basket. Her eyes had that benign, intelligent note of suffering one associates with old Europe, the gleam of enquiry one connects to the well-ordered streets of Vienna. She kept her grey hair in a bun and enjoyed gathering up the loose strands and storing them behind her ears. She stood to attention with her hands clasped: Schubert's Piano Sonata for Four Hands was coming from a record player that sat on top of a bookcase.

We walked over the rug and stood for a moment at the window. Man was something to be proud of, no? Each of the buildings was significant in itself, but together they were a projection of power and social brilliance that shone in the day and made illuminated pathways at night. Tall buildings cannot be built by ants or squirrels or dogs: they mark the high point of human aspiration, the pinnacle of man's ability to master the world's materials. Once they are up they are up and only man can take them down. Marilyn liked to order herself at the window before sitting down; she merely nodded at Dr Kris and turned again to the window, the vast, changing world.

The doctor had her routines and playing music between sessions was one of them. After a minute or so of the patient's being in the room she would walk, rather delicately, rather interestingly, to the bookcase and shut the phonograph off. Dr Kris was the kind of small-boned person who did everything just so. Were she not as efficient, as alive in her small and particular ways, it might have appeared the world was about to crush her hoard of sensitivity, but in fact she was good at living amid the world's bigness and very good at choosing her roles and finding her place. In the minds of her patients, the music was part of that. Marilyn found it aggressive. Coming into the room she often felt she might be swallowed up by the music's rather too potent indication of someone else's well-being. Dr Kris must have been aware of this possibility, but she played the music anyway. In fact, she was quite competitive when it came to the battle of selves that took place in the comfort of her rooms. I jumped up and sat on a cushioned windowseat; it was beautifully done, the windowseat I mean, upholstered in a bold grey-and-white-striped wool dhurri, with a vase of white tulips standing on the ledge. 'Take a chair if you prefer it, Marilyn,' said Dr Kris.

'I can't think of anything. It's useless. I've been trying to learn some lines for Lee. I can't think.'

'Sit down.'

Marilyn took off her sunglasses, removed her wig and sat down in a wonderful armchair, the sort of chair one used to find at Charleston, an expanse of cream-coloured cotton, rubbed and worn, covered in tiny, almost invisible grey roses. 'Do you find, Marilyn, that you must rehearse for these sessions?'

'No,' she said. 'Not rehearse. But I have to be able to think, right? It's often that way before the housekeeper arrives, for some people: they have to tidy up. Well, I guess I feel like that coming here. I've got to get my head straight.'

'Am I your audience?'

'No, you're my shrink. I don't have to wear make-up for you to recognise me.'

In decorative terms, the room spoke of a relationship between fadedness and vibrancy: the rugs were extremely good rugs, displaying colours that might have been common only to two villages in the north of Afghanistan a hundred or more years ago, but the fadedness of the material brought a nice philosophical edge to the room. All the parts worked together in this way, to dignify, to calm, to amuse, to deepen the tone, making a conversation of the most quiet kind. The glass bookcases, the rosewood side-tables, had come from Germany between the wars, and to Marianne Kris's mind they gave a dimension of wisdom and learning to the weathered prettiness of the room. Virginia Woolf would have been at home in such a place: the painted wooden birds and the tin toys, the ships-in-a-bottle, the damaged mirrors. They all spoke of the journey a person might make to become themselves. In many ways it was not a suitable room in which to conduct psychoanalysis, seeming so redolent of one woman's achievements. Even the lampshades were tokens of Marianne's awakening. The flowers underlined her good-natured sentiment and the paperweights fed her appetite for pleasure and hard work. Her eye could wander among these things, lighting on what was solid, what had survived. In the corner stood an eighteenth-century desk with a small blue painting by Paul Klee hanging above it.

Kris and her famous husband had escaped something I couldn't understand. And here she was in broad daylight, her hands covered in graphite smears and pencil dust, sitting at the centre of an environment she had made. She lifted and laid down her objects with a patience that seemed to give everything its due – a glass of water, a silver letter-opener, a spider plant with a tangerine beside it on a plate. Everything in the room, and in the dangerous world beyond the room, inclined towards Dr Kris's sensibility, her steady conception of reality, which made even her own psychological confusions appear as a kind of blessing to her patients. She knew who she was, she knew where she came from, she knew what she liked, and she lived pretty much as she had hoped. She would not have experienced these certainties as certainties, but to the people who visited her consulting room, Dr Kris had a definite talent for tethering herself to the world of herself. Other people, most of her patients, were much better at being more people, but none was so good at being herself as she was. That was how it seemed. This room was the domain, shall we say, of her subjectivity. The sort of place where one might easily feel absent among all this evidence of someone else's presence. Yes, the room was comfortable, but by years, and by degrees, it could become the kind of room that made you question the comforts in your own life.

Dr Kris lifted a pencil from an old stone jug and slowly sharpened it, using a sharpener from a foreign museum. The delicacy of the action, though typical, annoyed Marilyn: it seemed to indicate an over-sufficiency of personal content-ment. In fact, Dr Kris was still grieving for her husband who had passed away a few years before, but Marilyn was fixated on how the analyst seemed to cope. It had never occurred to her that they were both in the persuading game. The doctor held the pencil between her fingers like someone who had spent a lifetime with pencils, and who could master them, direct them, keep them sharp, make them do what she wanted. 'I guess it's not really possible to be Anna Christie,' said Marilyn, 'without *him* coming up and when *he* comes up then I have to talk about *him* as well, which is hard, you know? Lee says I should use all that and, of course, I try my best but half the time when I'm acting I just want to scream.'

'I must ask you, Marilyn. Do you experience your father as a source of prohibition, perhaps?'

'Uh, I didn't know him. In the play her father is standing over her. He wants to tell her who she can marry and who's a bad guy.'

'So, in the play *Anna Christie* the father is a source of prohibition. Maybe even of jealousy.'

'I guess so. It's by Eugene O'Neill.'

'Yes. I know the play. I saw it once with my husband in London.'

Marilyn took a deep breath. 'Her father can't tell her what to do.'

'And your own father . . .'

'He's dead, see? He can't stop me from doing anything. He couldn't stop me from marrying Arthur.'

'No, but it's interesting you mention one playwright in order to understand another, no?'

'I'm not trying to understand Eugene O'Neill. And I'm not trying to understand Arthur Miller. I'm trying to understand Anna – or I'm trying to understand why playing Anna is so terrible for me.'

'Okay, Marilyn. This is good. Just because your father is not alive, it doesn't mean he is no longer a source of prohibition.

He may be that. And equally he may be a source of something else, something unlikely, say, perpetual approval?'

'I always thought he would like me.'

'Who?'

'My father. If he had known me. I think he'd have liked me.'

'You do? Tell me about that.'

'Well. I thought he would like me more than other people. Not for sex. Not for sex reasons. That he'd know I was smart and everything, I guess.'

'You idealise your father, no? You idealise him as someone who idealises you.'

'That's right. Isn't that what fathers are for?'

'If you say so. But I'm interested in what the play is saying to you at this time.'

'It's a great play.'

'Why?'

'Because it allows me to be a serious actress.'

'This is your definition of a great play? Is *Hamlet* a great play for this reason, Marilyn?'

'Yes. Well, partly I guess. I would love to play Ophelia.'

'But let us return to the father. In the play your character is struggling to transfer the inhibited sexual feelings for the father onto the legitimate sexual feelings for a husband, okay?'

'I guess.'

'This is normal, Marilyn. This is what we do. Our husbands replace our fathers.'

'Not if we don't want them to.'

'No?'

'Not if we can't bear it, huh? In that movie last year, you know, the Cukor picture. We sang a song called "My Heart

Belongs to Daddy".'

'Why do you say "we" – "we sang a song". Wasn't it you who sang the song?'

'Yup. I sang the song.'

'Right.'

'Well, it took twenty-three takes. I kept crying. Isn't that something? I didn't even know my father.'

'But you want to know him.'

'I guess.'

'And that is a form of knowledge, Marilyn. A very pressing kind of knowledge. Desire. Yes. Desire may be the most pressing kind of knowledge there is.'

'My father's dead, doctor.'

My fated companion was irked by her analyst. More irked than she had ever been before: she sometimes had fantasies during these sessions that she, Marilyn, was the analyst, asking Dr Kris the questions her cleverness protected her from asking of herself. 'I know your sister Margarethe was an actress,' Marilyn wanted to say to her. 'Did you ever imagine your father preferred your sister to you?'

'No, Marilyn. I never considered that.'

'Is that because you wanted to sleep with your father or kill your sister?' Marilyn believed her shrink's world was made of tinder; it comforted her to imagine Dr Kris had the same kinds of problem she had. It would only take a little flame and all the comforts of Marianne's life would be consumed.

'I never considered that, Marilyn. Not at all.'

There were several old clocks in Dr Kris's room but none of them made a sound. As the voices bent and doubled and provoked and choked back – the customary motions of the talking cure – the room's objects maintained a state of perfect detachment, though, curiously, the patients often felt they were being watched. At one point that day Marilyn turned and clicked her fingers at me and it was obvious she needed comfort. I leapt on her lap and Dr Kris gave me one of her experienced looks, which always had a hint of narcissism. She went into a little aria of remembrance about Dr Freud and her place among the psychoanalytic royalty of Vienna. The lady's father, Oskar Rie, was a paediatrician and a friend of Freud's, sending the great man a case of dark wine every Christmas. She was busy telling Marilyn this, not for the first time, when a tiny spider crept across the front of the desk and gave me that charming E. B. White look, a very New York spider with its slick legs and its neighbourhood smarts. It had lazy, pot-smoking eyes, too, the little beatnik spider walking in front of me.

'Ahh, put a smile on it,' said the spider. 'This is where she does her counter-transference bit. Listen to her: her father, her father, Freud, Freud. They wrote a book together about children, haven't you heard? Aaaaah, shurrup already. Her father studied children, geddit? She writes about child psychology. You do the math.'

'But what about the music? The pictures? The goddamn Latin translation of Winnie the Pooh?'

'The one lying next to the desk there, on the floor. Yeah. I was over there this morning. All her clients see that book and feel intimidated.'

'Right.'

'I mean, Jesus Christ – *Winnie Ille Pu*? What's a person supposed to do with that information?'

'My girl has her troubles, but she always comes out of here with a dozen more.'

'Why does she come, bro?'

'For the conversation. She likes having somebody intelligent to talk to. But she often feels quite annoyed.'

'No wonder. I'm telling ya. You should see the number she does on some of these dudes. The whole room's a stage set and this woman, she smart, she nice, but she fluffs it up like crazy, man. You just watch the show here baby, it's all about her. She means well, but, boy, some people just exhaust the spirit, you know what I mean?'

'She's talking about herself. Is that not against the rules or something?' The spider just rolled his eight eyes and resumed his dainty walk over a set of Art Deco ink-wells.

'Just watch the show,' he said.

'My friend Anna Freud, the friend of my childhood, she never married. My friend may have enjoyed her father's brilliance too much. I think we were all intoxicated by his brilliance. I was one of his patients.' The fact is, though, that Marilyn liked this lore: it was intellectual gossip and Marilyn loved taking it back to Mr Strasberg. Much of what passed for psychoanalysis at the Actors Studio was more in the vein of gossip about analysts and writers, and it made them feel better, just as it did Marilyn, that the same dramas existed for the brilliant people of Europe as existed for those born in America. 'My husband would have been greatly interested in your little problem of Anna Christie,' she said.

'Don't let her patronise you like that,' I said, but my owner just patted me with her soft hand. 'That's so out of line, you know. Every word of it. I can't believe you're paying this woman to force her self-importance on you and her music and her good taste and her goddamn paperweights! Then, to top it all, she tries to get you to think painfully hard about the men in your life by – guess what? – talking ceaselessly and infuriatingly about the wonderful men in *her* life.'

'Say, let's be quiet, Maf,' Marilyn said, patting me again. 'He gets a bit antsy in closed rooms.'

'My friend Anna loved her dogs. Freud more understood the value of having a dog in the therapy room. He himself was addicted to his chows.' Dr Kris rose from her desk and straightened her cardigan. She walked to the tallest of the bookshelves and gingerly picked a volume from the middle shelf. 'My husband was a curator of sculpture and fine arts when we married,' she said. 'In the Kunsthistorisches Museum in Vienna.'

'Cultured men.'

'Who are you referring to?'

'Your husband. I guess he was a very cultured man.'

'Yes of course. I believe he was the first of those to marry, shall we say . . . the interests of psychoanalysis with the instincts of fine art.'

'Marry?'

'Yes, I walked into that.'

There were days when Dr Kris's fastidious nature wasn't quite as fastidious as it might have been. Patients often found her neuroses entertaining, and, at the same time, soothing: wasn't it nice to have an analyst whose hands shook more than one's own? In sessions with Marilyn, Dr Kris was often quietly uncovered in ways Marilyn did well to ignore. She became a lonely woman entombed by her past, eager to talk about what had mattered and what was gone. One imagined that was why she played classical music between sessions, to bring her back to her coping self, to feed the historical ego, returning her again to the chief graces of the confected

107

life. Marilyn sometimes listened to her as if it was a sort of penance. Her skirt was cutting into her waist; she fidgeted. She remembered often feeling the same discomfort as a child.

'My husband worked for many years to investigate the nature of caricature and facial expression in art and he published on that subject.' Marilyn looked down at me on her lap and made one of her comic faces, the one that made her beautiful lips into a perfectly round O. 'Do you see yourself as dealing in facial expressions for a living?'

'Sure. But I'm keen to broaden my repertoire.'

'You are angry at my question?'

'It was crude, Dr Kris. But never mind. Crude is fine. I guess I'm pretty used to crude.'

'That is interesting. Caricature seeks to discover a likeness in deformity. You feel these faces you are required to make are always sexual faces.'

'All faces are sexual faces.'

'Okay. We will work with that.'

'Dr Kris, why don't you just show me the thing in the book you're holding. I know that is what you want to do and I want you to do it, too.'

'I think you are experiencing anger today, Marilyn.'

'And I think you are.' I licked her hand and nosed her until she clapped me. I looked along a shelf and was baffled by the self-assurance suggested by its contents. There was a Buddha smiling at the sad turn history had taken. I always found it hard to take the Buddha seriously: his fat simple face that always seems so delighted at the prospect of eternity.

Dr Kris opened the book she had taken from the shelf, a bound volume of the *Journal of the American Psychoanalytic Association*. It appeared heavy and had many scraps of paper stuck between its pages. When the doctor laid the volume flat we could see the words 'Ernst Kris' and the year at the head of the page, '1956'. As my owner stroked me I began to experience something of what she was feeling at that moment: a certainty, and not an unpleasant certainty, really a freeing one, that the analyst was trying to undermine her. That was all. Marilyn had told Dr Kris her story a long time ago and the doctor had been very good at drawing it out from deeper and still deeper reserves, treating Marilyn as an injured child. And now the process had changed course and Marilyn was required to suffer a series of assaults on her 'personal myth'. In fact she was quite eager to be undermined: that winter she had got to the end of her old satisfactions, and now wished above all to be free of herself. Over the months I had noticed a change in the colours of her thoughts, as if her mind had changed season. She was taking more drugs and was behaving as if it might be good to outwit the demands and expectations of being herself. She was dropping old friends and looking for a new part: that's right, she was playing at being a serious actress, the biggest acting role of her life. And this meant she was walking very close to the edge of sanity all the time, manipulating her reality to meet the demands of some terrible, unknowable ideal. I watched it and I saw the tears and the little panics at bedtime. But I also saw the new steeliness: the determination that came over her, as if things must change, or things must end. 'Caricature is a comfort to oneself and others,' said Dr Kris. 'But it may also constitute a denial or a distortion of true selfhood. Perhaps Anna Christie relies on men to tell her who she is. Perhaps she wishes to be something unto herself, not merely a daughter or a wife, no?'

'I like that,' said Marilyn.

'People. I mean women. I mean children too. We might often rely on men and then resent them quite deeply for our reliance on them.'

'Is that Anna's problem?'

'Perhaps. But is it *your* problem?'

I looked at Marilyn as she leaned into the desk a little and breathed in that thoughtful way. Say it, I said. I will not be happy until you say it. Go on. As your only puppy I demand that you use your voice. Marilyn smiled. 'And maybe it's your problem too, Dr Kris.'

Good girl.

And what did the analyst do, the daughter of the great paediatrician Oskar Rie, the childhood friend of Anna Freud and patient of Freud himself, what did she do in response to my owner's point? She arranged the pencils in her pot and walked to the window, where she adjusted the wooden blinds and replaced an Indian cushion. Dr Kris turned with a serene expression and when she spoke it was obvious she was quoting from the book sitting open on her desk some yards away. 'My starting point is a more specific clinical experience,' she said. Marilyn squeezed me without much movement: that's what people do with their animals, they hug them, they squeeze them, but in actual fact they are really at that moment hugging themselves. 'It refers to a small group of individuals,' continued Dr Kris, 'whose biographical self-image is particularly firmly knit and embraces all periods of their lives from childhood on. Their personal history is not only, as one might expect, an essential part of their self-representation, but has become a treasured possession to which the patient is attached with a peculiar devotion.' Marilyn stood up and placed me on the armchair. She lifted the black wig and the sunglasses. Dr Kris went aggressively on. 'This attachment reflects the fact that the autobiographical self-image has become heir to important early fantasies, which it preserves.'

'John Huston's making a film of Freud's life,' said my owner while putting on her coat. 'He wants me for Cecily. She's based on Anna O. Do you think that's a good idea?'

'No, I don't,' said Dr Kris, without hesitation. 'I think it is a most terrible idea altogether.'

'Gee,' said Marilyn. 'I guess that's decisive.'*

By this point, Dr Kris had returned to her desk and was staring down at the book. She looked up. 'We are stopping early?' she said.

'I guess,' said Marilyn. 'I have work to do.'

'Okay, Marilyn.' After a second she continued to read out loud from the book in front of her. 'The patient's conduct of life', she said, 'could best be viewed as a re-enactment of part of the repressed fantasies, which had found their abode in their autobiographical constructions.'

'Abode is good,' said Marilyn.

Out in the lobby, waiting for the elevator, a sudden cold breeze came up from the park to refresh us. The snow would return tomorrow. I wanted to be back in New York in the years before the buildings, before the cars and the modern painters and the expensive shrinks, back in the days of Dutch

---

* After several attempts to persuade my owner, the part was finally accepted by Susannah York. Jean-Paul Sartre, who wrote the original screenplay, was very keen on Marilyn. He didn't get his way and neither did Marilyn. So much for *Les Chemins de la liberté*.

coins and single ships in the harbour. Marilyn mouthed a few of her lines and dabbed her eyes and giggled. She put me inside the top of her coat and we waited for the elevator to come, the music already beginning to play behind us in the doctor's room.

Eight

If adventure is the rogue's element, then movement is his oxygen. I had scampered and hirpled and rolled and begged, I had barked that day, I had run myself raw after tramps and cabs and helium balloons that carried the word 'Esso'. In the afternoon I was finding new verbs to inhabit, just as the actors in 44th Street were rubbing their hair and wishing they were Marlon Brando. There's a lot to be said for actors: they show humans what they are, though few of them can truly cope with the task. I have an image of Mrs Higgens in the kitchen at Charleston, arranging bluebells in a yellow vase. I see them whenever I consider an actor's genius: the bluebells were real enough and damp with dew, yet they seemed, in that house, to be waiting for their transformation into art, which took weeks. By the time the paint was dry the actual blooms had withered to nothing. To create something permanent the young actors would have to use up everything they had.

At that time in America, the raising of the personal could feel like a moment of historical proportions. In many ways that is the story of my life. All of those young acting people, like me, had come from elsewhere, but you heard their voices becoming American, becoming modern, joining themselves in those years to a new view of space and sex and money and art. Mr Strasberg filled the converted church on 44th Street with memories of the Moscow Art Theatre. Everything seemed so personal to Mr Strasberg, his eyes still filled with sadness about his brother Zalmon who died in the influenza epidemic of 1918. At the converted church on 44th Street, you heard the optimistic new voices struggling through the hallway, the sons and daughters of elsewhere. They had found their soil and named their source. They were American. In those corridors, and others like it, I felt the pressure of fresh voices adding themselves to a great tradition. And I have to say I felt myself to be part of the pressure.

Here was the voice of Ishmael summoning the ferocity of some God; the voice of Walt Whitman singing itself and the open road; Fitzgerald's voice, warbling sweet truths to the spirit of the age; Gertrude Stein and Bugs Bunny, pulling gags out of the hat; Mr Ed, the talking horse who arrived on television in 1961 and added his prints to the long wagon-trail of American rhetoric; Huck Finn and Stuart Little, Elvis Presley and Emily Dickinson, Holden Caulfield and Tweetie Pie, Sal Paradise and Neal Cassady, Daffy Duck and Harold Arlen and John Kennedy and Augie March. American born. Fully voiced. It has never been easy for us Trotskyists to face, but it was America, dear, golden, childish America, that joined the narrative of personal ambition to the myth of a common consciousness, making a hymn, oh yes, to the future, the spirit, and the rolling land. It was all about hope. Billions of creatures closed their eyes at night wondering if the world would still be there in the morning. The Cold War was magical. It brought us into company with the vitality of the everyday in a context of mutually assured destruction. And some of us found our voices there, at the apex of ruin. I know I saw its contours and its warpedness and now join my voice to its knots and grooves. Standing in that corridor, I realised that a new notion had wormed its way into the American grain: it was un-Homeric; it brought a new urgency to our travels. The notion was this: you can't go home again.

Mr Strasberg came into the rehearsal space. Here he was, the guru, the magician, the mangy old cartoon cat. He was nervous about his own femininity, perhaps that was why he often spoke in verse, but in secret he had studied Colette and sought to think like a cat whenever possible. The students, gleeful and breathless with promise, sat in rows and examined Strasberg's whiskery face. What was he thinking in those seconds before he spoke, they wondered? I'll tell you, shall I? It rolled to me like a polished dime across the resined floorboards. He was thinking of Kiki-la-Doucette, Colette's cat, who roamed the green-walled rooms of her apartment in the rue de Courcelles, depositing its dainty mess on the parquet floor. The atmosphere in the Paris apartment was bitter as Lee recalled it. Unhappy.* When Lee wanted to achieve a sense of intelligent peace, he would attempt to access a memory of snow as it fell in Paris on the last day of 1908. He remembered a letter of Colette's where she spoke of the snow falling, 'like a chenille veil, powdery and vanilla on the tongue', and he considered this as he looked at the beautiful people sitting down before him in the Actors

* Mr Strasberg remembered Natalie Barney saying that Colette chose her animals for their resemblance to herself. She later gave Kiki the starring role in her novel *Dialogues de bêtes*, a masterpiece of the form, I believe.

Studio. I was being looked after by a nice gentleman called Kevin McCarthy. I sat on his lap and watched Mr Strasberg begin to address the class, his eyes lifted ever so slightly in exaltation as his last thought trailed away, the thought of Colette out in the Paris snow with her pets, playing, as she wrote, 'like three mad women in the deserted streets'.

'I have a voice too,' I said to Kevin. 'It's been getting bigger and better for months.'

I must confess I laughed a second later. Sitting on Mr McCarthy's lap, I caught his memory of something my owner had said to him. 'Lee taught me how to breathe as an actor,' she'd said. 'I mean, there are other things breathing is useful for, or so I've heard.'

'Hold tight, little guy,' said Kevin.

Lee Strasberg brought his eyes down from the ceiling and placed them directly on me, so I snuggled down, and he got going.

MR STRASBERG'S INTRODUCTION

For this is our glory, dear actors, dear friends:
To make ourselves equal to living portents.
On occasion we falter, at times we forget,
But heaven remains in the standard we set.
We seek to capture the mysteries of time,
Belief and so on,
The common sublime.

Imagination is the god of all,
Do you hear that, Henry, Marilyn, Paul?
Show nothing you know of the scene in advance,
Just come home alone, as if from a dance,

116

To find newness pealing like golden bells,
From a place somewhere inside of yourselves.
That is the system, the Method, the scheme:
Hard work and so on,
But source your dream.

On the Lower East Side, kicking my heels,
I once spent my days in a world like O'Neill's.
The bars, the docks, the immigrant ether,
It made us sign up as the spirit's keeper.
Even now I can smell the wig-maker's glue,
Memory and so on,
It makes us true.

Do not debase the silence with applause.
Acting is being private in public because
The art of experiencing is the art of life,
Not representing Garbo, or a man and wife,
But total consciousness is the only aim,
Feeling and so on,
The human again.

They found it painful not to clap. This was Strasberg at his famous, sentimental best, exultant and prodigious, with large tears sparkling in his ruined eyes. He was a model of how to move people with the sheer scale and power of personal emotion: he didn't have better arguments than other teachers, purer lines or more original ideas, but he had deeper reserves of feeling, and he could draw them instantly to the surface in ways that struck the group as the very soul of charisma. He sought to persuade not with the subtlety of his case but with the size of his feelings, the technique everywhere of the vivid leader and the effective bully. But however lovingly he spoke of his actors and their potential, there was always a hint of bad temper behind it. Like all gods and many Americans, his invocation to success concealed a horrid rage at the idea of failure. The day they staged scenes from *Anna Christie* he was like an old king presenting his crown jewels. Mr Strasberg had never been so happy to be himself. He sat down.

A large white cupboard stands in the corner of the cabin. On its door is a mirror hanging on a nail. In the centre is a table with two cane-bottomed chairs. A dilapidated, wicker rocker, painted brown, is also by the table. There is a newspaper. The sound of a steamer's whistle is heard in the distance. Burke looks over the table at his rival Chris and says, 'We'll be seeing who'll win in the end – me or you.' Then Chris looks to Anna and says, 'You stay right here, Anna, you hear!' And in that moment Marilyn suddenly assembled Anna in actual time: she was fiddling with the hem of her skirt and tears filled her eyes and when she opened her mouth a string of saliva appeared for a second. She said nothing. Her consciousness seeming trapped between saying something and not saying it. She was thinking of a time years before on the beach at Santa Monica: there was salt on her lips from swimming and there was sand on the arm of Tommy Zahn. His arm was warm with the sun and he smelled so young and so completely like California. He said, 'Norma Jeane. Did they put your mother in the sanatorium?'

'Say, what am I, anyway?' Anna says.

Mat Burke: ''Tis not what you are, 'tis what you're going

to be this day – and that's wedded to me before night comes. Hurry up now with your dressing.' A flurry of words and Marilyn was thinking of Jim Dougherty telling her no decent girl works in a factory while her husband is away. They were living on Catalina Island. She heard the sea and again tasted the salt. The salt tasted like copper, like money. It occurred to her that she had always been a prostitute. Burke: '. . . she's taking my orders from this out, not yours.'

Anna laughs. 'Orders is good!'

She walks round the table and while she's walking she strokes her hair and loses patience. Marilyn's voice had disappeared into Anna: she feels she is vibrating with Anna and she is sad inside with Anna. She remembers her childhood friend Alice Tuttle and how much more ready for life Alice was than everybody else. She was too young for boys. Then the face of the girl disappears. Marilyn recalls a car Norma Jeane rescued from repossession by posing nude for a calendar. They paid her fifty dollars. Tom Kelley took the picture. She had to do other stuff, but the steering wheel was warmer than Tommy Zahn's arm. The memories pass in seconds. She catches sight of Anna in the mirror as she passes her: she pauses to nip a hair from her tongue. 'You can go to hell, both of you!' says Anna. 'You're just like all the rest of them – you two! Gawd, you'd think I was a piece of furniture! I'll show you! Sit down now! Sit down and let me talk for a minute. You're all wrong, see? Listen to me!'

She gets angry. She wants to break off a piece of the table. *The Misfits* comes into her mind and the sand at the edge of the desert in Reno and the brutality of that place and falling out of love. It was Arthur: he was married to his typewriter not to me. And that character, *Roslyn*. What was she? If that's how he sees me then I'm not for him and he's not for me. Some sex-pot. Some floozy. Playwrights are all shmucks wanting women to drown. They want them to drown and choke and end up dead. 'I'm going to tell you a funny story so pay attention,' says Anna. 'I've been meaning to turn it loose on him every time he'd get my goat with his bull about keeping me safe inland.'

She spoke and cried and tore at herself and mocked the air. 'I want to tell you two guys something. You was going on's if one of you had got to own me. But nobody owns me, see?' And she says the line as if, more than anything, she has always wanted to be owned by someone. But not like that. She has long since forgotten about forgetting her lines: she discovers each one with the thought that lives there. She hangs over the table and at one point gently kisses the wood.* One of the foster families had a good table in the hall and the man came to her room one night and it is all here, a part of Anna's wish to speak. She imagines a creak on the stairs and the salt again. 'It wasn't none of my fault,' shouts Anna. 'I hated him worse'n hell, and he knew it. But he was big and strong.' She points to Burke. 'Like you.' Some of the audience began to cry: is Anna asking for punishment or release from something terrible? 'That was why I ran away from the farm,' she says. 'That was what made me . . . a nurse girl in St Paul.'

The man Kevin was tense: he squeezed me at the top of each line, his tension rhyming with the tension in the play. 'If you'd ever been a regular father . . .' Anna says.

---

* She also thought of Garbo. She imagined her playing of Anna was a footnote to Garbo and a joining of hands with the vanished actress.

Marilyn unfurls herself. The audience could feel this delicate unmooring, this very human movement, and they could observe this person in search of a person to become, following Anna's meagre shadow out from the page and into some strange, new, living reality. There are only a few chairs and props, but Anna appears to magnify the space and set us down in the broad world beyond ourselves. For creatures who like that sort of thing, it was a little miracle, something I wouldn't want to take for granted during this account of my adventures. I've noticed that people cover themselves in material comforts to conceal their fears, but Marilyn dived into the centre of those fears and made it her work to find out what sort of person she might be. She played the part. Most people never go near the task and never know themselves. Most people imagine that being themselves is a perfect alibi for not being something better.

The barge and the harbour were terribly real. It was hard not to think of the boats against the wind in Fitzgerald's novel and I smiled to remember the sway of that passage. That was the line of American literature most enjoyed by my rusticated friend Trotsky: he detected right there the zeal of liberty and imagined it to be fraudulent. (One of the things all the literary dogs like about Trotsky, by the way, is the notion that the country's best literary critic could have been a natural world leader.) Marilyn had gone beyond herself: her Anna Christie came over like a liberated soul, a person saying no to some popular savagery, saying yes to idealism. I looked along the row and saw Mr Strasberg weeping into his hands and the audience holding its breath. She looked at us. 'Will you believe it,' Anna said, 'if I tell you that loving you has made me – clean?'

None of the audience knew the story Stanislavsky used to tell about the dog that came to his rehearsals. The dog would sleep through the sessions but would always wake up and appear at the door just as it was time to go. The Great Russian Ham said this was because the dog always responded to the moment the actors returned to speaking in normal voices. For all their truth-seeking, the players would always be something other than themselves while acting, and the dog could hear the change.* This seemed so germane to my interests that I sat on the metal chair for a long time thinking about it and the group buzzed around the studio doing congratulations and kisses.

The well-wishers were packed into Strasberg's office, the famous ones and the political types, Shelley Winters, Kim Stanley – 'wonderful, honey, what a knockout' – and a dozen others, including a studious young plant from the FBI. Marilyn sat on a chaise longue drinking champagne: in the aftermath of her triumph she was beautifully draped and relaxed, drink in hand, cigarette trailing smoke to the stained ceiling. Sitting at her feet I was happily aware of how much we resembled Georges Clairin's painting of Sarah Bernhardt in the Musée de la Ville de Paris. Ms Bernhardt is pictured semi-recumbent on a velvet sofa, her lupine borzoi lying on the floor beside her, both lady and dog serene as they stare out, knowing they must be the focal point of the people's amazement.

---

* I love Stanislavsky's dog, mainly because his behaviour opposes that horribly crude notion of my species set forth by Mr Pavlov. Whenever I think of the scientist's salivating fools, so machine-like in their reflexes, it makes me ashamed. Russian dogs of the period, like their owners, were not so happily enslaved. And Stanislavsky's dog had an artist's intuition.

Marilyn's fame made people giddy. After the class a little party developed across the street, the actors getting loud in a neighbourhood bar. Mr Strasberg came sidling into the place, putting his hands up like a man who was happy to say he didn't know anything about bars. His wife Paula was there and she fiddled with her purse. 'A small beer, bubee?' she said, fluttering a sheaf of dollars at the bartender.

'That's right,' he said, smiling. 'Like Prince Hal in the Boar's Head Tavern. It is no felony to drink small beer.'

'Everything is in Shakespeare, right?' said a bright young kid, bulky-headed, not good-looking, full of spittle and admiration for the theatre. He studied Shakespeare and Ibsen all day long and half the night in a cold-water apartment on MacDougal Street.

'Ah, the Bard,' said Strasberg. He liked to be playful in a playful situation, but the teacher was vain of his learning as much as his passion. It was his habit to pass off his mistakes as if they made him more interesting and more reliable, an English affectation he had picked up years before. 'I think I may just have confused the Henry plays,' he said. 'Such is the way of supposed expertise, young man.' The boy nodded and sipped from his beer. He was preparing another salvo. The guru detected as much and he winked and moved towards the main table where Marilyn was sitting. Strasberg had the leader's instinct for self-preservation: he wasn't likely to squander his bon mots just like that, on one student. Before he entered into his inspirational mode Strasberg's vanity demanded a very good house.

The group round the table were discussing how NBC had recently banned an eight-minute sketch from *The Art Carney Show* because it spoofed the President-Elect. 'Nothing at all should be allowed to stand outside comedy,' said Paula. 'It is absurd.'

'I dunno,' said the actor Paul, who had played Anna Christie's father. 'Nothing is sacred if you start taking off the President and his wife. Some things are just worth being solemn about.'

'Wow,' said Marilyn. 'Somebody tickle him.'

'That's just plain wrong,' said Ms Winters. 'Just plain wrong, goddamnit. Look here, Paul. There's absolutely nothing that ain't funny if you think about it. Nothing should be banned for being funny.'

'Certainly comedy is the, um – the most difficult of the dramatic forms to get right,' said Marilyn. She looked towards Mr Strasberg.

'That's right,' he said. 'We were just talking about Shakespeare over there. Myself and this young man.' He nodded to the fellow as if to confirm that he had made a good decision for both of them. 'And Shakespeare knew that comedy if anything was a raising of the tragic to meet the dimensions of the truly human.'

'Holy Kazooey, Lee,' Marilyn said. 'I'm gonna ask you to say that to Billy Wilder next time he makes me dance my ass off and trip over my ukulele.' The group laughed and clinked glasses and swayed into new bits of conversation, then Marilyn brought them together again by lifting me onto the table.

'Ah-ha,' said Strasberg. 'The very dog. It is Crab himself.'

'Who?'

'Crab – the only dog to have a real part in the whole of Shakespeare. A comical turn, no less, in *The Two Gentlemen of Verona*. He has been called the biggest scene-stealer in

English literature. See how he yaps at me. And he turns to you and to you.'

'Don't be cruel, Lee.'

'Not cruel. He's a joyful dog. Come, Crab: tell us whether friendship or love is the better thing.'

'Don't be cruel to Marilyn's dog, bubee,' said Paula at the edge of the table. 'He's fretting.'

'No, I'm not. I'm not fretting, you *floy*. You upside-down bat.'

'See his soft muzzle. He frowns,' said Strasberg, getting into his Shakespeare voice. ' "I think Crab my dog be the sourest-natured dog that lives: my mother weeping, my father wailing, my sister crying, our maid howling, our cat wringing her hands, and all our house in a great perplexity, yet did not this cruel-hearted cur shed one tear." ' He clasped my chin. ' "He is a stone, a very pebble-stone, and has no more pity in him than a dog: a Jew would have wept to have seen our parting." '

'Gevalt!' cried Mrs Strasberg.

The young Shakespeare scholar from MacDougal Street stood up with his glass, suddenly beaming with actorliness. ' "I am the dog," ' he quoted. ' "No, the dog is himself, and I am the dog – oh, the dog is me, and I am myself; ay, so, so." ' Strasberg waved his hand over the table and laid a finger on my collar.

'Now the dog all this while sheds not a tear,' he said, 'nor speaks a word; but see how I lay the dust with my tears.'

'You're very devout,' said Marilyn to the young Shakespearean. She scrutinised him, thinking aloud. 'Why don't you smile at stupid, happy old me?' The boy turned bright grey. The pendant light was hot, a spotlight, and my paws felt soft on the sticky table. Suddenly I felt my eyes must be darting here and there to find shelter from the thunder at the edge of the heath. A hovel. I could feel the cold blast on my eyeballs and the damp in my bones. 'Poor Maf's a-cold,' I said to them, my audience, my friends the actors in their moment of glee. I reached inwards. All the way in. I recalled some humiliation I once suffered at the hands of Evelyn Waugh and a croquet ball. I must have been the merest puppy and was pootling on the lawn at Bushey Lodge, where Mr Connolly lived. Yes: I suppose I was gambolling. Evelyn was making a point, a facetious point, naturally, about the ugliness of George Eliot, and when I tried to correct him along Latin principles he knocked a croquet ball across the lawn at vicious speed and it struck me in the centre of my infant forehead. The episode came back as a sense memory. I used it to deepen my performance on the table at the back of Jack's Bar. I think the Method got to me: I was shivering with cold and forgot myself for a second.

'Fetch some water for the little mutt,' said Strasberg. 'He'll be going crazy with all this noise.'

'Uh,' said Mrs Strasberg. 'The noise of bars would leave you insensible. Morbid places.'

'We were talking about comedy,' said Shelley. An entertaining New York publisher I once met said that Shelley Winters was the kind of woman who brings out the homosexual in all of us. She certainly lived in defiance of her own vulnerability. I only met her a couple of times, but I could see she was always keen to give people the details about themselves – give them their character, as Mummy Duff, mother of my Scottish breeder, used to say – and one suspected most of her bullying was either unconscious or else

126

came under that dreadful heading True Friendship. 'What about you, Paul? You haven't cracked a smile since 1932.'

'That's right – comedy,' said Paul, ignoring her, but certainly fated to brood about her remarks later. 'You gotta work out the politics of the joke. I mean, Freud, right? At the beginning of comedy the idea was to have a whole bunch of actors leaping around the stage wearing huge padded penises.'

'Fertility!' said Strasberg.

'Is that what it was?' said Marilyn. She looked like a child again and she bit into her lip.

'The Greeks played the comedies after three days of tragedy,' he said.

'That's right,' said Mrs Strasberg. 'Comedy was the appendage. Right? Light relief after so much horror.'

'The appendage,' said her husband. 'Very good, Paula. Very good, the appendage.'

'I guess I wouldn't want to be a joke,' said Marilyn. 'It's so easy to become a joke.' She spoke in a whisper.

'You have that gossamer quality that Garbo had as a comedienne,' said Strasberg. He loved to flatter Marilyn, because he believed what he said, and because he loved to see her glow so visibly among her colleagues. (It also enlarged him to see how much she needed his approval.) 'It is always a matter of intelligence and instinct.'

'And intention!' I said. 'George Orwell said that every joke is a tiny revolution.'

'Don't forget, when you talk about comedy,' said Mrs Strasberg, 'that one has to fight as much for its truths as for any truth on earth. A hundred thousand people were placed in the Gulag for telling jokes. That's the only point I want to make.'

'And Khrushchev has released them, right – the comedians I mean?'

'Yes,' said Mrs Strasberg. 'He released them from prison the same month he sent the tanks into Hungary.'

'It will always be a big image,' said Ms Winters. 'The image of those comedy writers out on strike. We campaigned a little for Wallace after the war, didn't we, Marilyn? We were just kids. And you'd see these comedy guys huffing and puffing. These were great writers.'

'Yeah,' said Marilyn. 'I dated one of them. The guy who worked at UPA.'

'The cartoonist!'

'Handsome guy. Too many wives.'

'This is West Coast talk now,' said Strasberg to the guy from McDougal Street.

'Hold on a minute, Lee,' said Ms Winters. 'These guys had walked out on Disney back then. They were strikers.'

'Socialists,' said Marilyn.

'It was about style,' I said. I leapt onto my owner's lap. 'It was an argument about style. Your men thought Disney was promoting the idea that animation should mimic cinema reality, an imitation of real life. These guys believed that was the wrong aesthetic: they wanted to let comedy and politics have a romance, you see, on the plane of new design, new character, graphic freedom. United Productions of America was a model for how art and social awareness could improve reality.'

'Their cartoons had a message,' said Ms Winters.

'They certainly did,' said Marilyn. 'A message? They were pink all the way through.'

'Well,' said Winters. 'The Committee came down on top of them like a grand piano.'

'I can't believe we're talking about cartoons,' said Lee Strasberg in his Uncle Vanya mode.

'Oh, shush, you old goat,' I said. 'If it's not bleeding from the eyes and tripping downstage carrying a giant egg-timer you think it must be frivolous.' Marilyn placed me back on the table. Strasberg was fidgeting. He didn't really know anything about comedy and he liked to think that art was really beyond politics. He always thought the words 'popular culture' had a whiff of gunpowder about them.

'UPA lost its brightest workers in a week,' said Ms Winters. 'Anybody with any sort of communist affiliation. They stopped producing social conscience stuff altogether. Yet everybody now copies their style.'

'Wow,' said Marilyn, her thoughts drifting. 'He was such a sweet guy.'

A waiter came with another round of drinks and I was reminded of a certain English habit that I deplored – the upper orders arguing in favour of radical politics while their servants set down their tea in front of them. Marilyn turned to Paula as the conversation turned to Clifford Odets. I snuggled into a corner of Marilyn's coat and fell asleep. I don't know for how long, but when I woke up I noticed many of the group had left and Marilyn was fizzy. It was the end of a conversation and Shelley Winters was looking lovingly at Marilyn as she tried to be helpful. 'Some actors are nobody,' said Shelley, 'they don't exist at all. Like Laurence Olivier. He doesn't actually exist as a person. Even his wife says so. That's what makes him such a good actor. And I say this as a great compliment to you, honey – the greatest compliment in the world: you are too much of a person to be a great actress. You have an existence.'

'That's nice, I guess.'

'Yes, you are somebody. She's called Norma Jeane.'

'Oh.'

'She's a beautiful thing,' said Ms Winters. 'But she can only be herself. That's all I'm . . . that's the thing I'm trying to say.'

They were both drunk I think. After a moment my fated companion said the most perplexing thing. She said: 'The best way for me to find myself as a person is to prove to myself that I'm an actress.'

'But you're already a person, darling. Too much of a person. You will always be a star and you'll always work. I'm your friend and what I'm saying is for your own good. What you do is not acting – it's being. You should be proud you have too much substance to do what they do.'

'Who's they?'

'Those people.' She paused. 'Garbo. Marlon. There's nothing there. Absolutely nothing. Zilch.'

Marilyn ate her soup and thought of Mr Strasberg, who had talked about comedy but who seldom laughed. All evening he had sat at the table like one of Colette's ancient cats, his chin cupped in his hand, those small, cold nostrils dilated by his violent purring.

Outside it was dark. We were both huddled into Marilyn's coat and the neon down the street was fuzzy blue. Marilyn was crying when Charlie appeared. She had seen him a few times since the night at the Copacabana, but always in passing, a wave on the way into a town car or a blown kiss from some window. But tonight he was outside the Actors Studio and he came up to ask if she was all right. 'Hello, Charlie,' she said. She was pleased to see him. She had a headache as she walked up the sidewalk and she felt she had lost her bearings, the tears a little unsure.

'Let me help you, Marilyn. Can I get you a cab?'

'Would you do that for me, Charlie?' He skipped off and in a few minutes a yellow cab came to a stop right in front of her Ferragamos. Charlie came up behind the cab with the street light splashing on his face. 'It was a long class today, huh? Are you sure you're okay? Don't need anything?'

She touched his chin. 'You're a sweet kid, Charlie.'

'What about Staten Island?' he said. 'We talked about it the night of the premiere, remember? I said I'd show you Staten Island. We can eat hotdogs.'

'Gee,' she said. 'A ferryboat.'

'What d'ya say?'

'I'd like that, Charlie.'

'How about Monday?'

'Monday?'

'Yeah. Let's go to Staten Island on Monday.'

Nine

They didn't like dogs at Kenneth's, the hairdressing salon on 54th Street. Not that it bothered me a great deal: Kenneth was one of those men with a large petted moustache and a mind like a pecan pie, sticky and dense. Kenneth always imagined he was about four minutes away from ruling the world, standing in a pair of plaid trousers, his scissors ready to dive osprey-like into the hair of some turbulent matron. Usually he stood in that very pose ready to *warple* a new piece of gossip into existence, but the day we came in he was very huffy. 'Even for you Marilon, dahling. For you, even, my dahling Marilon, I cannot have animals in the salon. Even seeing him! Even looking at him, please!'

'O come on, sugar. No more than five minutes. I need you to comb this out.'

'Marilon. It breaks my heart. You call me up and I come here and we are not even open yet and already you are saying to me "dogs".'

'Five minutes, I promise you.'

The whole point of this was Samson, the salon's late cairn terrier puppy. Poor Samson. He had an altercation with a laundry van and didn't come back to life. Kenneth turned his back mumbling the kind of complaints that sound like prayers.

Marilyn sat down and I stayed by the front door, Kenneth giving me hateful looks as he went to work and blinked back tears. It was a strange process in the chair over there: she was asking him to de-Marilynise her for a day of what she called 'normality'. (This last period in New York involved many such efforts.) She could just have washed her hair in the apartment, but that wasn't her style of de-styling: she wanted the ritual breakdown, the taking apart of last night's heroine. On the wall there was a photograph of Samson carrying rollers in his teeth; they say he was a working animal at Kenneth's in full-time employment. I suppose that should have made me feel more of his pain, but human sentiment takes a very heavy toll on one's natural empathy. The whole process of de-Marilynising took much longer than she said it would – involving cold cream, lashes, the endless tying of a Bloomingdale's scarf – so I closed my eyes and thought of other working animals. My head was full of Trompette in *Germinal*, that sad, hard-working French horse, feeling its way forward in a culture where darkness prevailed and only darkness had meaning.

From the ferryboat we watched the passing of the *Queen Elizabeth* bound for Southampton. There was something in the Cunard ship's great majesty, in its two grey funnels gliding over the Bay, that made one imagine Europe must be a firm retort to the comedy of America. But no. The matter of the passing ship opened up a difference between Charlie and Marilyn. She held me with one hand and shielded her eyes with the other. 'They're going in exactly the wrong direction,' said Charlie.

'I wouldn't say so,' she said. 'The nice people will be sitting down with silver forks in an hour. They'll be drinking cold wine and thinking of the nightingale that sang in Berkeley Square.'

'Your ideas are very beautiful, Marilyn. But ludicrous.'

'Well, that's what people say. But I think those people are heading toward a little culture, no?'

'I don't think so. They're leaving the culture behind. The best of Europe lives here now.'

Marilyn was thinking of Yves Montand. She was thinking of darkly clever French movies. She always thought Europeans were sniffy with her and felt compelled to give them credit for that. But Charlie was thinking of the Jews: the great escape, the miracle of survival. Charlie was an interesting new type in those days. He had the confidence, the brio, the spiritual brawn of literate young American Jews whelped on Bellow and the first book by Philip Roth. He could magic certainty out of his parents' doubts; he could sleep with girls and drive cars and think about the condition of his people in a culture of waste. Charlie craved. Charlie yearned. He soaked up history and sensuality and spoke of the intricate dangers to world peace: Jesus Christ, Charlie was ready for anything in 1961. He was a junior editor in publishing. He made his point about the ship and Europe, but what he mostly wanted to do was kick a thousand survival myths down the field of a lighted stadium. Good old Charlie. He breezed into the elevator at the Viking Press each day with a copy of *Partisan Review* in the pocket of his windbreaker. Ruby-cheeked and ready to go, he travelled up to the eleventh floor, strode past the sexy girls with history behind him and a dick in his pants. His dark eyes were happy and naive as he made his way down the corridor, winking at himself, dwelling on the existential purity of a life of crime and the untold mysteries of the orgasm. He had read all Mailer's essays. He cared for jazz, movies, and was moved by the psychic terrorism of the Bomb. Charlie was far into *Henderson the Rain King* and the familiar old voice within, which says 'I want, I want, I want . . . raving and demanding, making a chaos, desiring, desiring, and disappointed continually.' One day at a breakfast joint he tried to talk to my owner about the book's symbols. 'Gevalt,' said Marilyn. 'Don't talk to me about symbols. Aren't they things you clash together?'

Charlie was especially sweet on the movies. As I said, for two years he and five friends had made it their business to shadow my companion around Manhattan. Not in a creepy way: they were fans, and Marilyn felt they looked after her when she was on the East Coast. It was true she hadn't seen so much of him recently: he was growing up. On the ferryboat to Staten Island, she felt tickled to be with him in an ordinary way, so clever and respectful, so clean and modern and alive, the Charlies of the world. The boat seemed to slow as we passed Ellis Island and I must admit I felt a stab of pain at the memory of my quarantine. It wouldn't be long before we were California-bound again. Meanwhile, what a lovely day we had in the soft breeze with Charlie and his vast opinions about everything. Ellis Island was in a state of decay with long grass around the buildings and the windows broken. 'So many languages were spoken there once,' Charlie said. 'In those halls and corridors. So many. But they were all saying the same thing, weren't they? *Let me start again*.'

'I guess that's true,' she said.

'Like Irving Howe said, quoting one of the immigrants: "America was in everybody's mouth".'

Marilyn put her arms behind her on the railing and the

wind blew the tails of her headscarf as she smiled. She was looking back at Manhattan. 'It's a place to get lost in. It's a place where you can disappear,' she said. 'And doesn't everybody want that eventually?' The boat moved on and the wastes of Ellis Island were quickly supplanted by the stone cartoon of Liberty, thousands of starlings wheeling over the statue, forming a grey elastic cloud around her head. From the deck of the ferryboat, I could hear the birds: they weren't murmuring at all, they were joshing as a single choir, poking fun at the human notion of liberty. 'They call that freedom?' The starlings made the observation into an occasion for self-celebration. Birds are always talking out of charity to themselves, snapping, preening, touting the superiority of their own experience. They pitied people to ennoble themselves. That was my thought as the boat rode into the foam.

'Arthur's brother Kermit always said their family left Poland clutching sewing machines,' Marilyn said. 'That's a fact. Their father Isidore is a dream of a man. When he was a kid he turned up on Ellis Island with a scab on his head the size of a silver dollar.'

'My people were the same,' said Charlie. 'Garments. They made coats. They lost it all in the Depression. How does that sound? If immigration taught my people how to be capitalists, the Depression taught us how to be leftists.'

Marilyn put me on a leash and I walked around the deck quoits.

'To understand the pure good of America you have to have been a communist in your youth,' said Charlie. 'You have to have felt, at least once, that after a certain point money-making is aggression. It murders people.'

'That's the way Arthur talks in his plays. But I don't know about real life. He always seemed pretty interested in money to me.'

'That's the way it is. You hate it and you love it. You hate loving it. You love hating it.'

'Hey, buster,' I said, licking his trouser leg. 'Stick to being a fan of the movies. You don't know the half of what people want. You young guys wouldn't know a cause if it slapped you in the face!'

'Okay, wise guy,' she said. 'What else is true?'

'Garments,' he said. 'You throw a little survivors' guilt in among all those American rags and you've got yourself a national literature.'

'Ha! The cheek,' I said.

'Arthur used to read Bashevis Singer to me,' said Marilyn. 'I converted, you know?'

'To Singer?'

'To the whole cannoli.'

'Good for you,' Charlie said. 'Now we're equal.' She laughed and then hid her laughter, afraid she might be recognised. 'Those dockyards over there have stories to tell,' he continued. 'We all have stories to tell and they're never the ones your family wanted.'

'That's for sure.'

They looked over at the chemical plants of New Jersey. The photographer Sam Shaw once told her they only produced chlorine and cyanide. My memory gave me a little gust of almonds and evil, a memory of something I'd absorbed about Hitler feeding poison to his dog Blondi. I suddenly felt grateful for Charlie and his generation, the things they might do to take the world forward. The pair talked about

137

California and Marilyn's forthcoming trip to Mexico for her divorce. It seemed to her that Charlie was always sizing her up for an education, but she found that cute in someone so fundamentally green. 'None of us has our own names,' he said. 'You're not you. I'm not me. Nobody in America is who they are.'

'What do your parents call you?'

'Gedaliah. The Jews are my unconscious,' he said. 'My parents were wage slaves. They scrubbed and cleaned and now they are proud to say they know nothing of the working class.'

'Gee,' she said.

'They deny the workers. They say they don't know anything of such people.'

'Well,' she said. 'I guess we all grow.'

'That's right. We all grow. I saw some pages of Bellow's new work-in-progress. Do you know what one of the characters says? He says, "He sometimes imagined he was an industry that manufactured personal history." That's what it says in his next book, Marilyn. I'm not kidding – it's me. That's me talking. It's the story of my entire life.'

'Oh, Charlie,' she said. 'That's cute. You're twenty-three years old. You don't know what the story of your life is.' She reflected for a moment and showed me thoughts are stories. She always did that. She showed me encounters are stories and moments sagas. The ferry made its way up the Bay and nature suddenly seemed awake to us, to them, to Charlie and Marilyn and their laughter and their passing camaraderie, the little flag at the end of the boat snapping in pointless allegiance.

'Do you really think Kennedy will make all the difference?' Charlie said.

'I hope so. It would be swell, wouldn't it, just to have a guy who's on your side?'

'Yup.'

'It feels like a natural change.'

'Nature might be a mentality,' he said. 'Everything changes. Change is ordained. If Kennedy hadn't come along we might have invented him. No question.'

'That's tough,' she said. 'It can't be easy living up to people's hopes, like that, don't you think? So many hopes?' She looked out and remembered Anna Christie.

'I don't know,' said Charlie. 'We manufacture hope. That's just the way it is over there.'

He gestured towards New Jersey.

'What a game,' she said.

'People love it,' Charlie said, smiling again. 'Hoping and believing. That's just what people love in Linoleumville.' Charlie took out a pack of Twinkies. Good man. He gave me two in a row. Good man. Underneath all his thinking and quoting, Charlie just wished more girls would kiss him. He stroked me for a moment with displaced affection. 'In *Henderson*,' he said, almost wistfully, 'the character says a person might reason with an English dog.'

'I'm not English,' I said. 'I'm Scottish. An ancestor of mine is known to have licked the face of his dead owner at Culloden.'

Nationalities. Don't get me started. I had to explain to a squirrel in Battery Park that dogs need no translation from one language to another – that is simply another human problem, and a problem for Manhattan squirrels apparently. We hear expression very clearly, as if it was being played on a series of wonderful drums. I didn't have much luck explaining to the squirrel that drumming was a native American tradition.

A week later, she travelled to Mexico to divorce Arthur. At first Victor the doorman was going to look after me, then his wife got a temperature and he was forced to spend the week boiling kettles in Queens. Then May Reis, Marilyn's secretary, said she would stay at 444, but Marilyn needed her on the trip, she needed May's professional loyalty as well as her loyally disapproving face, so in the end the three of us headed south on an extremely bumpy plane. As we boarded, the navigator chucked my chin: I had begun to think of myself as one of those fluffy companions, those charming vertebrates that are known to chaperone elegant individuals across the globe. Like Leoncico, for instance, the yellow hound that belonged to Vasco Núñez de Balboa and sniffed along at his side as he discovered the Isthmus of Panama. Leoncico's voice had a similar background to mine, though history fails to record whether there was anything Scottish in his pedigree. There was more tolerance in his moral character than there was in his master's. The dog protected him against everything except his own viciousness. (Typical problem, I have to say.) He even climbed into a barrel with Balboa to escape his owner's enemies. Maud Gonne's chaperone was actually called Chaperone, nicely enough, a grey marmoset filled with Celtic lore and Hellenic rhymes, poems, for the most part, to the impotence of human passion.* Alas, the little primate was not set to cavort with his owner through

---

* Marmosets are known for their nationalism. Miss Gonne needed no encouragement in that department, but the beast made her worse.

the years of her national widowhood. Gonne took him on a spying trip to St Petersburg where the cold put a quick end to his life. Thinking of marmosets as companions, there was also poor Mitz, 'that horrid little monkey' as Vanessa Bell used to call the animal, who accompanied Virginia and Leonard Woolf through Germany in 1935. According to Vanessa, the rise of the Nazis was nothing compared to the increasing power of Mitz, who made the Woolfs quite ill with parental angst. Vanessa was always happy to report how jealous her sister had been of the little beast's powers of concentration. 'He always behaved as if the world were a question,' said Virginia.

These creatures were on my mind as the plane chugged over Hanover, Pennsylvania, and the thought of them continued to grow and yap in my sleep, as we passed the Blue Ridge Mountains and the Sinks of Gandy in West Virginia. We sat in the big tin bird, leaving a trail above the Cumberland River in south-eastern Kentucky. I saw the world down there in my sleep, the open fields, the farmhouses, and the faces at the farmhouse table in the chirrupy shade of the evening. We passed over Memphis, Tennessee, and DeGray Lake, Arkansas. I thought perhaps I could be a navigator when I grew up. Anyhow, soon we were flying over miles of empty space, single houses standing in the middle of nowhere, then we roared above Franklin and Hopkins, a place called Rains. My journey came to an end at Dallas Love Field.

I was delighted with the ensuing chaos and its resolution. One of the reasons I love Trotsky is because he took so well to being a picaroon, travelling the earth looking for a place to dwell and work, encountering new people and fresh enemies in Turkey and France and Norway and Mexico.

At Dallas, the authorities forbade me a seat on the Mexico plane. Wrong forms, no permission, quarantine issues, what a riot. (I was reminded of Noël Coward's first encounter with American Customs. 'Little Lamb, who made thee?' he said to the grumpy official, and all hell broke loose.) May Reis tried to call the Mexican Ambassador, but then a helpful woman from the airline said she knew some dog-sitters. My owner and May were only going to be in Mexico for one day to tie up the divorce. I felt sad but I knew I'd get my chance to go to Mexico before too long: it was written.* While we waited for the dog-sitters to come I managed to knock over a bucket of detergent in the airport lounge. Marilyn was mournful, sitting at the bar with May and a martini. The television was lined and fuzzy, but it showed pictures of the very thing that was on her mind that day: the inauguration of Senator Kennedy as the thirty-fifth President of the United States.

The Russian novel sat on the counter. She filed her nails and she watched and drank, just like any white girl in America. A man in a business suit picked up a cigarette butt from the floor of the bar and smoked it. The people on the television were wearing heavy coats. You could see the white clouds of Kennedy's breath as he spoke. 'Man holds in his mortal hands the power to abolish all forms of human poverty and all forms of human life,' he said. Marilyn suspended the glass an inch from her lips and noticed the businessman bending down to lift another butt from the

* Every dog must go to Mexico at least once before he dies. It is said to be the place where we are most at home. This was said to me by one of the Duffs in the earliest days of my puphood, and it stuck. Not every dog makes it there, but it is our dream project. It is our Mecca, our Never Land, our Xanadu.

floor. She began to get nervous and then she smiled most perfectly. 'You know, May,' she said, 'I think I could live very happily on the streets. Like a bum, I mean. Don't you think I'd be . . . you know, resourceful?'

'I think you'd hate it, Marilyn.' But I loved the idea of Marilyn turning her face to the wall and refusing all luxury. Before we parted, I had that last image of a fur-coated Marilyn as Diogenes of Sinope, refusing all comforts while the street dogs looked on in admiration.

Raymond and Arlene were the two young dog-sitters, fairly daft the pair of them, beautiful and cool, into beer and sweaters and necking in cars. Raymond was holding up the *Dallas Morning News* as we walked back outside. 'This is too darn crazy,' he was saying. 'This dawg's too crazy. This jaaab.' He looked away from the paper for a second.

'D'ya see that lady's face?' asked Arlene.

'I saw she was lookin' away. The ol' lady was doin' everythin'. D'ya think she was somebody?'

'I'm thinking she was,' said Arlene. 'I'm thinkin' she was really somebody. Her coat hangin' off her shoulders like that, like she's somebody.' Raymond went back to his paper and I got to tune into Arlene as she walked in silence and chewed gum. 'I sure wish we could meet somebody,' she said.

'New Ross, Ireland,' Raymond read. 'The people of this tiny coastal village where John F. Kennedy's ancestors once lived danced on the Charles Street Pier last Friday night to celebrate the inauguration of their favourite son.'

'That's neat,' she said.

'It was from the Charles Street Pier', he continued, 'that President Kennedy's great-grandfather set sail to seek his fortune in the new world. Friday night there were bonfires, a torchlight procession, songs, jigs.' He looked up. 'What's jigs?' he asked.

'Dances. Dancin'. Like all them Irish people dancin' together.'

'. . . and good cheer. And at the hour of the actual Inauguration the Stars and Stripes was raised alongside the Irish tricolour by Kennedy's fourth cousin, James Kennedy of Duganstown.'

She put me down on the back seat of the car, next to a generator and a heap of empty bottles. I licked a Lone Star label and then chewed on a ticket from the Jefferson Drive-In for a movie called *The House of Usher*. I liked Raymond and Arlene instantly, which was more than a little promiscuous of me given I was only passing through. But the rule for us picaroons says that a rogue will always like a rogue. They moved up the highway looking for trouble, my tousled dogs, my friends, powered by *l'esprit humain*. I'm sure they could scarcely spell their own names, but that can be quite charming of an afternoon, when the sun is high and the world is yours. It turned out the kids were very happy to be making some extra cash, courtesy of Arlene's uncle Arnold, who ran an agency fixing people's problems. Two days before they had delivered two giant bags of ice to a funeral parlour in Duncanville. Last night it was cups: seventy paper cups for a doctor's house party in Lake Highlands. But mostly what the kids did was steal – they were shameless and quite accomplished thieves. All the beer was stolen, apparently, and when they stopped at gas stations or drug stores they had a tendency to bring back items of temporary usefulness. Arlene was especially brilliant at bringing home the non-bacon: plastic sunglasses and barbecue instruments being

144

the sort of thing she would chortle over before tossing them onto the back seat.

'*Yeck!*'

'Am sorry, li'l pup. That was jest me bein' clumsy now, wasnit? Beg your pard'n.'

We drove south and came to a town called DeSoto, not at all large, the sound of distant cowbells competing with the car engine, and they put me on a leash and came out to see what there was to steal. Waiting for them, I looked up and saw a pair of sneakers dangling from the wire between two telegraph poles. From Judah's Jot-em-Down Store, a grinning Raymond made off with a fishing reel and a packet of household candles, and at Mrs Gallagher's Grocery across the street, Arlene nabbed two fan magazines and a bottle of purple nail varnish. The trunk of the car was full of stolen items, but they also had a sack of Scamp and they poured the biscuits into a bowl for me out in the parking lot. Arlene had the cheek to go back into Mrs Gallagher's asking for some water for the dog. '*Yam yam*,' I said. 'All property is theft and hallelujah for the young.'

I will never forget that night in Texas. First they met up with all these teenagers: Joyce, who was shameless, Margie, who was brainless, Scott, who was brainless and horny, Hintze, who was horny and scientific, and Eddie Kimble, who was more or less psychotic. When Raymond stopped the car they all came tripping out of Kimble's house, some in Bermuda shorts and others in brand new jeans, the boys carrying four-packs of beer and pitchers of some grape-juice concoction. Kimble was antsy about his share. 'Hot damn, this here's a whole nuther thing,' said Hintze. He was swigging from the pitcher as he sat on the back seat.

'Nu-uh.'

'Ah pipe down, Kimble. You gettin' your turn. Here's the stuff am gone be looking after.'

'You talkin' 'bout that li'l dawg?' said Margie.

'Nu-uh, I aint, Miss Plug Ugly. I'm braggin' 'bout this here jungle juice. Kimble made it.'

'Give it here, Hintze!'

The Margie girl rubbed me around the ears and put me on her lap. 'Hey, Arlene. Look at this li'l feller. You had him all day?'

'All day. All night,' said Raymond. He liked to think he was the daddy of the group.

'No way, man.'

'What?'

'Pass the juice.'

'What?'

'Arlene, the li'l dawg here's like a gnat in a rainstorm. Can't we drop him off somewhere?'

'He's bin dropped off somewhere. With us,' said Raymond looking in the rearview mirror.

'He's fixin' ta bite your hand off,' said Kimble. He lit a cigarette and looked sideways with his puffy eyes, looking all crazy towards Margie and me. 'He's one agger-vated dawg I'm tellin' ya, and you, girl, are one sorry-ass babysitter tonight. You better keep this li'l chicken far 'way from them flying saucers! This pony gone be shit-scared.'

'Am more worried about you,' she said.

'Yeah, pass that here, you maniac,' said Arlene. She twisted the radio dial and everybody laughed at nothing while taking large, acrid swigs, the vapour in the car becoming so dense you could lick it off the windows. It was dark outside and the cicadas were *veep-veeping*. Their wild conversational gambits rolled around the car from window to leatherette seats, the young people saying things then unsaying them, clicking their fingers against the beat, spewing cigarette smoke and feeling embarrassed about nothing in particular, while Raymond wound down the window and countless small essences escaped into the trees and the lighted houses, the voice of Eddie Cochran falling behind us on the road to Cedar Hill.

Over the town, the TV antennas blinked like fireflies. The Texas sky seemed placid enough but grave, too. People were talking and the sound they made was burnished by yet more of the insect noises. Together they made a happy sound in the grassy amphitheatre of the hill. This was, they said, the highest point in the state between Red River and the Gulf of Mexico, and the height, the fireflies, the cicadas, the flash of cigarette lighters and the sudden gleam of tilted beer bottles and of moisture in the eyes of maybe a hundred or so young people, brought the evening into line with some great Aztec evening of yore. That's what I thought as I watched them peering and necking up there at the edge of Cedar Hill State Park: they were watching the sky in the full flow of their youth and in the face of the changes that their youth would bring about, but the gesture was old, the instinct to look up was old and the hope of awe was older still. They all sat on the grass and I liked them and ambled among the sneakers looking for something to eat.

Joyce was telling Hintze that she once saw one from the top of the rollercoaster at the Schaeffer Carnival. It was long like a cigar and definitely wasn't a weather observation balloon or any old thing like that. Hintze tried to feed me a piece of beef jerky from his pocket but I left it on the grass and he frowned. 'My dogs'd cross the county to git some of this larrupin' stuff,' he said. 'Hey, Raymo. What kinda upper-crust hound dog you got here? The ole cuss won't even eat his jerky.'

'He's a good 'un,' said Raymond. 'He's one of them dawgs from New York.'

'Some business-lady's rascal,' said Arlene. 'And what a cute little fella all the same with his dirty old collar.'

'We think his owner is somebody. Ain't that right, Arlene?'

'Sure. A lady from New York. Some kinda person from New York with shades on.'

'Well, it's the easiest ten bucks you ever made, brother,' said Kimble, now chugging the last of the pitcher and looking up.

'We won't be gettin' no ten,' said Arlene. 'Uncle Arnold will hit us with five if we're lucky.' I walked over their knees and ducked beneath the plumes of smoke. 'Ole rascal,' said Arlene, kissing my nose while the smell of a dozen camp-fires rose on the breeze.

'Feline,' I said.

There was something in Arlene that smarted for rhythm and rhyme, her brown eyes perhaps, the sense that dwelled in her nervous smile that life could never be easy. She wanted the heights of everything. She stroked my back and I felt a small yearning in her hands, the need for poetic glories in love and belonging. She looked at Raymond and he blew four perfect smoke-rings in the air before turning to wink at her, able to wink without doubts in his mind. I felt there was a story here, a story about these girls never leaving Cedar Hill. They were my opposite. They would never leave and

148

this stone cold fact felt like one of the lessons of the evening breeze.

'My daddy saw a heap of 'em,' said Margie. 'Flyin' saucers flyin' like ducks in formation. He saw 'em above Carswell Air Force Base. That's the truth. The honest-Gawd truth.'

'Darn right,' said Hintze. 'Elmo Dillon saw one of them land in the middle of his mamma's lawn. I'm talking some crazy-lookin' gizmo.' He sat up. 'It lands right there in the yard. Elmo says his mother passed away. Not that night but a hundred days later and she was babblin' in a hundred languages an' deluded and shit.'

The UFO hunt had all the kids on the hill looking the same way. They looked upwards and they pointed at stars and shooting debris. Many of them were tangled in one another's arms, others sat alone, with Christmas telescopes trained on an infinity of eyes they imagined to be looking back at them from the blue-black sky.

'Deluded is right,' said Eddie Kimble. 'It's all hoaxes my friend. You know what I'm thinkin'? I'm thinkin' we should git from here and find ourselves a whole new basket of beers.'

'We're staying,' said Raymond.

'Do you think we're being watched?' asked Arlene. After a second Raymond turned and his expression told her she'd asked one of the great questions. He nodded. Yes indeed. He nodded like one who was forced to carry the wisdom of ages.

'Definitely, man,' he said. Raymond was wondering whether he might get work as a grocery clerk before the summer. It seemed the night to ask. Maybe they should stop by on the way back into town. Maybe he could run more errands for Arnold or look for a bar job in Fort Worth. Tips were good for bartending. Come the summer, it should be the Marine Corps: the air base at Corpus Christi. He'd never been anywhere. Maybe he would see places and tell them all about it. Far-away places.*

The sky was a bastard for secrets. I remember my keeper at the Griffith Park quarantine saying there were over five thousand pieces of astro-junk floating up there, broken engine parts and jettisoned fuel cylinders, the shiny detritus of our battle to master the cosmos. The kids felt planted and watched, but out there the space chimps of the United States were running out of oxygen and the astro-dogs of the USSR were passing through the solar system in a state of ample loneliness. Alien races would meet those thirsty dogs and take them in for questioning – tell us what you can, they'd say, about the strange beings who paint the walls of caves and send their fellow creatures into the boundless dark of space. I wonder if the Russian dogs care for Plutarch as much as I do. I can see the lost Laika opening her maw and planting the flag of comedy on the terra firma of Mars. 'Consider a monkey,' she might say. 'Because it cannot guard property like a dog, or endure weight like a horse, or plough land like cattle, abuse and sarcasm and jokes are heaped upon it.' Posidonius, in *The Fragments*, has exactly the same notion about monkeys. The choice of monkeys over dogs for use in the national space programme might begin to describe what Billy Wilder called the comic nature of American reality.

Hintze came up the hill with hotdogs. 'The top two's mine so keep your mitts off,' he said.

'Gawd, Hintze. Insane amount of mustard.'

---

* Years after Marilyn was gone, I saw a picture of Raymond's face on TV. It was a late-night special about soldiers lost in action in Vietnam.

'We say *moutarde* in France, dear Raymond.'

'Yeah. Blow me, Hintze.'

'Come on, guys. Let's get outta here,' said Kimble, flicking a cigarette butt down the hill. 'There ain't nothin' gonna show up there. No saucers. No damn UFOs. Let's go into town. This is a bust.' As Kimble was speaking, I kept my eyes up and believed that something would show. They all liked rockets but none of them understood how rockets had turned them into an endangered species. I wanted to see one, just for the adventure.

'No, it ain't a bust,' said Raymond. 'This is how you get to see them. You keep watchin'.'

'That's right. You keep watchin',' said Arlene. 'There's only nothin' there if you don't keep lookin'.' She lay back on the grass. Her eyes were fixed on the sky and her hands were crossed in front of her. I put my head on her lap and watched as the fireflies blinked above us, the Texan sky wide open and nothing happening.

Ten

Vita Sackville-West once spoke of her admiration for a French tapestry showing Ulysses being met on the doorstep by his dog, Argos. I can see the brown colour of the wanderer's tunic and the expression in his eyes when the dog recognises him. I felt I was playing both parts. It was the year of a song called 'A Sleepin' Bee': we heard it one night as we walked past a joint in Greenwich Village and the music summoned our sadness and our hopes at the same time. Marilyn wasn't well that season: to be precise, she had been in the doldrums and a danger to herself, sick with depression. I can't pretend that I ever truly understand what ailed my owner; it was the human thing, that burden of self-consciousness that weighs down the day. Since finishing with Arthur, I think she felt she might always be alone. She felt she was bound to fail at everything and end up mad like her mother. There were periods of weeks when Marilyn just sat in her bedroom staring at the wall, never washing and never getting dressed. She told her maid one day that the most reliable items in her life were her dressing gown and her socks. It was hard for me to feel I was making a difference: worries just went round in her mind like those records she played after it got dark.

At Dr Kris's suggestion, she was admitted to the Payne Whitney psychiatric clinic, a total disaster – it looked like her mother's institution – but I took up sentry duty when she was moved to a private room at the Columbia University Presbyterian Medical Center. I loved being her guardian, but I wasn't much good. She had been in her bedroom on East 57th Street with the curtains drawn for many weeks previously. She just wept. And during those long days and nights I absorbed her dark mood. It's not always easy to keep one's whimsical composure. So when I sat down by the bed at Columbia I was not so much like Argos as Garryowen, that mangy dog in Joyce's novel who waits for what the sky would drop in the way of drink. I wasn't exactly sitting there quoting the ranns and ballads of ancient Celtic bards, but I was gloomy, no mistake about it; I was like the old towser growling at the nurses.

Marilyn lay dreaming of her father. She lay in the well-made bed and she couldn't help passing her sadness on to me. '*Give us the paw! Give the paw, doggy! Good old doggy! Give the paw here! Give us the paw!*' That was the Irish nurses all right and non-stop. The sad talk circled in my head for weeks. 'All those who are interested in the spread of human culture among the lower animals (and their name is legion) should make a point of not missing the really marvellous exhibition of cynanthropy given by the famous old Irish red setter wolf dog formerly known by the SOBRIQUET of Garryowen.' That was James Joyce in his book, loved, admired, and not quite read by my owner, and, to the same degree, unloved and mostly unread by my former owner's sister, Virginia Woolf, who said the author went on like an undergraduate scratching his spots. Bitter, Virginia, like that, or so it was

153

implied in the kitchen at Charleston, a house where her memory lay as heavy as the stones in her pockets, Grace always said.

Marilyn sat up in the bed, her skin stressed, her eyes clear, and she looked over at the window to see the snow was melting down on the streets. People need people, and they came and went, publicists, actor friends, and Dr Kris one day in a beautiful grey cardigan. She brought roses. 'I'm sorry Marilyn. I did a terrible thing. That place was wrong for you and I know it now.' The winter freeze appeared to linger in Marilyn just then, because the eyes she turned from the window were unforgiving.

'Dr Kris,' she said. 'I guess you miss your husband very much, don't you?'

'Why this question?'

'Yes. You must miss him very much. And your father, too, I guess. Do you miss your father?'

'Marilyn.'

'Goodbye, Marianne.' The therapist stood at the side of the bed for a second, frostbitten, lost for words. Yet already Dr Kris was arranging the favourable terms of her self-pity. She pursed her lips and made a note to herself about individuals who think terminally. Her sister's face fluttered through her mind, but she banished it, feeling stronger by the time she reached the door and closed it behind her.

By degrees I could get onto the bed, first hopping on a chair, then paddling among the blankets and scampering onto her, Marilyn's fingers welcoming me. For long weeks she was propped up in bed reading Freud's *Collected Letters*. Everything she thought and touched, including me, was infected by the old boy's way of going on, as if the book

154

was offering a signal of comfort about unhappiness and the battle we endure with ourselves. It makes us feel better to know that suffering is both common and routine: not only common but intellectually respectable, something that fails, for all the pain, to reduce a creature's appeal. In that way the book comforted Marilyn through several weeks and I picked up some language and a few bad tropes. Of course, we're all slightly too much like ourselves, and I found myself, during her reading of the Freud letters, taking the greatest interest in my own kind. The things that intrigued me most were not to do with the death drive, whatever that is, or the early tendency towards bum-worship, which canines know well enough, but were chiefly to do with Freud's deeply affectionate silliness when it came to the comings and goings of his pet chow Jo-Fi.

In the apartment at Berggasse 19, Freud had begun to resent his wife's slow-burning malice. Martha had all the cardinal virtues, but some vital part of her was disturbed by Freud's commitment to his work. She couldn't wash a cup without seeing it as an act of self-sacrifice, which becomes quite exhausting after a number of years. Freud tried to remember her abilities, her tenderness, her former beauty, to recognise how much of herself she must have held back in order to live with such a man and love him. But as time passed she had grown secretly dependent on religion, and, increasingly, she was able to experience none of the old pride or comfort in her husband's preoccupations. Her silence formed a gloomy prospectus. He sometimes went from room to room in a state of confusion, and, of course, he blamed his own mother, which is a natural place for a man to start if he is shopping for someone to blame. Martha had a point, by the way: the man was not merely a hard worker but an embalmer, a museum-keeper, and that study was the great tomb of their lives. He said very little about any of it, but you could find the story between the lines of the letters, among the unsaid things.

For Freud, reliable companionship came at that time in the form of Jo-Fi, who appeared to share his instincts. The dog would lie on the rug or pad around his treatment room, always giving Freud a clue as to the mental state of his patients. Every old man requires a rescuing accomplice – or a saving lie, as Ibsen preferred – and for Freud it happened to be a fuzzy chow with tender and independent feelings. 'I miss her now almost as much as my cigar,' he wrote in one of his educated swoons. 'She is a charming creature, so interesting in her feminine characteristics . . . wild, impulsive, and yet not so dependent as dogs often are.'

What a story Jo-Fi could have told, if her mind had given itself to the manufacture of personal history. The dog was an intuitive genius in the room, signalling by her manners the exact degree of a patient's anxiety. At the end of fifty minutes the dog would yawn and stretch; if she'd been wearing a watch she would have pointed at it, so keen was she to ensure the old man was not worn down. Martha of course decided not to like Jo-Fi. She had her reasons. When Freud went to Berlin for medical treatment she put the dog in kennels and Freud wrote pathetic little missives, beautiful really, asking if anyone was visiting the abandoned dog. And once back among the antique statues in his study, Freud turned to Jo-Fi to give him comfort from his aching jaw. He allowed her to lie on a frayed blanket, next to a white bowl for water that sat on the floor beneath a cabinet of

Egyptian gods. He wasn't well and the dog knew it. 'It is as if she understood everything.'*

Marilyn read the *Letters* next to a vase of yellow roses, which stood beside her on the bedside cabinet. When it comes to the story of people's lives, isn't it strange that we seldom know them in their quiet, reading moments? Freud wrote to his friend Marie Bonaparte of 'the affection without ambivalence, that feeling of an infinite affinity, of an undisputed solidarity' he felt for the dog. I suppose it was Mme Bonaparte who invented the idea of the psycho-analytic house party, patients and doctors mingling over lunch and whispering in the garden as waiters came round with little toasted breads smeared with foie gras. And I suppose Freud was lonely inside his own life, lonely amid the neatly upholstered world of his domestic loyalties. The dog answered a private summons. That is often the way. The princess Bonaparte wrote a book about her own sweet chow, Topsy, and Freud seemed to love it as he loved his sculptures, his grave-robbings, his tokens of extinction. The man had an unusual appetite for hungry selves, and the story of Topsy appeared to meet his needs in the raw. The matter set up new opportunities and new associations. He would spend several weeks translating 'Topsy' with his daughter Anna. He was clocking in for love, perhaps, and it turned out to be his most personal work.

Nobody in Freud's family ever understood how he had

---

* Kafka said, 'All knowledge – the totality of all questions and answers – is contained in the dog.' This is typical Kafka overstatement, of course. I'm afraid it is part of the Prague wizard's charm always to over-endow the meek. If Kafka had spent time with Dr Freud, I wonder if they might have sought to out-dog one another.

come to know Spanish. The story has to do with his oldest friend from school, the bold Silberstein, who stirred a great deal of affection in Freud, especially as the doctor entered his old age. Silberstein wrote a letter addressing Freud by a name he had used when they were bosom buddies: Cipión, the name of the second dog in Cervantes' wonderful tale *El Coloquio de los Perros*, 'The Conversation of the Dogs'. The two boys had appropriated the names Cipión and Berganza, the dogs who engage in a philosophical dialogue as they lie outside the door of a famous hospital. For Cervantes, it was an early shot in the battle for the novel,* but for Freud it was something altogether more intimate and local, the story bringing to mind the brotherly love and affection that had made him happy in his early days. The boys learned enough Spanish so they could speak as the dogs. '*Tu fidel Cipión, perro en el Hospital de Sevilla,*' wrote the young Freud in closing those humorous letters. He and his friend were the Academia Cartellane, a secret society of boyhood and doghood, a part of Freud's life that was lost to the past and

---

* I am bound to say it opened a great tradition, a habit of style and substance, where animals speak of humans. Of course, the tradition is older than Cervantes, but he made it a cornerstone of what is called prose fiction. The habit may have come and gone, mainly gone, but along the way it has earned a place in the annals of instruction and entertainment. For George Orwell, it was a realist's strategy. For Mrs Woolf, it was a way of having fun with her poetic impulse, making a joke of the describable. They would have pointed to others – Swift, of course. But it is the Russians who have proved most loyal to the great tradition: Chekhov, with his little Pomeranian at Yalta who sees how the woman's beauty excites the man's hatred; Gogol, with his little dogs nattering in the street; and Tolstoy, who manages to tell one of his stories from the point of view of a not-very-nice horse, 'Strider'.

buried under adult requirements. Silberstein became a wise old banker. And Freud continued to imagine him as his boyhood *amigo*, the lives ahead of them unknown. There would always be nostalgia concealed in Spanish words. He would whisper them to Jo-Fi. He spoke them to Anna, too, the daughter he called 'puppy'.

On her last day at Columbia-Presbyterian, Marilyn talked on the phone for hours and then her friend Ralph Roberts came to take her home. He was accompanied by a smart young publicity girl from Arthur Jacobs' office called Pat, who had a certain college freshness about her. Some of the press guys had gathered outside, apparently, but Marilyn looked healthy and she was ready for the questions and the flashes. She lifted a camel-coloured coat from the bed and I stayed on in the room for a second when they walked out. A field of light was coming through the cold window. Marilyn had left Freud's *Letters* on the cabinet beside the bed.

They forgot me for a full five minutes. I walked over and lay on a bare mattress in a room across the hallway. There were bedbugs. I saw them and immediately assumed they were little Karamazovs. I don't know whether it was the general environment, or the condition of the people they'd been close to, but the bedbugs had a perfectly Russian attitude, seeming to doubt the reliability of everything. 'We admit it is our time,' said one of the bugs in a mournful way. 'Russian values, if we may speak of anything so nebulous and bourgeois as values, are understood, in America as elsewhere, to be a central feature in what we might call the great duality and contradiction of the age.' He meant the Cold War. 'The Americans envy us. They are fascinated by Russian literature.'

'And what has that to do with you?' (Sorry to have been so rational, but on these visits I'd spent a lot of time around very rational young doctors. And the times were paranoid: I thought they must be spies.)

'We are weaned in hospitals. In flop houses. In asylums. In cheap hotels and in housing projects. Our soul is Russian.'

'But you are Americans, right?'

'No,' said a tiny voice. 'We are bedbugs.'

I was glad to be back on Sutton Place. 'You is bad and bad enough!' said Vincent the doorman as he walked me around the streets one nearly spring-like day. 'My, how you've grown. You is one fat li'l puppy.' Vince seemed to know all the old ladies in the area, not just remembering their names – Miss Olsen, Mrs Taymor – but remembering their dogs' names as well, all those Luckys, Butches, and Maximilian Schoenberg the Thirds. 'And how's your Claudius today,' he would stop and ask. 'Ripe as a week-old nectarine, I'd say. Lively as a sack of polecats, I'd say.'

'Why do you talk like that?' I said. 'Why do you talk like some wide-eyed fictional black man, some daddy of the cotton fields?'

'Ah, Maf Honey. You is *sunny* today.'

'Oh, stop it. Can you hear me? Have you ever listened to your voice, Vince?'

'Sunny side up and no mistake!'

Vince once said something that Grace Higgens used to say upstairs at Charleston and Mrs Duff on the farm in Scotland used to say it, too. He said, 'Don't ask me. I'm just the dogsbody.' That kind of talk made me growl with confusion. In those years your politics was the story of how you defined

160

the individual against the power of the state. The whole thing became slightly hysterical, as things did with people, at a book party I attended with Marilyn later that day. The common obsession back then was totalitarianism, and for some reason – I don't know, my private education, the life and opinions of your average dog – I always located the struggle between the individual and the state in the kitchens and on the backstairs, in the lobbies, houses, and apartments where we lived. Also on the streets where we walked. But the workers didn't always agree. They didn't talk as if they agreed. As Trotsky once said of some haphazard victims, they had a tendency to increase the term of their own captivity.

Yet Vincent had a full understanding of everyday comedy. He worshipped the writings and cartoons of James Thurber, a gentleman from the *New Yorker* who managed to understand dogs (and people) a lot better than most dogs (and most people). Thurber had gone so far into Vincent's mind that the doorman had Thurber-like thoughts, seeing people as alarming creatures and dogs as questing beasts. After we came back from our walk we still had to wait an hour for Marilyn to come down to the lobby. Marilyn was late for everything: it was her creed, her prerogative, her style, and her revenge.* Vince was a connoisseur of other people's lateness. He gave me a dish of water and then sat in his big chair to look at a library book, a story called 'Extinct Animals of Bermuda'.

There was some kind of demonstration on the Upper

* I never understood why people made such a fuss about her lateness. When Gladys Deacon, the future duchess of Marlborough, was an hour and a half late in coming to an appointment with the playwright Jean Giraudoux, he felt that this was 'the minimum time to wait for someone of her beauty'.

East Side, so the car had to go fifteen blocks downtown, cut across, and climb back up in the direction of the Plaza Hotel. It should have been a simple journey, but no journeys are ever simple. Anyway it was a lovely evening, the sort of fresh April evening when men of thirty suddenly realise they should go and buy their girlfriend a ring. At one point we got stuck in traffic trying to join Fifth Avenue and Marilyn suddenly asked the driver to stop. She fished in her pocketbook for a quarter, stepped out of the car – my owner in chiffon dress and mink – and asked the first man she saw to do her a favour. The man took his hat off when she stepped up to him. The driver lowered the window. The man was in a state of what they call disbelief. 'Holy smoke,' he was saying. 'Are you who I think you are?'

'I think so,' said Marilyn. 'Are you?'

'Holy smoke,' he said again. And then he said, 'I'm William Ebert. I don't know why I'm telling you that.'

'Would you be a pal?' she said. 'Would you do something for me? I need to get back into this car.' She held out the quarter and he took it right away. 'Could you call the Plaza Hotel? The Oak Room. And just say Marilyn is going to be late but is on the way. We're trying to hurry. The message is for Carson McCullers. Could you do that for me?'

'Sure,' said the guy. 'Holy smoke. Give me that name again.' He laid down his briefcase, took a pen from his top pocket and wrote it down, then he handed the pen and the piece of paper to Marilyn.

'Could you write "To Jenny"?'

'Is she your sweetheart?'

'I want her to be,' he said. 'Her name's Jennifer.' Marilyn pulled the front of her coat around her after she'd written her name, as she handed back the pen and paper. People began to stop and point.

'She's a lucky girl,' said Marilyn, stepping back to the car and blowing him one of her kisses. The car horns were beeping. The man shouted back at her as she stepped in beside me.

'The Oak Room, right?'

'Thank you, William,' she said.

'I'll do it. I'll do it right now,' he said.

By the New York Public Library I saw two butterflies going round the head of a stone lion. They landed on the bridge of his nose before dancing above the steps and stopping on a small tree by the roadside. The female was brown and the male was blue, shy of his orange chevrons. I put my face up to the open window and listened to them. The evening was moving into amorous dusk, but I could see the butterflies clearly and they spoke in the manner of Nabokov. 'Translucent friend, I am sea-sick with longing. I admire your wings the colour of sapphire and your tiny breath, the ballet of your movements in the pensive air.'

'Come,' said the other. 'Let's tom-peep along the hedges.'

'We will find an arbour in flame-flower.'

'Tomorrow. Yes.'

'There will be poplars, apples . . .'

'A suburban Sunday.'

'Yes.'

'There are small houses. Moist gardens.'

'Let us go there.'

They lifted off and the blue one caught my eye as they passed right over my head. 'Take care of her, *mon brave*,' he said.

'I will,' I said. 'I'll try.'

And with that the butterflies looped over the taxi cabs to disappear against the silver bulk of the buildings. So far so good, the Lupine Blues lost in the sky above Manhattan.

The last bit of the journey was boring. Marilyn looked briefly at her Russian novel, put it down on the seat between us and took out her mirror, fixing her lipstick and smoothing a dot of cream into the skin around her *preoccupeyes*, as I used to call her blue, worried eyes. So I used my time in the traffic to think of my Top Ten Dogs of All Time. The list changes from week to week according to which trait is uppermost in my mind – was loyalty the virtue of the week, or was it cleverness, bravery, athletic ability, or my old favourite, pure goodness?

GREYFRIARS BOBBY

A Skye terrier from Edinburgh. His owner was a night-watchman and when something happened to him – okay, he died – Bobby visited his grave at Greyfriars Church for fourteen years. Bobby was a kind of saint, really. And sainthood is the kind of fame you want.

LASSIE

A brilliant collie. 'Greenall Bridge is in the country of Yorkshire, and of all places in the world it is here that the dog is really king.' That was Eric Knight, the author who first found Lassie in his head. She was then found by the people at MGM. Pal was the star who acted her. Pal made the character real and the role made Pal real. That is what happens in great acting. Sometimes Lassie got confused about who she was. No wonder, as she was always played by male dogs.

JO-FI

A world-inflecting chow from Paris. Managed to put Freud's patients at their ease with Freud, while also managing to put Freud at his ease with Freud, a very much harder job.

SNOOPY

A very wise beagle. A novelist at heart. One of those that puts the create part into creature – a wonderful reader of Tolstoy. Apparently, he didn't say much for the first two years of his life, which makes him very human.

LAIKA

A brave Russian soul. Laika was a stray on the streets of Moscow, a stray as we all are, and was rocketed into space on *Sputnik 2* in November 1957. She never came back, but she learned what her owners never could. Her death-capsule orbited the world 2,570 times before it burned up on re-entering the earth's atmosphere. I believe her memoirs would constitute a masterpiece to rival *David Copperfield*.

FLUSH

London spaniels seldom had the sense to bite Robert Browning. This one did, and kept Virginia Woolf sane during an especially truculent season of the mind. *Flush* shows us at once how to live on several planes of experience, which is a gift to art and a gift to good sense.

LADY

An American cocker spaniel, the girl of my dreams. She appears in a wonderful Marxist fantasy from Disney called *Lady and the Tramp*. She was typecast as the love object, but I always saw beyond that, appreciating the rare gifts of this most perfect canine being. If only she had met me things would be different.

BALTO

A Siberian husky. He took exquisite revenge on the notion that stupidity comes with servitude – and, in so doing, he ridiculed the instinct of people to rank themselves above other people, and other animals – by tramping a long way to save some human beings from diphtheria. His statue stands in Central Park to remind passing strangers that their dogs are probably kinder than they are. Some say that another dog, Togo, did most of the leg-work and that Balto just got all the glory. I choose to believe what I want to believe, which is a dog's prerogative.

PELLÉAS

A complete riot of a dog – a bulldog – owned by Maurice Maeterlinck – a riot of a Belgian. His master was a hero of the simpler magics, making beauty and truth from a basic belief in the possibility of consciousness. Pelléas was the inspiration for a great deal of tender, unforgettable prose on the part of the old man, who understood the wisdom of California. Pelléas is the great and ceaseless muse, with a powerful forehead like that of Socrates or Verlaine. 'His intelligent eyes opened to look upon the world,' wrote Maeterlinck, 'to love mankind, then closed again on the cruel secrets of death.'

BISOU

A cairn terrier who lived in Montmartre, Bisou watched

the birth of modern painting. She was painted by Renoir one sunny day while playing with a model wearing a yellow hat adorned with fresh poppies. The people around Bisou imagined she was a silent witness, if any witness at all: in fact she was the most absorbent creature of her age, and, it is reported, a speaker to rival Oscar Wilde.

Eleven

In the Oak Room at the Plaza, the waiters tried to conceal their love of my owner and their loathing of me, which for a moment shook my faith in the working man. But after a while they saw the light and fed me a little plate of morsels, placing it next to me on the banquette. The girls were drinking Dom Pérignon. It was merely a private drink, a little relaxer, before they set off together for a book party they'd agreed to attend uptown. 'Pre-drinks drinks,' is what Marilyn called them.

'Mercy, if he ain't the Colt .45 of Monroeville, Alabama,' said Miss McCullers, 'larkin' aroun' Europe with them nice ladies and their rich husbands. Babe Paley and Gloria Vanderbilt and Carol Marcus and y'all. He's playing y'all like a bullfrog plays the summer pond. You should watch it. You should watch his tongue if you're fixin' to see the winter months.'

'Oh, we know about Truman's tongue,' said Marilyn into her glass. 'He's wicked.'

'Worse than that. He'd drown his own mother for ten minutes with a princess. Not even a princess, a lousy duchess. A lady-in-waiting. Gawd knows, the darn cousin of a lady-in-waiting.'

'Oh, Carson. Aren't you just a tiny bit jealous? I mean, he's a joke, right? But he's a good joke and good jokes are hard to find.'

'Why would I be jealous, dear? He stole all that writin' from me and Bill Faulkner.'*

'I hear tell he's mighty good on a yacht,' said Marilyn.

'Quit impersonatin' me,' said Miss McCullers. 'I'd sooner walk the plank as sit on a yacht. Telling ya'. Truman nearabout killed everybody who was ever nice to him and that's the damn truth.'

'He stole your work?'

'Yes, dear. He stole that little fag novel from me and Bill Faulkner and Eudora Welty. The rest he got from Tennessee Williams.'

'And what about *Breakfast at Tiffany's?*'

'He stole that from you, dear.'

'So they say.'

'Yes. From you he up and stole it. And from Carol Marcus and Slim Keith. That was the story he stole, and the attitude he done stole the same way. The style, well, honey, the style he stole from me and Christopher Isherwood, right'n front of our eyes.'

'Heavens.'

'When you reck'n on Truman, he's really jest a redneck pansy impressed by the smart folks. He's a rag-doll, jest waitin' to be picked up by any spoiled girl who happ'ns to be passin' by lookin' for a darn plaything.'

'Well, nobody's saying he's Proust.'

* This was a little self-regarding of Carson. Mr Capote had in fact stolen much more from Colette and Jane Bowles.

'Next time he comes your way, you skedaddle now dear, you hear me? He'll cuss you behind yo' back like tomorrow's never comin'.'

'Carson, Carson. Come, come.'

'You'll see if I'm wrong, dear. That little bitch hung his momma out to dry. He hung Katherine Ann Porter and Newton Arvin out to dry. You know what he said about Greta Garbo? He said he happened to go up there to her apartment and she has a Picasso in there, but Truman says she so stupid she hung the Picasso upside down.'

Marilyn shrieked. I jumped onto my feet at the size of her laughter and she covered her mouth. 'Oh, my,' she said. 'He must be the most wicked man who ever did live.'

'Quit impersonatin' me. And he ain't no man. Don't kid yourself on that score. Yo' just naive about men.'

Carson had a cane hooked over the back of her chair and her face was white. She was only forty-four years old, ten years older than Marilyn, but from her face and her manner one might have imagined she was much older. Lillian Hellman said that Carson wallowed in her illness – and that was the kind of thing Lillian Hellman would say – but nobody, not even Carson, could deny she was conscious at all times of being 'efflicted'. She even understood how sometimes she used it to gain control over others, that being a 'burden' or a 'handful' was often a nice way of making sure you weren't forgotten. For much of the time in the Oak Room, Carson spoke about the surgery she had had on her wrist, about a second operation due to happen in July and then there was her novel. 'My. I guess that's something to get excited about,' said Marilyn. 'Do you know what it's going to be called?'

'*Clock Without Hands*.'

'That's beautiful, huh? Did you steal that from Truman?'

'No, dear. From Faulkner.'

The thing that the girls really had in common, though, was their doctors: they had both spent time with analysts who were child psychologists. Marilyn smiled sexily at the waiter and he poured the last of the champagne into their glasses. 'Dr Kris put me into the Payne Whitney,' said Marilyn. 'It was horrible, Carson. Really awful. You know the Dangerous Floor? They put me up there with locks on the doors. Like I was crazy. My mother's been in a ton of those places. I can't help her and she can't help me.'

'Then you're even, dear.' Marilyn drank the whole glass of champagne down in one go. 'But Payne Whitney,' said Carson. 'That's shocking, dear. They did the same to me in 1948. That's how long they've been that way with poor efflicted people.' Carson shuddered so her bangs shook on her forehead; she lifted another cigarette, her hands trembling around a chipped gold lighter.

'Carson, do you live alone?'

'I live with the people I create,' she said. She didn't say it in a regal way, but very simply, as if she was just giving her friend an important fact.

'My analyst's father was a big wheel in Vienna,' said Marilyn. 'A friend of Freud's. And her husband was a big wheel in the psychology of art. She thought I was crazy for leaving Arthur.'

'Is that why she put you in the bin, honey?'

'I think maybe. I mean, I know I needed help. Maybe a lot of help. There's no point denying I've been . . . well . . . I've been sad, Carson. I didn't think I could be so sad . . . so . . . you know, lost.'

'Take your time, child.'

'Yes. I've been so very blue. Too blue to cope, I guess. I would wake up and think everything . . . was just, well . . . dust.'

'That's the end of the road, honey. Or the beginning.' Marilyn shivered and went on speaking.

'Anyhow. I guess the shrink was angry at me, putting me in that place.'

They discussed it further, Carson wincing now and then and holding her cigarette over the ashtray, her fingers stained yellow, shaking. Marilyn loved talking to Carson because sometimes, just in the middle of their time together, after the gossip and the teasing, a moment would arrive when everything came together, when all the stuff that mattered to each of them came spilling into a chat about books. As you know, Marilyn had been reading the same novel for months, *The Brothers Karamazov*, and she felt Carson was the only person who would understand how to talk to her about it, and how to allow her to talk about it as well. Marilyn lifted me onto her lap, a sign of her nervousness. 'Do you know that article of Freud's, the one about Dostoevsky and parricide?'

People often lose their accent when they talk about books. I'd noticed it in others, but in Carson it was dead obvious. 'Naturally,' she said. ' "Four things may be distinguished in the rich personality of Dostoevsky: the artist, the neurotic, the moralist, and the sinner." '

'You know it?'

'I'm afraid I do,' said Carson. 'And some of my friends'd say that's no surprise at all.'

Marilyn coughed quietly. 'Well, Lee says he thinks I would make a wonderful Grushenka.'

'He's right, honey.'

'Thank you, Carson. Thank you for saying that.'

'Go on, dear.'

'Well, I've been reading the novel. It takes a lot of reading. For me, anyhow, it does.'

'Oh, for anybody.'

'And I'm trying to figure out how a girl would want to be with a man who wanted to kill his father. I mean: killing your father . . .'

'We all kill our fathers, dear. That's what we do. Then if we're fortunate we find someone to put in his place.'

'Some people love their fathers,' said Marilyn. 'Some people love their fathers all their lives.'

'Loving, murdering. It's all the same.'

'Oh, Carson. I can't talk to you today. Even for me, that's just too perverse. I won't say another word.'

'Perverse, honey? They give me awards for that.'

The waiter put another dish of olives on the table and Carson just ate them up, one by one, until the dish was a grave of sticks and stones. I could smell some lovely things coming from the kitchen, but I just sat there, I'm afraid, growling at some of the passers-by, who were staring. Some of the women wore ballgowns, great balloonings of tulle, and others came in yellow or purple trouser suits from Jax. Marilyn felt about Carson the way she often felt about the Strasbergs, the way she used to feel about Arthur. She liked their thoughts. She liked their thoughts the way people liked her face. Carson began to speak as if Freud's essay on Dostoevsky and the falling sickness was really a treatise on her own problems. Marilyn put her hand under her chin and listened. Egotism is sometimes a very entertaining disease.

'Grushenka's a darn case,' Carson said. 'You know the novelist had the mentality of a criminal? All the good ones do, my dear. We are racked with guilt about the things we do in our dreams. Not just in dreams. They say poor Dostoevsky may have assaulted a young girl years before. He was king of the neurotics, sweet man. Wrote a great book, though, my God, and beastly too, just beastly. That man could imagine anything.'

Marilyn lowered her voice. 'Grushenka's another way for the men to deal with their neurosis, right?'

'By fucking her? Oh yes, my dear.' Marilyn took out a book and showed a page, an underlining.

'He writes that the earliest doctors called copulation the little epilepsy.'

'*Le petit mal*. Darn right. Grushenka has real passions. She has authenticity, by God. She has innocence. And these men'll seek to quench their neurosis any which way they can. Not that she helps herself any. She thinks she's a drink of water when really she's a drought.'

'Gee,' said Marilyn. 'Lee would love that.'

'But remember we had fathers, too, dear. And so did Grushenka and little Ophelia. The girls have fathers too and they have mothers, God help us. God help everybody.'

'I never knew my father,' said Marilyn.

'Well, child,' said Carson, putting the last olive stone into the dish. 'Never knowing your daddy has its problems, but at least it means you'll never lose him.' Marilyn asked for the check and the girls began to collect their things. For each of them, the hour they spent at the Oak Room would be the best part of the evening. But now they were due uptown: they were already late for a cocktail party, though Carson

174

said those book parties only got going when people had stayed past their welcome.

The party was at Alfred Kazin's place on Riverside Drive, an apartment with books piled on the stove, ice heaped in the bath, tapenade smeared on the crackers, the English huddled in the hallway, and the beatniks on the fire escape. I have to tell you it wasn't a natural haven of cocktail-party talk. Carson was sitting in a large armchair next to a record player, which she soon asked to be turned down, and Marilyn, radiant with champagne, was spirited through the rooms by invisible hands. Mr Kazin wasn't in love with dogs, you could tell, but Carson is from the South where dogs are understood to be among the beacons of high culture, and I was soon tolerated. (Not long after we arrived, I noticed that almost everyone appeared to be discussing the current number of *Partisan Review*.) Mr Kazin had a connection with Carson that was sentimentally intense: he was humbled by her manners and her talent, her small boy's face that made him nervous. Whenever he was around her, he found himself quietly hatching plans to compliment her. She didn't say much back, simply spitting a little tobacco, watching him with her suspicious eyes. 'Mary McCarthy mentions you in April's issue,' he said. 'She says you and Jean Stafford carry the torch for the writing of sensibility today.' Mr Kazin's eyes narrowed every time he was about to launch an idea. 'You know how it is with Mary. She wants everything cut and diced. She imagines the new crowd, her, young Updike, are like mimics, actors, where an abundance of care is used in the mechanics of the imitation. She likes it that way.'

'Well,' said Carson. 'I'm damn sure Mary knows well enough what she's talking about.'

'She has the tendency to be overawed by her own discriminations,' he said.

'I don't know,' said Carson, 'but I'd say that was the critic's prerogative.'

I thought of Mr Connolly and was excited for a moment to imagine he might be there. (He wasn't.) At the same time a man called Marius Bewley tripped up quite homosexually. He was with a man who smoked a pipe as if he were playing a cello, Bewley's large moon face appearing through the fug. Bewley glanced at his friend. 'I've never seen a briar do such sterling work,' he said. Carson sniggered and gladly accepted a martini proffered by sensitive fingers.

'Marius, we were just discussing Mary's piece about character in fiction.'

'Oh, yes. All that hissing jargon. Mary assumes that comic characters are by definition real, while serious people like myself are figments. My dears, I am no less real than Leopold Bloom. I may be averse to cheap soap and the tang of urine, but I am real. Touch me if you like.'

'Damn right,' said Carson. 'You're as real as Edith Sitwell.' She laughed, she coughed, until two grey spots appeared on her cheeks. She thought Bewley the very spice of literature.

'I'm as real as Jay Gatsby, dear. And much more serious than Dame Edith. Do you want to know what Randall said about Mary McCarthy? He said, "torn animals are removed at sunset from that smile".'

'Ha! That's the funniest thing I heard in munts,' said Carson. 'Munts.'

'She means "months",' said Mr Kazin.

176

'Am I not objectively existent?' said Mr Bewley.

'You're on far, sister.'

'She means "fire",' said Mr Kazin.

'I met her brother,' I said. 'His name is Kevin. I sat on his lap at the Actors Studio.'

'Now look at that little white dog.' Mr Bewley sighed and shook his head. 'Oh, to be young and innocent again.' Mr Kazin lifted me up and walked me through the crowd to get to the kitchen, where a dish of water was kindly made available. I was up on the draining board. Next to me, leaning against the stove, a Dr Annan of King's College, Cambridge, was speaking to a poet about the doctor's recent evidence in the *Lady Chatterley* trial. 'Dwight MacDonald wrote about it in *Partisan Review*,' he said. A hand reached between us and lifted a bottle of vermouth.

'I did indeed,' said Mr MacDonald, his cuff all wet from being dipped in my dish. 'Hello, Noel. That was a very sprightly performance in Court Number One.'

'Oh, one has to do one's bit,' said Dr Annan. 'Now, have you met my friend . . .'

'Frank O'Hara,' said the poet, putting out his hand in a cramped way.

'Oh, yes,' said MacDonald. 'I read Kenneth Koch's piece about you in the last issue.'

'It was a sweet article,' said O'Hara shyly. A poet from the fire escape made O'Hara smile by calling him a square and a beauty. I looked round at the sound of the cracked voice. The man had whiskers and was more like a lion than a cat, a big poet of the jungle with his chunky spectacles and holy whispers. It was Allen Ginsberg. He was drinking wine from a jug and offering 'revelations' to people asking about his

177

long poem, a thing I was bound to like called 'Howl'. He was excited about life and he had his own boisterous crowd, other poets, a drunk from Times Square with a bashed face. Last thing I saw on the fire escape was Ginsberg attacking Columbia University and taking a young man's face in his hands, kissing him and saying, with no small degree of relish, 'Trust is an intimate conspiracy. *Shantih. Shantih.* Trust is Mae West's asshole.'

'Is that in your poem?' said the young man.

'Nope,' said the poet. 'It's just for you.'

'Sweet?' said MacDonald to O'Hara. 'He said you were the best writer about New York alive.'

'That's very sweet,' said O'Hara.

I rested my head and surveyed the room. 'Why do critics always look like unhappy rabbits?' I thought.

Kazin tickled me under the chin and put me down on the floor. It was great just to walk among the shoes: there were lace-ups and heels, sandals and boutique boots, some of them like beautiful drawings I had recently seen in the magazines. I followed the trail of Chanel No. 5 in the hope of finding Marilyn. I passed a great many people, some of them touching hands and all of them gripping drinks, the youngest ones' eyes now and then flashing with terror. I passed one pair and looked up to see a man called Jacob trying to be kind to a girl of eager solemnity. 'A good magazine, Susan – it was Susan, right? – is not only about what it puts in but about what it keeps out.'

'Ah,' she said, this Susan, 'the natural despotism of literary selection. I like it very much.' Her eyes appeared to darken with excitement. 'I am writing something about the comedy of high seriousness, not an essay so much as a series of jottings. A cascade of *pensées*.'

'And what do they indicate, these jottings?'

'That the world is an aesthetic phenomenon. It's about a sensibility, the idea that there is a good taste of bad taste.'

'So it's about Oscar Wilde?'

'Oscar, yes. But also Tiffany lamps. The novels of Ronald Firbank. Schoedsack's *King Kong*.'

'So it's about innocence?'

'Perhaps,' she said, making a mental note. 'But also about seriousness, a seriousness that fails. It is also about extravagance, empathy, and the glorification of character. Life as theatre.'

'So it's about homosexuals?'

'Not all Jews are liberals and not all queers are artistic.'

'Most are, if they are good at what they do. Good at who they are.'

'That's very funny.'

'Thank you, young lady. Pass the ashtray. Can you give me another example of the thing you're talking about?'

'Garbo's face. *The Wings of the Dove*. The rhetoric of de Gaulle. The Brown Derby restaurant on Sunset Boulevard.'

'That's four examples.'

'I think I've had too many martinis,' she said.

'You'll find the Brown Derby is on Wilshire,' I said.

'Shoo that dog away,' said Susan. 'I don't trust dogs, the way they sniff.'

Half a room later I stopped at the ankles of a woman with several holes in her stockings. She was very loud and wearing a pair of reptile-skin shoes by François Pinet. I absorbed without hesitation that she was Lillian Hellman. She was smoking a long cigarette and dangling a glass of vodka down by her side, splashing my nose. I licked up the

179

puddle of booze at her feet, then sat under a nest of tables to eavesdrop. She was tougher on the editors of the magazine than she was on Josef Stalin, and I soon found I wanted to bite her. The woman was totally in love with herself, which was bad enough, but she also disliked Marilyn because of Arthur – she was waiting for her chance to say something nasty – and it was clear she considered herself to have been the greater hero before the Committee.* In the time I spent under the tables, she found something vile to say about everybody she mentioned. First it was Marilyn: 'So vulgar you wouldn't believe it. They say she killed Clark Gable stone dead with her lateness on *The Misfits*.' Then it was the magazine: 'Don't make me laugh. *Partisan Review* is the house journal of the nation's liberal cowardice.'

'Why are you here, then?' asked a nice-looking painter called Robert Motherwell.

'I like to feast with my enemies, darling.'

Then it was Norman Mailer. 'He's been looking for someone to stab for years. And Adele was looking for years for someone to stab her. They were perfect together. Existential hero, my ass. Norman couldn't fight his way out of a pillowcase. His career is over.'

'That's harsh,' said Mr Podhoretz, gliding up. 'Norman's honest.'

---

* Lillian Hellman appeared before the House Committee on Un-American Activities in 1950. She invented her life, which is reasonable, but she also invented a good line she claimed to have said under interrogation. 'I cannot and will not cut my conscience to fit this year's fashions.' No such line was uttered, except by Lillian at parties. Arthur Miller appeared before the Committee in 1957. Marilyn had accompanied him to the hearing in Washington.

'Honest, my ass,' she said.

'You know something, Lillian. You ought to try just for once being generous. Norman's in trouble and he's been good to you.'

'Good to me, my ass.'

'No. He was good to you and he was good to Dash when he was ill. You should be ashamed to go talking like that.'

'I haven't been out since Dash died.'

'Well,' he said. 'I'll put it down to that. You know what Degas said of Whistler? He said he behaved as if he had no talent.'

'That's just the worst thing you can say about an artist.'

'Well, Lillian. Think about it.'

'Aren't you the moral arbiter,' she said. 'I might believe you, Norman, if *Commentary* magazine ever gets up and says a single brave thing before it dies. Why don't you just go back to troubling those pot-smokers?'

'People change, Lillian.'

'You won't, Norman. You'll be licking people's self-inflicted wounds for them until Doomsday.'

She then engaged a nice little man called F. W. Dupee in a discussion of the Cold War. Miss Hellman believed it was all invented by the CIA to keep Russian people poor and American people stupid. 'We have no national style,' she said. 'The government in this country wouldn't give you a nickel for what you people call high culture.'

'That's not true,' said Dupee. 'The government takes a great interest in high culture. Even the bad bits of government care about it. Everybody in this city can take it for granted that politics and high culture have everything to do with one another.'

'Rubbish,' she said. 'Wishful thinking.' Stephen Spender, a cat sloping among cats, grazed past her and she sent a dirty look like a harpoon into his back. 'We are living through a period when the American government has no real consciousness of intellectual life at all.'

'I'm afraid that's wrong,' said Dupee. 'The war between capitalism and socialism happening now is basically an ontological debate. It's an argument about how people can live in society. We locate that debate in culture, and that is America's instinct.'

'You're dreaming, honey.'

'This is a new era for America,' said one of the editorial assistants, called Jane.

'Get me another vodka stinger, honey,' said Miss Hellman with a boiling face. She turned. 'You are all addled Trotskyists, as dictated by lunacy. I'm sorry to say Comrade Trotsky is a traitor. I was glad I opposed his application for American asylum.'

Everything went blank and I just launched myself from under the tables and sank my teeth into her nylon-clad ankle. She screamed loudly and people stepped back from her. 'Help! I'm being attacked! *Ohhhh*. They're attacking me!' she said. I didn't hang on for long and Mr Kazin was there in an instant, lifting me up. 'Is that *Mrs Miller's* dog?' she shouted.

'No fuss, Lillian.'

'Is it? Goddammit. The dog bit me for telling the truth. I'll sue.'

'No fuss, I said.' He examined her ankle. 'There are no cuts and it's all over. Don't fuss, Lillian. Not even a scratch. This is a swell party and he's just a little dog. Hot in here for a dog. Ann! Could someone open a window?'

When Mr Kazin placed me back on the floor, a number of his friends patted me. Many of the *Partisan Review* wives were in fact widows: their husbands were totally preoccupied with each other, and the wives for the most part remained un-introduced, abandoned by the door, where they tried not to seem tetchy. There were exceptions of course among these women, but not many. The area around Columbia and Riverside Drive formed a society – a world of social ease that Kazin resented – and it was the wives who did the crockery-borrowing, the pattern-swapping, the passing back and forth of kids' clothes. Most of these wives didn't have anything to do with the 'smart women': they were frightened of their tongues and their independence and happy not to be like that. I wandered out from that hall of pretty shoes, and was soon among the brogues. A young man had a girl up against the bathroom door: they were sharing a cigarette and a love of Samuel Beckett. 'Hellman's play is about consumerist madness,' he said. 'It just closed at the Hudson. Well, it's about the brutality of shopping, but, hell, she's the biggest shopper in the business. She's the only Stalinist in the history of the world to have done a . . . you know, starred in an ad-spot for mink coats.'

'God. She's quite fierce, isn't she?' said the girl. 'Old Scaly Bird.'

My head turned and I took two paces through the forest of legs. Ted Solotaroff was talking to an intense young man with hurt eyes. At first I thought it was Charlie, the leader of the Monroe Six, this being the sort of party Charlie might steal into as a young staffer at the Viking Press. He had the same intensity and self-involvement as Charlie, similar interests, but he was much smaller and didn't find things funny. He was talking about a story of Isaac Rosenfeld's called 'Red Wolf'. 'In some ways I think it's a real pity,' the young fellow said. 'He was never gonna be Saul Bellow. I mean, they were friends and everything. They both thought they were going to be Bellow, but only Bellow has a shot at it.'

'Even that isn't guaranteed,' said Solotaroff. 'It's all a struggle. Have you read Saul's Africa novel?'

'Crazy stuff.'

'You bet. Anyhow, that Rosenfeld story. Story's narrated by a dog, right? Well, that's him doing Kafka. He can't get over Kafka.'

'Oh, give us a break fellas,' I said.

Following the perfume trail, I found Marilyn in the bedroom up against a white bookcase. She was standing with Lionel Trilling and his wife Diana, while Irving Howe sat looking up at them from the arm of some William Morris upholstery. My owner had that lovely, strange, underwater look on her face and she was listening intently. I stood in the shadow-box of the doorway, when it occurred to me that this was a play and with a certain taste in my mouth, a taste of Hellman, I could see myself as the author. As Cicero said, 'honour encourages the arts'.

TRILLING *is wearing an elegant sports jacket, a dark tie, holding a pipe at an angle to his thoughts.* DIANA *is wearing a midnight-blue dress with a jacket over the top, a brooch pinned on her breast as if to guarantee her dignity. Her lips are stained grey, but I guess that's just a dog seeing red.* MR HOWE *is wearing light trousers, a pair of soft shoes, and a cotton jacket with pencils sticking out of his top pocket. The room has a strong sense of the setting sun.*

The sound of Dizzy Gillespie comes from another room.

TRILLING [*careful, noble, unassailable*]: Let us call it the romance of culture.

DIANA: No, Lionel.

TRILLING: No?

DIANA: I simply can't believe we have enough reason to begin thinking of art as a narcotic.

TRILLING: One might do better to insist on the notion that no work of art can ever be divorced from its effect. *The Brothers Karamazov* is no kind of narcotic, but for the sensitive reader it may nevertheless possess a homeopathic character. Tragedy's function is to prepare us, to inure us, as human beings, as a society even, to what we may experience as the pain of life.

DIANA: So art is simply an escape?

TRILLING [*patiently*]: No. An engagement.

MR HOWE [*cheerfully*]: The very opposite of escape. The very opposite!

TRILLING: In comedy we find reality. We find the essence of man as a living creature.

MR HOWE: Too true!

DIANA [*to* MARILYN]: Mr Kazin believes that Dostoevsky is the master critic of our civilisation.

MR HOWE [*very shyly*]: Is that so?

DIANA: Do you mean, is it the case? I would say it is arguable, yes. Let's see what Lionel says.

TRILLING [*looking at* MARILYN]: In the essay of Freud's you mentioned a few minutes ago, 'Dostoevsky and Parricide', Freud says that psychoanalysis can have no real purchase on the artist. Yet he understands Dostoevsky to be a very

185

great writer indeed, and a high-culture prophet, who could summon the forces at work not only in man but in civilisation itself. But you are interested in Grushenka, and I must say I believe that is where the author's genius actually finds its bearings, in the blend of tragedy and comedy that informs his rendering of the secondary characters in that powerful work.

MARILYN: Do you think she's funny?

TRILLING: Anything truly alive is funny.

MARILYN: Really?

DIANA: Khrushchev is funny? Leopold and Loeb? Adolf . . .

TRILLING: Khrushchev is not *unfunny*.

MARILYN: He came to the studio. When was it, last year, the year before? They had a dinner in the commissary at Fox. I thought he was very funny. Kooky. I mean odd, but I liked him. He once told Nixon all shopkeepers were thieves. Nixon grew up in a shop, or something.

TRILLING: There you have it.

[As DIANA *looks towards the window,* MR HOWE *fiddles with the pencils in his top pocket.* DIANA *sips her martini. She looks as if she's biting the insides of her cheeks.*]

MR HOWE: Yes. Dostoevsky and Dickens are writers who show us the comedy of realism, the tragedy of intellectual life, the wonders of psychology. Each of them is a prophet and his religion is humanity.

DIANA [*smiling*]: Very good, Irving. Very good indeed.

MR HOWE: The work is full of buffoonery.

MARILYN [*almost hurt*]: But I'm sure *The Brothers Karamazov* is very serious.

MR HOWE: It is serious.

TRILLING: There's nothing so serious as comedy.

DIANA: Go on, Irving.

MR HOWE: The novel is political to the marrow of its bones. In the world of Dostoevsky, no one is spared, but there is a supreme consolation: no one is excluded. Like Dickens, he populates his books with true people. Dickens sets in motion a line of episodes: the *pícaro* is defined by his energy and his voice, and he moves from adventure to adventure, each cluster of incidents bringing him into relation with a new set of characters. Via Fielding, the great influence on Dickens was the picaresque. A novel must not only reveal the world but it must be a world. Show me a good novel and I will show you a centre of vibrancy. Why, this dog could write a novel and I would read it tomorrow. It would no doubt be a piratical compilation from the works of old Spanish masters. Old British masters. So be it. Let's have it. We need more of this. Where are today's comic novels? It is the heartbeat of the form. That's how society might be examined and our examinations, God save us, might even prove to be entertaining. That's my argument.

DIANA: Well, it's not much of an argument.

MARILYN: I think it's neat.

DIANA: Neat?

MARILYN: Sure. I think it's neat.

DIANA: You have lost me, Irving. Are you suggesting that it might benefit our . . . our national literature, if works were to be conceived by workers and servants, and by . . . by dogs?'

MR HOWE: *The Brothers Karamazov* is really the story of the domestic servants. All great stories are about the servants.

TRILLING: That's outrageous.

MR HOWE: I mean, even *King Lear* – it's the Fool's story. And

The Brothers K. is Smerdyakov's story.
[*I yapped with excitement and put myself into the play.*]
DIANA: Oh, look. It's the hero of the hour.

At least Irving Howe was agile and open in his absurdity. (Perhaps too open: I think he was standing too close to me, picking up my propaganda, the taste of my experience, my will to power.) Mr Trilling, on the other hand, was a puzzle of a much less benign sort. There was something sinister in Trilling's immense composure. People appeared to be awed by his carefulness, his patient discrimination, his gentle unwillingness to say too much or to think too little before speaking. His manner concealed fear and so did his faith in culture: there was dirt and uncertainty out in the world. Mr Trilling knew it, and his project was to make his defences impregnable. Not even his wife could quicken his cool blood, though God knows she made a good effort. While appearing to share in her husband's dignity, Diana in fact exerted a powerful drain on it, subtly challenging his sense of himself while wishing to appear its curator. (Not that women are obliged to protect their husband's gifts, but Diana wanted to, and she wasn't aware of the hostility it generated in her.) There was something wrong with Mrs Trilling that caused her to deny, when it came to other people, those qualities she knew she lacked herself: it was merely a survival ritual. She needed to feel superior in order to feel alive, that was all. Lionel, meanwhile, had made a fetish of his own moral percipience, his body a vehicle of serene motion, a machine that concealed its efforts and its exhaustions. He wasn't to blame for anything except his need to be blameless. All these things became obvious as the Trillings inched around each other with their super-alert conversation, rewarding the bystanders with their attention while making it clear that their marriage was all the social intercourse they could ever wish for. In her own mind, everything Mrs Trilling knew about her husband gave her licence both to doubt him and to defend him, and she knew that he had only recently forgiven Mr Howe for an article the latter wrote in 1954, about the intellect and power. Some essential human conflict was crystallised in her marriage to Lionel, but she found she was almost happy, which her private self told her was quite sufficient. She looked down at her shoes: blue, with a heel, a prim little bow on the front. Mr Trilling, meanwhile, was thinking how well – relatively well, almost well – his wife was coping at the party, given Kazin's unforgotten criticism of her psychoanalytical approach to D. H. Lawrence. Marilyn remarked to herself how very smart these people were and how decisive they seemed about everything. 'I'm afraid we've rather been monopolising Miss Monroe,' said Diana as Mr Kazin came into the room, leading a bright and portly Edmund Wilson, who was sniffing into a handkerchief and holding a glass of whisky.

'As we speak, Lillian is telling Carson she knows nothing about the South,' said Alfred. 'She is saying Carson has never been to New Orleans.'

'The *convergence* of the twain,' said Wilson like a grand and busy bumble bee.

'I don't know if you've met Miss Monroe,' said Diana, always polishing the silverware.

'Hello, madam.'

Marilyn put out her hand. 'Charmed, I'm sure.' Wilson tapped his tummy and looked at Lionel. It was like the meeting in the forest between Mary and Elizabeth in *Mary Stuart*: each bowed almost imperceptibly and Wilson coughed. Schiller himself might have coughed at the throat-tickling buzz which Wilson felt passing through his body as he gulped his whisky and began to talk. As people often do around dogs, they used me as the excuse for a little small talk, and you could see instantly that neither man was built for small talk. 'When Henry James was old and tired,' Wilson said, 'he could be seen moving down the High Street in Rye with his dog Maximilian trotting behind him.'

'Ah, yes,' Trilling said. 'The dog that may embody the finer feelings. I believe Maximilian was the long-lived Tosca's successor. Edel wrote that Maximilian appeared to have some of James's authority.' Lionel looked around as if it all came naturally. 'Is Leon here?'

'I don't know,' Wilson said. Then he paused. 'How are the Groves?'

'Of Academe? At the same time vexing and propitious. We are running a course.'

'Great books?'

'That's right. We aim to rehearse the old lost belief in the virtue and power of rationality. We count on order, decorum, and good sense to see us through.' Everyone chuckled except Marilyn.

'And you will add Freud, just to keep in touch with human frailty?'

'Naturally: *Civilisation and Its Discontents*.'

'Lucky them. Lucky students. I see all the little gods will be present and correct.'

'Yes, Edmund. We dare not expect, in the first term at any rate, to bring ourselves to Arnold's "fullness of spiritual perfection", but we will do our best with the small talents at our disposal.' Wilson swayed. He looked quickly at Mr Kazin.

'It won't wash, Alfie!' he said.

'Edmund.' The old man turned back to Professor Trilling and narrowed his eyes.

'Is the course in any sense American?'

'In every sense.'

'Really?'

'Yes. In every sense American. It is the spirit that moves us, Edmund. We are Americans teaching young Americans how to read.'

Irving Howe shook his head.

'No, Irving. They won't be marching,' said Trilling. Alfred Kazin shook his head. Trilling turned to him. 'No, Alfie. They won't be looking for something to get angry about. They will attempt to understand the place of moral authority in modern literature. They shall learn how to read and if they succeed at that then they will learn how to live their lives. We intend to look at Diderot.'

Wilson took another slug from his glass. 'It's not American, Lionel. It's English. It's French. It's German. And it's more English than anything.' Mr Howe took a step back, behind the sofa, as if to distance himself from anything that sounded like patriotism.

As they proceeded to a gentle dispute – gentle on the surface, raging underneath – my ears twitched and I could hear all the voices at the party. The sound was that of old Europe boiled down to its modern sap, the sons and daughters of immigrants claiming America's newness for themselves. Carson was Lula Carson Smith; Marilyn was Norma Jeane Baker; Mr Trilling was Lionel Mordecai, just as our old friend

Lee Strasberg was Israel Strassberg. They were like children in the little garden of America, alert to something new in themselves and excited to be in an environment that might readily shape itself in accordance with their wishes, each of them investing all the while in a quantity of forgetting. Marilyn looked over her glass and felt they were all like the people in Arthur's plays, only kinder, better suited to go places, with greater spirit. She was finally glad that part of her life was over. Yet she supposed she might always be on the lookout for what made couples work and what made couples fail. Tonight she had a fresh and simple thought: the couples who survive as couples tend not to get caught up in provoking each other with negative remarks. The truth of it was quite moving. I've seen some people, not far into their marriages, produce unhelpful statements, not to say hateful ones, indelible ones, on an industrial scale. Not the Trillings, though. Their quarrels were silent. Jamesian. They saved their hateful statements for other people, and even those would be wrapped in a doily made of the finest lace and scented with a vapour of good manners. But it didn't always work. As usual, Diana was first to break.

'France? England? That's nice, coming from the author of *Axel's Castle*. You know, Edmund. I think all that work you've been doing on American battles has gone to your head. Are you losing your mind? Or is it drink?' This was Diana at her least controlled and Lionel sought to silence her with a single word and a bow of his head.

'Diana,' he said.

'Look, Lionel,' said Wilson. 'I'm sure Mrs Trilling has an argument. She usually does. She's not wrong, by the way. I've had enough whisky to refloat the Confederate vessels sunk at Gwynn's Island.' Wilson suddenly seemed unsteady on his feet and he stepped on my tail. I squeaked but nobody noticed. 'Work, work,' he added. 'It kills the appetite for social display.'

'C-come now, Edmund,' said Kazin. (The old habits were beginning to show.) Wilson looked at him with jowly contempt and the pity he reserved for immigrants who set too much stock by American ideals and promises. There was a touch of old Brooklyn, of Brownsville, in Mr Kazin's attitudes, Wilson thought, just as there was an element of City College in his determination always to be ready with the correct answer. Wilson drained the glass and the ice clinked his teeth. Professor Trilling had travelled back to himself, to the place where other people's bad behaviour merely confirmed his own certainty about how he himself must behave. Nevertheless, he wondered if he had kept Mr Kazin out of Columbia for good reasons, or just because he thought one Jew was enough.

'I'm not making myself understood,' said Wilson. 'I am a ghost sometimes to my own opinions. I merely meant to say how unfortunate I find it that British values enjoy such automatic genuflection.'

'Perhaps at *la plage des intellectuels*, they are. Perhaps in Wellfleet,' said Irving Howe. 'There's Stephen Spender over there. He's constantly thinking of Englishmen who were truly great.'

'Stephen, yes,' said Wilson. 'Like so many Englishmen, he doesn't know where he is going but he always knows the quickest way to get there.' Lionel looked at Diana and pointed to his watch. Marilyn was thinking she must have bored the people, but she felt a nice cool breeze coming from the window. 'I'm afraid the British are the blind leaders of the blind,' Wilson said with his eyes almost closed, 'and quite despicable for that. All those second-rate painters, academics, with their high, thin voices. Despicable.'

Wilson leaned down at this point and placed his empty glass on the floor. He did it very slowly as the people around him were dispersing. 'Don't mind me, I'm just a citizen of falsehood,' I said. He ignored me as he heaved his weight onto his back foot and grappled with the glass. It wasn't too late, I said to myself, there's still time, and then I jigged forward and made an effort to bite the fingers of his trailing hand. 'OWWW!' he said, most eloquently, 'the buggering hound is at me!'

'Take that,' I said. 'The patriotic gore. I'll show you, vile man! I'll show you to undersnizzle my people.'

'Ow, ow,' he said. 'The vicious cur.' He was inspecting his pink sausage fingers. He went quiet and his eyes were closed again. 'Ow. The ineluctable modality of the tactile,' he said.

'Maf! I don't know what to say,' said Marilyn, lifting me up and looking to her hosts. 'He's usually so, um, reliable and not at all like this.'

'I wouldn't worry about it,' said Mrs Trilling at the door. 'It was a pleasure to meet you. Your little dog has the most exquisite critical taste. We must find a place for him on the faculty.'

When we got to 444 that night it was obvious from the behaviour of my owner that I was in deep disgrace. I tried to nudge her, make up to her, but she was listless with thoughts, regrets, and I'm sure she was busy deciding to take me with her less often in future. She sat down on a brass vanity stool and peeled off each of her false eyelashes in turn. Lena the housekeeper was ironing clothes and laying them in two giant suitcases. 'Lena, would you be a dream and take Maf down to the park?' said Marilyn. 'He's been very bad. I'm sick of him.' Marilyn bit her lip and picked up a grey notebook she often took with her when she was working with Mr Strasberg. 'He's been . . . *wilfully* insubordinate,' she said.

'Really, Miss Monroe?'

'Yes. He bit two people at a party this evening. Two big shots.'

'Naughty Maf!'

Marilyn brushed out her hair, before pausing and resting the brush on her lap. I looked at her and realised this was our love story, too. I guessed I would never feel so close to anybody in my life. Not just because of the feeling she gave me, but the other things. I believe she taught me everything about what it took to have empathy. I believe she was like Keats in that way: her small efforts spoke of beauty and truth, in ways that made her eternal. Watching her, listening to her thoughts, I was in love. She formed everything about me, including my sense of the novel. Even in anger, she looked at me and I understood the storyteller's vocation. 'A novel must be what only a novel can be – it must dream, it must open the mind.' She took *The Brothers Karamazov* out of her bag and examined the back cover, sticking out her bottom lip and blowing upwards like a child to clear the hair from her eyes. It was weird to think all those people had opinions about Arthur.

A cool breeze was coming off the river. I felt bad, not ashamed, just egotistical and unhelpful, the kind of dog you wouldn't want to share your life with, like one of those mutts in Conan Doyle. Lena tied a scarf around her head and from the back she looked like Marilyn: I wondered what her own domestic life was like, her husband at home and her children sleeping by now, the house very clean I supposed. Her family thought her work was so glamorous, the sort of work you could talk about to people who liked news. The Greensboro Bridge lights were strung like lights on a Christmas tree. God, I felt misunderstood. Picked-on. Some animals are respected for their artistic conscience, like Congo, the talented chimp, who painted pictures admired by the likes of Miró and Picasso.*

A dachshund came sniffing round the bench as his owner smoked a cigarette, the dog more jowly and misanthropic than Edmund Wilson. Then another came, a Dobermann as handsome as any dog in Landseer. 'They never know who they are or what they want.'

'Who's that, skipper?' said the Dobermann, giving me the eyes of friendship.

'Them,' said the dachshund. 'People.'

'Ah, to hell with that,' said my friend. 'I've had three dinners today and I'm not complaining. Nice night out here. Let people own their troubles. Have a heart. What's with the sad face, buddy?'

'I got on the wrong side of the old girl,' I said. 'I took a chunk out of a bore at a party. Two bores. What the hell?

---

* Incidentally, Congo did not return the compliment. The chimp considered himself a social realist and accused Miró of fashioning 'subconscious Catalan doodles'. In May 1960, I saw Congo on television with Desmond Morris. The naturalist was busy talking about abstract impressionism when Congo, dabbing the canvas in a rhythmical way, mumbled that the picture was in fact a portrait of his late mother.

They were asking for it. Anyhow, she bawled me out. Then in the car home she starts going on about how she misses her last dog, Hugo. The ex-husband took my predecessor to live in Connecticut.'

'That's too bad,' said the Dobermann. 'To get hit with the old dog routine. I mean, that's tough.'

'I knew the old dog,' said the dachshund with a heavy expression. 'Hugo. Boring as a week in Amagansett. Bit of a pedagogue. Loved Ibsen.'

'Oh, *can* it, Marty,' said my friend. 'Can't you see our friend's suffering over here. He's caught a dose of the old self-pity, if I'm not mistaken.'

'Just a bit,' I said. 'My owner's been in hospital. She's terrific, though. Smart as buttons.'

'Ah, self-pity. The great romance.'

'Tell me about it,' said the jowly dachshund.

'Love your accent,' said the Dobermann, with a little lick at my ear and a sweet harrumph. 'Just remember you're in good company. Biting, I mean. Don't do it too much or it'll start affecting the dinners. There's always consequences if you bite. Remember Cardinal Wolsey's dog called Urian? He bit the hand of Pope Clement VII. He caused the Reformation. That's what my boss says, anyhow.'

'Seriously?'

'Absolutely. Hey, have you ever met the Queen of England?'

'No,' I said. 'But the owner has. She's got a million corgis or something. I have to say: I'm sad tonight. She won't forget it easily. She gets hurt. What do you do with a person like that?'

'Ride it out, buddy. We know people love their dogs even when they try not to.'

'Learn to loathe them,' said the jowly dachshund, pacing before the fence. 'Life is better in the doghouse. They're not our friends. Don't fall for any of that "man's best friend" baloney.'

'Ahh, shurrup,' said my friend. He turned to me. 'Forgive him. He lives with a guy who can't stop putting up buildings. The guy's got an edifice complex. The owner worries a lot, that's the deal.'

'I'm sure it'll pass,' I said. 'But tonight I'm Citron, the dog on trial in *Les Plaideurs*. Did you ever get Racine?'

'Nah,' he said. 'My owner's a priest over at Our Lady of Peace. Nice guy. Cares a lot for detective stories. Private eyes, that kind of thing. I don't think Racine would do it for him.'

A little street cat paused above the sandbox. 'The Puppiad,' she said. Her tongue seemed gymnastic as she spoke her Alexandrines, and she licked her face and twitched her ears.

> The dog steals a capon and finds himself in court,
> Before the judge Dandin, I'm happy to report.
> So punctiliously he pontificated,
> That the Norman mob were instantly elated.

> The puppies were brought in to plead their father's case,
> But who will beg for you, young Maf, in your disgrace?
> You need an advocate, why not Swifty Lazar?
> To get you out of jail, and tell you who you are.

Lena picked me up and kissed me on the head. 'Okay, Maf Honey. Bedtime.'

'Goodnight fellas,' I said over her shoulder. The dogs nodded and sniffed the ground around the bench, the river shining at their backs and a horn sounding over the East River.

Twelve

Wilshire Boulevard. In the parking lot of a Jack-in-the-Box chicken joint, a young marketing guy was interviewing people about their buying habits. 'We was middle class before we had a car,' said a bald Phil Silvers-type with chickeny fingers. The Gray Line tour had pulled up behind the man and you could hardly hear him for the grunting of the bus.

'What – straight purchase?' asked the guy with the clipboard.

'I don't know. All I can tell you is my family got cars and didn't think anything about it. Nice cars. My folks got a small house and a big car on the same day.'

'Where?'

'Pasadena. My father worked for the US Termite Control Corporation.'

'They bought a car and a house?'

'Yes, sir. My mom and pop took me and my sisters down to Knott's Berry Farm and Ghost Town to celebrate the new house and the new car. You know, down in Buena Park? We had a chicken dinner then, too.'

'You did?'

'Yes, sir. We did. And we stayed in a motel down that way to celebrate.'

'You celebrated the new house by staying in a motel?'

'Indeed we did, sir. My father'd been in the army. South Pacific. He came back to California and he said he wanted a house and a car and a washing machine, and that's what we got. So, we had a celebration the night everything came through. We took the car and went to a motel with a swimming pool.'

You can't drive on Wilshire without thinking of the Roman Empire. Maybe just in the summer, when a layer of warped heat hovers over the road, the straight road that goes from civilisation to the sea. I thought of grapes. I thought of olives. I thought of tough guys in sandals. There was also a sense that the humid day might give way at any moment to annihilation, not Gaulish arrows but Russian missiles, raining down on the scene of enjoyment from a perfect blue sky. The palm trees shivered in the midday sun. Marilyn had me on her lap in the back of this long black car and we were cheerful, ready for chicken in a bun. 'The last thing like this I'm going to eat, okay buddy?'

'You look great,' I said. She did, she looked great, ready for sunshine and melody.

'I've got a picture to make. I'm losing all that New York puppy fat, okay puppy?'

On the way to Doheny Drive that day, she asked Rudy, her driver from the Carey Limousine Company, to stop at Mullen & Bluett so that she could buy some new bedclothes. 'I guess it's sad to be buying sheets just for yourself,' she said. 'But that's the way it is, Rudy. That's the way it is.' On the door of the apartment the nameplate said 'Marjorie Stengel', which was actually the name of Montgomery Clift's secretary. She had to keep the world back. She never had a fan in LA to compare with someone like Charlie in New York, no one clever and full of the future like him. Some of her possessions were in boxes, otherwise the Doheny apartment was an empty space with a bed and a few books. On an upturned orange crate she laid a pile of scripts. The New York sojourn had awakened her once again to her potential, which is a happy place to land when things have been rough. That's what she thought. Marilyn ate bok choi, drank water, and looked after her skin.

Her beautician worked out of two rooms on Sunset Boulevard. She was Madame Rupa, a woman who found it hard to believe an animal who lived in Hollywood was not a veteran of showbusiness. 'Can you make a dance or do a song for me?' said Madame Rupa.

'He's very silent,' said Marilyn.

'No talent?'

'I guess he's thoughtful.'

'That's no good! We want dancing. Acting! Can he cry like Shirley MacLaine or speak a few words like the horse on television?' There was music playing in the room, a song called 'Ae Mere Pyare Watan', a patriotic song from a film called *Kabuliwala*. 'A beautiful song about how we miss our homeland when we are far away,' said Madame Rupa, mixing a special mask for Marilyn out of Bayer aspirin. She would crush the pills in an old, traditional-looking mortar, adding water until the mixture was creamy. 'Bayer Works Wonders!' said Madame Rupa.

'Gee,' said Marilyn. 'We know a few face-aches who could use this, don't we Maf Honey?'

'Dozens,' I said.

'Dr Kris!' said Marilyn. She was laughing as she lay back on the bench.

'Paula Strasberg,' I said.

'Richard Nixon!'

'Mrs Trilling!'

'Arthur. What d'ya think, Maf? *Arthur*.'

Sometimes it made me sad that she couldn't hear me. Marilyn chuckled, her eyes peeping out from the white stuff. She stroked me. She was none the wiser. Madame Rupa just stared at us from the beaded curtain, her brow furrowing in the company of two more crazies. She was none the wiser either. She instituted sanity by talking more about the song that still played, its sitars melting into the air conditioning. 'The words are Dari,' she said. 'From Afghanistan. I salute the breeze that has passed from your valleys, it says. I will kiss anyone who can mention your name.' She loved reading the crime pages of the *LA Times*. That is where she turned when the songs and the stories ran out.

There were so many nice places to pee in LA. I mean, if you have to pee you have to pee, and why not next to the swimming pool at the Château Marmont, right? When Marilyn lived in Doheny my favourite place was the corner of Cynthia and Doheny, where a giant jacaranda hung over the road. Over those weeks back in Los Angeles, the Doheny apartment filled up with belongings: the first thing I recall being brought in was a large bronze bust of Carl Sandburg. She brought some records and as many clothes as would fit in two trunks, which her friend Ralph drove all the way from New York in his old Buick. I noticed the apartment was brighter and so was she: her moody New York books were left behind, as if they had taught her everything they could. No Fitzgerald any more. No Carson. No Camus. Only one of the Dostoevskys. This was the beginning of Marilyn's last period. She was in her final months, and the only books she tended to keep on the shelves were children's books, Beatrix Potter, Dodie Smith, *Peter Pan*, the books she imagined were meant for her alone. 'It didn't fail,' she said about New York to one of her friends. 'It will always be there, right?'

Gloria Lovell, Sinatra's assistant, lived in the same apartment block. She knew me from my first weeks in America – it was Gloria who arranged the handover with Mrs Gurdin in Sherman Oaks – and now she was the nicest neighbour in the world, coming in with sausage casseroles and all sorts of love. The trouble with Frank's people was never Frank's people, it was always Frank, who at that time was so puffed up and antsy about the Kennedys he was constantly a bag of nerves. 'Such a great find, your dog,' said Gloria. 'Little Maf. The only helpful present Frank ever gave anybody.'

'Did you know the people Natalie's mother got him from, the breeders I mean?' asked Marilyn.

'I'm not sure. English wackos is all Natalie said to me.' Marilyn looked down at me in her arms and half-closed her eyes.

'I take him every place,' she said. 'He's my mascot.'

'You're going to see Natalie,' said Gloria. 'Frank's putting together a little thing on Friday.'

I was assuredly part of the life of the boulevard. Frank's thing was a private dinner at Musso & Frank's. Natalie was there that night and I got the feeling Sinatra was just showing off his favourite girls to a hoodlum chum of his, Frank DeSimone, who wore glasses and called himself 'Frank's Attorney'. It was just the five of us. They say Frank's Attorney killed Hooky Rothman in broad daylight, in back of Mickey Cohen's haberdashery shop on Sunset. He was sharp on the dressing front: silk tie, English suit. At Musso & Frank's, Sinatra was giving out about the late Whittaker Chambers, telling everybody what a shmuck he had been, what a phoney. At the same time he ordered the girls' food for them, insisting they try this or that dish from the menu. 'Listen, honey. You gotta have this zucchini, okay. You're having it. I'm talking fried.' He looked up at the waiter. 'Tell Bob the oil has to be fresh.'

'Could I just have rice pudding?' said Marilyn.

'What, you crazy? Huh?' He looked at the other Frank and shrugged. 'These dames. Did you hear that? Can you believe that, Frank? They don't know how to eat food, these girls. They don't know how to live. They want to eat dessert before they've had fish. They won't eat pasta. What a goof. Hey, Clyde! Do me a favour. Bring this lady the Shrimp Louie and a salad deluxe. After that the spaghetti with meat sauce.'

'Wow, Frankie. I can't eat so much food,' said Marilyn. Natalie laughed nervously and proceeded to knock over a bourbon highball. 'What a klutz,' said Frank. 'Can you believe that? Can you get these girls? What a klutz.'

'I'll have the baked apple,' said the Attorney. Everything he said was spoken with a menacing softness. Sinatra looked at him. It was odd to see Frank saying nothing.

'You won't have the grenadine of beef?'

'I'll have the baked apple.'

I wished for a second that one of the girls had the gumption to answer back to Sinatra. He was a bully. Yet there were no moans or dismal sobs at the restaurant that night, just a kind of fearfulness on the part of Marilyn and Natalie. Sinatra picked a thread off his tie and smiled like a smile can fix things. 'Chambers,' he said. 'What a fink. Can you believe him? He testified in '48. He's the kinda guy who made people crazy in this country, I swear to God. He ratted out his best friends.'

'This is a great country, Frank,' said the Attorney.

'No argument.'

'A great country. Some people, maybe they would like the communists to run the show, huh? Maybe some people would like these guys who hate the baby Jesus to come and take over our schools, huh? You know something Frank, I love being an American. It makes me cry. I don't want to be told how to live by some goddamn Russian communist.'

Marilyn stroked me on the seat beside her. I felt the urge to pass on some information. 'Whittaker Chambers translated *Bambi*,' I said. She stroked me again.

'Did you know Whittaker Chambers translated *Bambi*?' she said. (Wow, I thought. Now, we're getting somewhere.) She tossed her blonde hair. 'Yeah, he was a very interesting writer.'

'Who cares about any goddamn writer?' said Sinatra. 'A snitch and a writer! What a cube. Maybe they should have given him the Congressional Medal. Did you hear that? He did *Bambi*!'

'A swell story, that,' said the Attorney. 'My children cry at that story. I love that story. Usually I don't like animals. I hate animals.' He nodded downwards. 'Tell you the truth, I usually hate dogs. I'm giving you a free pass because you're a very good-looking girl. I loathe dog-lovers. Most of them are cowards who haven't got the guts to bite people themselves.'

'Holy Jess!' went Frank. 'Dog-lovers!'

Marilyn was getting drunk and so was Natalie. They were both nervous of Sinatra and Sinatra was nervous of his attorney and it just wasn't fun to be with them at Musso & Frank's. Natalie began talking about Elia Kazan and the film they had just made, some squealing epic in which Natalie was able to put absolutely everything in about her mother. The girls went from Kazan to Strasberg to Marilyn's time in New York, Natalie doing that actor's thing of gently undermining her friend's sense of achievement. 'Oh, *Anna Christie*'s so overblown, don't you think?'

'Why, no,' said Marilyn. 'I think it's beautiful.'

'O'Neill's too hysterical. I mean, what do I know? But for me it's too much. It brings out the worst in most people, I swear to God.' She smiled. 'It asks for . . . how would you say? Brassy emotions.'

Marilyn's hand trembled as she moved to drop me under the table. I heard Sinatra asking Natalie what was new with her mother, and Natalie saying Mud was on the war path and her father had recently banned all the dogs from the house. 'He's drunk every day,' she said. 'And Muddah now thinks the Russians are in league with the UFOs.'

'She's a smart woman,' said the Attorney.

Despite their differences, I think Natalie had what her mother had in such splendidly extravagant proportions: not only the Slavic paranoia but a very determined sense of affliction. Maybe the greater part of it came from Nick Gurdin, the gun-slinging alcoholic of Sherman Oaks, but there was a sense that the bounty of America made that family delirious. It doesn't always do to compare one temporary owner with another, but a dog can't help dwelling on his material, so to speak, especially a journeying dog, and

206

I have to say the Gurdins were a sort of purgatory to me, a place where one felt in exile both from the possibility of happiness and the certainty of judgement. I had quite a nice time there, during my in-between life, but I can't bear to think how many dogs Mrs Gurdin must have sent out into the United States in a state of nervous exhaustion.

Sinatra had removed one of his shoes under the table, and he was nervously stubbing his toe into the clay tiles, the dust coming off on his sock. Natalie was getting into a real drunken flow about Muddah, the way she treated the help down in Sherman Oaks, the fact that Nick was so delusional he thought he was a lost son of the Romanovs. There was a frenzied element to her laughter. She looked from one person to the other with a craving in her eyes for reassurance, laughing again, at one point beginning to imitate the voice of the mother in the Kazan film. 'Now, Wilma Dean,' she said. 'I wanna talk to you. Boys don't respect a girl they can go all the way with. You and Bud haven't gone all the way, have you?'

'Jesus, honey. You are cranked,' said Sinatra. When she moved on from *Splendor in the Grass* and began talking about Bobby Kennedy, Sinatra eased off his other shoe. At the same time, the Attorney gently put his hand on Marilyn and began stroking her thigh. I put my head down and sniffed one of the empty shoes, which smelled of nothing. I had a sudden vision of *The Last Supper*, that nice painting by Titian, where the apostles appear much more generous when it comes to allowing scraps to fall off the table.

I am happy enough with the sea – was happy that time at New York harbour, when we went to Staten Island – so long as I can be among the little dogs on the deck, protected from the secret undulations by several tons of cast-iron vessel. But the actual water – no. I had a fear of deep water,* which was difficult in California because Marilyn loved the beach at Santa Monica and for her it brought to mind a happy experience of infancy. She was a strong swimmer and she found the place uncomplicated. As far as it goes, I've never really been much of a holidaymaker. Like all dogs, I take for granted a certain amount of sanctioned laziness, but beaches, tanning, ice-cream? To me the beach is an unfixed term on a roasting spit, a stifling penance, the water out there a border of pronounced anxiety. It's not always easy for a dog to know where self ends and owner starts, but my thing about water made me realise that Marilyn's fears were different from my own.

Late that summer I began to accept that I might never see New York again. Life in California was slower somehow and sweetly empty. Some afternoons, on the freeway, on the beach, your stomach could momentarily lurch with a steep sense that life was elsewhere. I came to understand it as a very California feeling – it came with the smog and the sun-kissed faces. We spent a lot of time down at Peter Lawford's beach house in Santa Monica, a lovely house, an outpost that once belonged to Louis B. Mayer. Normal individuals would get excited by the fact you could step straight onto the beach from Lawford's deck. Sometimes, Marilyn would

* It's possible this squeamishness is borrowed from a number of the people I met, especially Natalie Wood, but also, I understand, from an early personal trauma, the drowning of my Aunt Cressy in Loch Morlich, an event that occurred in the first weeks of my puphood. That was one family story: the habit of blanking it out for being morbid was another.

kick off her sandals and run onto the sand and immediately be confronted by a mental image of herself sixteen years before, blossoming into stardom in a bikini for some army photographer keen to make it in magazines. Peter was one of those English men who grow more perfectly English the further they are from England. (Marilyn had enjoyed many an earful about him from Frank. 'How does cheap, weak, sneak, and creep sound?') In himself, Lawford always felt like a comedy turn, an ersatz European, not quite natural when surrounded by all this natural American power. He had enough talent to turn it to his advantage, marrying the Prez's sister and everything, but he worried he was never as cool or as substantial as his friends, a very teenage thing to feel. Lawford's curse was the same as his blessing: he always wanted to be more like the people around him. When standing with Frank he wanted to be more like Frank, when drinking with the surfboys he wanted to be more like the surfboys. Marilyn and I contained multitudes, admittedly, but for Peter we were the easiest creatures in California.

Now we come to the President. Don't hold your breath for stunning revelations. I'm afraid I only met him one time, a warm night down there at the beach house, and my chief memory is that he was worried about his back and a local shortage of procaine. As far as Lawford was concerned, Jack was very straightforward in the brother-in-law department, a regular, bluff guy, happy to be with Peter and his friends so long as they were lots of fun and nice to his sister. The party was no more racy than usual. I guess people were giddier because of the President, drinking more, dancing more later on, exhibiting that strange confidence people exhibit when they realise they might be at the dead centre of the action.

Everybody's eyes were larger and probably darker than usual, engorged with power's immediate proximity, and every girl in the room came armed with a question. 'Mr President, what can we do to support President Ngo Dinh Diem in his fight against the Viet Cong,' said Angie Dickinson with a toss of her hair, a small furrow appearing on her brow as she 'did' serious.

'*Jack*,' he said. 'Call me Jack.'

Marilyn's make-up man Whitey Snyder had driven us down to the beach from Doheny. It was one of those gentle evenings when the palm trees suddenly make sense, the warm breeze whispering among the leaves on Santa Monica Boulevard. 'I think my father has been trying to call me, Whitey,' she said. 'There was a call from a hospital in Palm Springs.'

'What did they say?'

'They said his name was Mr Gifford. They said he wanted to get in touch with his daughter.'

The trees had lights on them and the shadow of the trees passed through the inside of the car. 'Do you think it's someone making a fool of me, Whitey?'

'You didn't ask to be put through?'

'Not yet. I couldn't. I took the number.' I put my head on her arm and she breathed with that quick, manufactured courage of hers, ready for anything, ready for the whole world. 'You know, I always forget I'm a daughter,' she said.

'You shouldn't, honey,' said Whitey. 'It's just too big a thing to forget.'

'I lied to my New York analyst,' she said casually. 'I told her my father was dead.'

'It's just too big a thing to forget,' he said.

We arrived at the party around 11 p.m., too late for supper but in very good time for scraps. It was a stand-up thing anyhow, which dogs understand, and Marilyn's arrival caused no fuss. Kim Novak smiled from the corner and said 'hi' with a pretty cascade of fingers. Lawford had that preposterous, theatrical, very English way of greeting old friends, where he pretended he had been waiting the whole night just for you. It was a trick he had learned from his father, Sir Sydney Lawford: how to exude passionate interest without a scintilla of real personal involvement. They say Peter's mother dressed her boy as a girl for the first ten years of his life, which explained a number of things about Peter quite neatly and sympathetically. He spent his life devising scenes of great moment that he could preside over whilst enjoying a secret absence. He beamed and took Marilyn by the hand. Someone gave her a glass of champagne and I stared up at Lawford with admiration. I loved him in *Son of Lassie*, the RAF pilot helped to safety across the snows of Norway by a dog whose eyes blazed with the strange existentialist thinking of Martin Heidegger. The dog was living for the moment, unsure whose side to be on, but Lawford made himself a likeable project and convinced the dog to gain its freedom by throwing off reason and morality. I gather this is not how the film is usually described, but I think Lawford must have agreed with my memory of it because he lifted me out of Marilyn's arms with a whoosh of recognition. 'Good Lord,' he said. 'You've brought the dog. Is this the Frank dog?'

Lawford had, in fact, met me several times before. In conversation, he liked to pretend not to know things, just to have something to ask. It was one of the ways that he showed himself to be upper-class.

'Yes. He's Maf.'

'Maf?'

'Yeah. Mafia.'

Lawford's handsome face creased up. 'Hello, Dreamboy,' he said. 'I happen to know three individuals who would absolutely love this little chap.' Marilyn laughed and moved her head like a person in a dream of themselves, putting out her hand to greet the people, the Democrats, the moneymen, who were quickly swimming around her.

Three children in pyjamas were sitting on the stairs. They were sharing a bowl of popcorn and beginning to look sleepy. 'I want it. I want it,' said Christopher, the eldest. The boy scrabbled down onto the carpet and tried to pick me up by the ears.

'No, me, Daddy. Me,' said Sydney.

'I'm not kissing him after you! Daddy. She's got cooties,' shouted Christopher.

'Dog,' said Victoria, the youngest.

Dogs love children: we love them for the purity of their narcissism. But children don't always love dogs. They love the look of us and our air of teddyness, the way we can seem so loyal and biddable and cute, but they always mistake us for fictions even as they feel the wet dash of our tongues on their laughing faces. Of course, we are no more loyal than children are innocent, but we try our best, aiming not to disappoint the little people in their conception of us as four-legged bundles of fluff and simplicity. To them we are funny things, made-up creatures, cartoon mixtures of texture and colour, who simply love being patted. It always struck me in Hollywood that dogs are probably less like that than people are, but who's going to argue with a child's wonder-seeking eyes, even if they appear amid a fusillade of poking and pulling and general dollying? 'This is Dreamboy, Marilyn's dog,' said Lawford to the children.

'*Mamallen* dog,' said the smallest. Christopher, the boy, cradled me and swung his arms from side to side. 'Oh, my darling, oh, my darling, oh, my darling, Clementine,' he sang in a yokel voice and with a cow's-lick the size of New Hampshire.

'Let's paint him blue!' said Sydney.

'You is Huckleberry Hound!'

'*Icklebelly Yow*,' said Victoria.

'Let's paint him blue!'

There was a certain amount of bouncing me up the stairs on two legs, Christopher chanting lines from a recent episode of their favourite cartoon. 'Scrubby brushes! Scrubby brushes! You wanna buy one of our new scrubby brushes?'

'Make him like a space dog,' said Sydney.

'*Beige dog*,' said the smallest.

'With a space helmet.'

'How 'bout that?' asked Christopher, placing a plastic drinking cup on my head.

All the while, Mr Lawford had been talking to a security guy. He turned round and his big smile reappeared. 'Would you look at these kids,' he said. 'Aren't they just wonderful?' I was lying in a basket of small hands and my head was wet. Looking up, I stared at Peter and remembered how close he had been to Lassie in that lovely story.

'Mr Lawford,' I said. 'Is the possibility of Being contingent on an acceptance of Mortality? I mean, is all experience an aspect of Time?'

'Come on, Christopher. Jolly along. Don't have the little

213

dog barking. Let him go now. It's bedtime.'

'But Daddy, it's fun.'

'I said enough, Christopher.' Mr Lawford pulled me free and the elder children booed. The baby chewed her cuff. Lawford frowned like a clown, as if his decision hurt him more than it hurt them, and they ran up the stairs and chuckled over the banister.

A lot of depressing shoes at the party. I mean mules. Everywhere I stepped it was D'antonio gold mesh sandals, or little English mules by Rayne. The men, if they were in the movie business, wore white shoes. The Harvard boys wore black oxfords with the laces at equal length. I walked past a great deal of flannel and seersucker, summer tones, until I came to the President's shoes, which were oxfords, of course. Very shiny.

I'd like to be able to say Marilyn and Kennedy had a big world-historical discussion, but they didn't, though they looked for a moment like they might. They got involved in a few rapid minutes of performance, an air of great significance hanging over them. They could never have been just any man and woman meeting in the corner of a party, it couldn't be imagined, especially not by them: their conversation was a meeting of private fantasies that would breed private fantasies, and my memory of their talk is of something dramatic lying just under the surface. Kennedy was drinking whisky and soda. He sat in a beautiful Charles Eames chair. There was a cushion at his back, and he tapped the plywood side of the chair for emphasis as he spoke to her. She was sitting on the chair's matching footstool, and I snuggled against her legs. Her hand was shaking ever so slightly as she stroked my coat. 'I think it safe to say he has the instincts of a riverboat gambler,' he said with a wide grin. They had been talking about the Vice-President, Mr Johnson.

'He's tough, huh?'

'He's Texan.'

'But does he have the liberal imagination?'

'Of course he does.' Kennedy paused. 'Well, that's an interesting question, Marilyn. I hadn't realised you cared so much for that kind of thing. Trilling and so on.'

'I did a little reading.'

'And Trilling? You know him?'

'Well, I don't know him. I just know he said something – he wrote it. About Fitzgerald, your namesake. He wrote a line about the "habitual music of Scott Fitzgerald's seriousness". That's the thing I most wish someone had written about me.'

'Is that right?'

'I guess so.'

'Those literary guys. One of them called me an "existential hero".'

I licked her arm. 'That'll be the day,' I said.

'Is that a compliment, Mr President?'

'I couldn't swear to it. I think it's more of a compliment to the person who wrote it. You're so sweet, Marilyn. You know something? I don't think you should worry so much.'

'I was born worrying.'

'Not about pipe-smokers, surely. You're bringing joy and wholesomeness to people's lives. That's the truth.'

'The whole truth and nothing but the truth?'

He grinned. 'So help me God.'

'Don't change the subject, Mr President. We were talking about civil rights.'

Just as stars are always the best star-fuckers, the needy are

215

often the very best at feeding the needy. The President and his new friend were locked onto each other that night, addressing each other's doubts, his sexual and hers intellectual, until everyone decided they must be a couple. Sitting by the patio windows at Lawford's house, they seemed to present such a heavenly coalition of natural accomplishments that no one could resist picturing them in each other's arms. This kind of thing gains force by desire and repetition, and those, like me, who like myths more than facts, will enjoy the notion of Marilyn and the President together. Yet they were only in each other's company a few times, on each occasion talking about themselves and politics in a public room, enjoying a fondness that history would consecrate into something larger than life. He tapped his opinions out on the side of the chair, answering her points, impressed at the way she listened, even as he wished to ask her about success. That was the President's interest in her, that's what really intrigued him. It had fascinated his father and it fascinated him: he wanted to understand the nature of fame. She had lived with it longer than he had and she had suffered by it too. He would never have kissed her in a room full of people; he was married to a dignified woman and was too political for spontaneity, but the closest he came was when he finally asked her, point blank, her pretty eyes open to his Boston carefulness, to tell him the thing that is concealed by fame.

'Gee,' she said. 'What a question. You think the answer is private pain, don't you?'

'Yes. I suppose I do.'

'Well, that's not the answer, Mr President. Fame doesn't conceal private pain, it only emphasises it. And I guess I might have had troubles even if I'd never left Van Nuys.'

'What, then?' he said. 'I'm interested.'

'Self-knowledge,' she said. 'Simple as that. The thing concealed by fame is self-knowledge.'

'We must speak again.' There was a thread hanging off the bottom of Kennedy's suit trousers and I wanted to play with it, pull it with my teeth and see how far it went before it snapped.

'Now, I answered your question. We had a deal. You should answer mine.'

'You want to know if I sprang Dr King from Reidsville state prison?'

'Well, yes. Lester Markel of the *New York Times* told me you and the Attorney General did a swell thing. He said you called up Mrs King when he was in that place, that prison. He said Mrs King was expecting a baby. You called to reassure her and word got round the community, the churches. Next thing folks are really paying attention. You did that, Mr President? You called that lady?'*

'You give me too much credit,' he said. 'We were walking on eggshells. But I have to tell you it was Harris Wofford, my campaign aide. We were taking big risks in the South – we had plenty of votes to lose and plenty of votes to gain. Even Dr King's father was supporting Nixon at that stage.'

'And Dr King had been arrested? For sitting down in a snack bar in Atlanta?'

'That's right. They had him in prison.'

'And you sprang him?'

'No. Well. Put it this way. We couldn't be seen to be

---

* I don't know why Marilyn said it was the guy at the *Times* who told her the story. It was Frank Sinatra who told her.

217

backing King in a Southern fight about segregation. That wouldn't have helped anybody.'

'But you wanted to, right?'

'Of course we wanted to. But we had to take it slowly. We were lighting fires in the morning and putting them out in the afternoon.' By this point in the conversation, I noticed the President had shifted forward in his chair and was now addressing a group of listeners, which signalled the end of his flirtation with my owner. 'We had people in jail,' he said. 'We had Klansmen in the fields. Dr King was in a maximum-security prison and Wofford had the idea that we should call Coretta. Just a few words. We had a few minutes at O'Hare so I just took the goddamn telephone and made a call.'

Marilyn drank more champagne and lay the glass down next to me. I licked the rim. Her eyes were wide open and she was drunk. I believe she had taken pills and was loose in herself. 'What did you say?' The President smiled like a veteran of many campaigns to win the approval of strangers.

'I said I understood it must be hard for her, expecting a baby and her husband in prison. I said we were thinking about her and Dr King.'

'Thatta boy,' said Marilyn. I think she was talking to me but I can't be sure.

'Bobby went ape,' he said. The President had taken pills too and they were working nicely for him. 'It was only thirteen days to the election. But then he got so angry that he called for King's release. He couldn't bear it that some lynch-law judge had committed a civil rights leader to hard labour. That was it. I made a phone call and Bobby made a phone call and it shaped up from there.' Peter Lawford leaned over Marilyn's shoulder and made like a leading reporter.

218

'It had a rather significant effect, no, on the Negro vote in the South?'

'Right. Rather significant is right.' He leaned over smiling and picked up his drink. 'And you know what King Sr said after that? You know what he said? He said he would now be voting for Kennedy even in the face of me being a Catholic and all.'

The party laughed. 'Can you believe that? Martin Luther King's father being such a bigot?' And then he looked at Marilyn again in a private way. 'Well,' he said. 'We all have fathers, don't we?'

People were sitting around the pool. Others were squeezing between the security men to walk on the beach and I followed. I sat down beside the young Mexicans who had been serving. Mexico was meant for me. The workers laughed and jibbed one another, reminding me of the young Texans who drove me to see the UFOs that time, the evening we listened to rock and roll. The waiters smoked pot and passed the thing back and forward on the sand. They stroked me and said, 'here, boy'. The air was mild and the sky was full of yellow streaks. The waiters hadn't expected the night to be so informal, but with their shiny skin and their white shirts, their bow ties, they seemed like they belonged. They talked about how sexy the film stars were, how amazing the food was and how cool the firearms of the security detail. But one of the waiters didn't want to have me on his lap, a young man from Watts named Jabril. He smoked the cannabis and it mingled with his own sweet scent, but he told the others he had no time for dogs.

I was happy listening to the fellows. The night sky grew inky and I drank as much as I could of the soft air. People are so busy with thoughts of paradise they fail to see they have been in paradise all the while. It had been for me a night of listening – a life of listening, and not being heard – and beside the Lawford house I remembered Plutarch, his beautiful essay 'On Listening to Lectures'. A female Jack Russell came racing across our sight-line and headed straight for the surf. I bolted out of the waiter's arms and chased her up to the roiling edge where the foam fizzed on the sand. I was always very slow to fall in love and quick to form my tactics of delay, but the Jack Russell made my heart swerve in the air like a tennis ball. Who was she?

I nodded back at the house and my young friends, the Mexicans. She glanced at me sideways, a rather perfect manipulation of her long lashes. 'Virtue has only one handle,' she said. 'The ears of the young.'

'They're nice,' I said. 'My kind of people.'

'You like Mexico?'

'Oh, yes,' I said. 'It's the ultimate destination. It's always been in my head. I think we're going there soon. A short adventure. That's the plan. I've heard my owner talking about it.'

'You're so lucky. I've never been.'

'Something happened to Trotsky there. I mean . . . he . . .'

'Yeah,' she said, a born realist. 'He died. Was he a friend of yours?'

'No, not a friend. He was before my time. My first owners loved him. You know how it is?'

'Yeah. They never leave you. First loves.'

We walked round each other, tenderly sniffing. Then we sat at the water's edge and I nudged her cheek and licked her ear. 'You be careful now, honey,' she said. 'I'm spoken for.'

'Where do you live?'

She walked a few steps and nodded up to the brightly lit houses beyond the cliffs. 'Pacific Palisades,' she said.

'Really?'

'You like writers, don't ya?' she said. 'I'm picking that up. I'm in the same boat. My grandparents knew all those writers.'

'Up there?'

'Yeah,' she said. 'Brecht. Mann. The Belgian one, Maeterlinck. He was a good listener.'

'I got him! I love him!'

'Yeah. He came to Hollywood to work in pictures. I think Samuel Goldwyn was just proud to have a Nobel Prizewinner on the payroll. Anyhow, Goldwyn puts him in a room. He's been in there for months. Maeterlinck decided to adapt his book *The Life of the Bee*. So he comes out of there waving a sheaf of paper and it is taken to the big man. An hour later, Goldwyn comes bursting out of his office shouting, "My God. The hero is a bee!" '

We both laughed. The night was funny and so is love. 'Well, so long,' she said. 'Enjoy your life, Maf. You're going to Mexico, huh? Where something happened.' She licked my chin and didn't waste any more time, running like blazes down the beach. At the other end, the dog's owner was clapping her thighs and mouthing words I couldn't hear. I think she was saying, 'Home, sweetheart. Home now.'

Marilyn carried her glass out of the party. I saw her coming towards me across the sand. She sang a few words and she sat looking out, liking the water and the distance, too. The song was happy. Nat King Cole, I think. Her lips were soft and her hair rolled back in those small blonde waves. The song was something she knew from her mother, who said it was once sung to her by the only man she ever loved. We weren't far from the pier. The ferris wheel was going round and its lights burned a hole in the dark.

Thirteen

We spent her last Christmas in Dr Greenson's house in Brentwood, roasting chestnuts and playing charades. There was a sense of things concluding in a spirit of possible renewal, which might, on balance, be the saddest sense in the whole world. She wasn't very much like a person at all by then, but like an element, or like those casual flocks of pigeons in Wallace Stevens who live in an old chaos of the sun. They make 'ambiguous undulations', as she did in those final months in Los Angeles, before going 'downward to darkness, on extended wings'.

Marilyn had put up a small tree in the Doheny apartment and she kept it there for months, watching the red shadow of its lights on the wall when she couldn't sleep. Over at the Greensons, things were happier and psychoanalysis was a way of life. They seemed comfortable basking in the global scale of its achievements. She often stayed after her sessions to have dinner with the family, peeling potatoes and drinking champagne, the clean, creative life of the house making her feel that things could be managed and things could be saved. I would be sat on the dining-room floor, eating from a sky-blue Tupperware bowl they kept specially for dogs. The bowl was some kind of anomaly because Hildi Greenson loved crockery. On the wall next to the breakfast bar hung four antique side-plates – 1900, I'd say – by Creil Montereau called 'L'Esprit des bêtes'. The bottom one showed two donkeys dressed as learned gentlemen with stand-up collars. One of them sits with his elbow on a large book, next to a Roman statue, and he is speaking. '*Sans nous,*' he says, '*que seraient devenues les merveilles de la science et les chefs-d'oeuvre de l'esprit humain.*'*

I have to say, I didn't love Dr Greenson. He was flamboyant in his judgements, somewhat previous in his convictions, and he adored stardom a little too much. For all his high-mindedness, he exhibited a rather tiresome mental softness. Yet he believed in Marilyn's 'potential' and was convinced that her sensitivity could become an asset to her talent, a theory that caused her to relate to him as a father. Now, I'm a dog and I see things in my own way and I have to tell you Dr Greenson was a little too entangled in his favourite role. The doctor was recommended to Marilyn by Marianne Kris in New York, who was only outdone in her father-worship by her childhood friend Anna Freud. These two women were close to Greenson, who was now treating my fated companion, whose own father was visible nowhere but present everywhere, like the perfect author and the worst kind of illness. Dr Greenson was happy to play father to them all. At the time I'm talking about, he was helping Anna to oppose John Huston's proposed film of her father's life, while helping Marianne publish some of her father's papers and get him his due. I was there on Franklin Street

* 'Without us, what would have become of the wonders of science and the masterpieces of the human spirit?'

the day Greenson said, as Dr Kris had, that it would be a mistake for Marilyn to accept the part in the Huston picture, the part based on Anna O.

'But why, when I feel I know her?' Marilyn said. 'The connection is strong, don't you think?'

'Leo Rosten just wrote a book about me,' he said. 'You should look at it, Marilyn. The novel is called *Captain Newman, MD*. It made a fiction of my life. I am quite happy with it – I understand art. I helped him with information. But it's a very serious undertaking to have your problems and your experience and maybe even your brilliance fictionalised, you see? Psychically speaking: it's a lot to take on. I know this is slightly different. But do you imagine that playing one of history's totemic hysterics would enhance your own feelings of well-being at this time?'

'This is different,' she said. 'It's not my story.'

'Yes and no.'

'You know, I yearn for a decent part.'

'We shall take our time, Marilyn. I have spoken to Anna Freud in London and she is convinced this movie is going to be a travesty. She wishes they would all drop dead, to tell you the truth.'

'Is that what they mean by the death-drive?'

'No, Marilyn. It's the life-drive. One must be able to protect one's own father, no?'

Greenson also banned me from the consulting rooms, both the one at his home and the one at his office in Roxbury Drive, saying he did not share Freud's belief that dogs were an aid to therapy. 'They have ears,' he said, with less paranoia than Marilyn assumed at the time. 'And they have eyes. I always feel the eyes. This little dog can wait downstairs with my daughter.' And so that particular cycle was complete, from daughter to daughter to daughter to daughter, the heavenly father upstairs with his patient and me and Joan in the kitchen with two bowls of pretzels and a TV that had to have the sound turned down low.

The godsend in all of this was Mrs Murray. She had actually owned the Greensons' house some time in the 1940s and had stayed in touch as their friend and helper. To Mrs Murray, interior decoration was a kind of religion, and given she was a Swedenborgian, the matter of hand-painted tiles and garden furniture took on the dimensions of a helio-spiritual quest. With Mrs Murray I always felt I had come towards the closing of a circle in my own journey: she was Scottish, somewhere, an arch decorator, a servant of psychoanalysis, a lover of animals, and a woman with a tremendous passion for the life and lore of Mexico. She was democratic or servile, depending on her mood. When Marilyn decided she needed a house like the Greensons, it was Mrs Murray who found it, just a few blocks away at 12305 Fifth Helena Drive. She agreed to become the housekeeper. Mrs Murray took me in her arms and told me in her whispering voice that everything always turns out perfectly in the end.

There's nothing so empty as an empty swimming pool. Mrs Murray came into the garden of the new house with her grizzled hair and her winged spectacles, her tiny eyes casting about for poetic improvements. I think she was a little like the Cheshire Cat in *Alice*, who didn't feel mad, or a dog, but who was capable of imaginative feats of her own. 'We have to *make* what little life we have, Maf Honey.'

'Nice you,' I said.

She was always in her garden slippers. She whispered

226

little religious confections while opening the door to the sun room or preparing the areas for the builders. She had a very clear idea of what we needed: a house like Dr Greenson's, a refuge from prying eyes. It was also a place where Marilyn could begin to know herself, gathering the strands of her life together and getting ready for happiness. That was the kind of thing a woman sometimes had to do in life, and it's never easy with husbands who walk off, but we do it, she said to herself, we do it and we thrive, is that not the way of it? Is that not right, Mafia Honey? Mrs Murray explained to me on our walkabouts that marriage is eternal and one's husband or wife is still one's husband or wife after divorce and even in the afterlife. 'If a person is unmarried, like you darling, then it is said that you will meet your wife for the first time in heaven.'

'Oh, goody,' I said.

This was all said in the smallest voice. Not since Vanessa Bell had I spent time with someone so perfectly devoted to her invented world. In Mrs Murray's opinion, her world was real and had God at the centre. 'All evils originate in mankind and should be shunned,' she said to me one day as she fitted a square of oatmeal-coloured carpet in the closet of the master bedroom. 'Good actions are of God.' And who could fail to love such a believer in the possibility of eternal lives? She made me a bed in the guest house on an old fur coat of Marilyn's that had been given to her by Arthur Miller. She opened a window and clipped back the bougainvillea vines that had become tangled among the bars. 'That's it,' she said, taking out a hankie from her sleeve, a hankie bearing a brown cross inside a grey circle. 'A person's fate after death is according to the character they acquired in life.' She coughed into the hankie. 'Those who loved the Lord or who loved being useful to others are very much in heaven.' The previous owners had fitted two tiles into the threshold of the house, saying '*Cursum Perficio*'.* That first week, the tiles felt nothing but my paws and Mrs Murray's carpet slippers.

Mrs Murray, for all her myopia and hush, was a big wheel in the self-consciousness industry. The Greensons had been dependent on her for a long time, her surprise meals, her gardening efforts, and her library cards – the way she could grasp practical problems, read up on them, dominate them, and then, at small expense and with muffled drums, solve them. She had become well-known in the Brentwood intellectual and artistic world as a purse-lipped solver of people's botherations, and I'm talking about people with a lot of botherations. (She could make calls you wouldn't believe, including to the Mexican Embassy, where, pulling strings, she got me a pass from quarantine, allowing me to come on the Mexico trip.) Mrs Murray would arrive with her things in a net bag and her small, consoling smile: she had secrets that glistened like mica in her solid nature, and she hovered at the edge of her employer's conscience, waiting for mistakes she could busy herself in rectifying without comment. The abandoning husband, John Murray, had been a Swedenborgian minister who became a carpenter in imitation of Christ. It seems he had little of Mrs Murray's domestic zeal so he disappeared into Mexico to organise workers' unions. He was never seen again, though I suspect, by now, he must be living somewhere in the suburbs of heaven with his wife, Mrs Murray.

* 'My journey is complete.'

She entered my owner's life and took charge of everything: house, car, medical appointments, dress fittings, laundry, fruit salads, and – most of all – what she called 'the demands of home decoration'. Caring about such business was part of my pedigree, but I found it hard to influence Mrs Murray. Her convictions were ingrained at the levels, shall we say, of personal grief and natural obsession, and I could only accompany her and yap quietly as she went about the making of our house in Fifth Helena Drive. As I said, her great model was the house she had sold to the Greensons, the one she had hoped to live in for ever with her husband John. The style of that house was Mexican and Mrs Murray would do it again, better this time, as if to show her skills had only improved with disappointment.

The trip to Mexico was arranged by Mrs Murray down to the very finest detail. It would be the perfect melding of politics and shopping. Marilyn, of course, wanted to find the materials for the new house, but she also wanted to see some people from New York who were now living in *la Patria*, working in the film industry or living the dream. It was the end of February 1962 and there was a true note of magic in the air as we arrived at the Continental Hilton. Marilyn was wearing one of her yellowish Pucci dresses and I remember a lovely breeze passing through the foyer, as if we had arrived at last in a world of perpetual spring.

Mrs Murray arranged for the bags to be taken to the rooms while Marilyn took me to a bar on the roof of the building. Three glasses of Dom Pérignon later, we stood and looked over Mexico with that sense of fulfilment that comes with arrival. I suddenly remembered, or picked up from my owner's memory, the sleazy little doctor in *The Asphalt Jungle*. He says Mexico City is a great place: the air is pure, it has great nightclubs and restaurants, a racetrack, and beautiful girls. 'I'm sorry to drag you so far away from your toys, Honey,' said my fated companion.

'Are you kidding?' I barked. 'This is *heaven*. My first owners, the Scottish ones, they told me Mexico is the home of freedom and *peyote*. I believe they had read Mr Huxley on the subject. I believe they had a healthy attitude towards the business of hallucination. My breeders saw life for what it was.'

'But isn't it swell?' she said, not hearing me. Then quietly: 'It's sure nice to be making a home.'

'A little part of here,' I said.

She broke some nachos in a white bowl. 'There you go, Snowball. We got everything we need.'

The look on her face was Mexico and the drumming of my heart was Mexico and so was the scent on the breeze. 'A book he read to me on that farm in Scotland,' I said. 'It was full of paintings and one of them showed the Aztec city rising from the water of the lake. Underneath, the words of Bernal Díaz from 1519. He was speaking of the moment they arrived in the city, "the day we saw what it was always in our minds to see, and our soldiers asked whether it was not all a dream".'

That night the Mexican film people threw a party for Marilyn at the Grand Hotel. We made our way there around six o'clock, when a flag was lowered in a huge solemn square, and it seemed part of the ongoing splendour of insurrection that history's cries for freedom and equality should lead in time to a bourgeois hotel. That is often the way with human struggles, I've noticed: they start in *barrios* and rowdy cafes and they end in the grand rooms of plush hotels, or in fetid palaces, bordered by guards and grey sofas. The contradiction

230

seemed very earthy at the Grand Hotel, very much at home, jungle vegetation and overhead fans working together to stir the air. 'Of course!' the manager seemed to say, there is a necessary distinction between the glorious masses and the chosen few. In one smiling sweep we moved from the pavement – the popping cameras, the beautiful faces shouting 'Maraleen, Maraleen' – to a staircase of white marble. The big shots of the Mexican film industry were looking over the banister, Marilyn lifting me, cocking her head, my eyes dazzled by the men's smiles and some bright Tiffany glass.

We ate like royalty. A man took me off to the kitchen and gave me a truffle omelette in a silver dish and I nearly cried with pleasure. The man had been a policeman but was now recovered. He made a joke to his comrades about me being *un guapo* and all the men in their white tunics laughed and passed me round. They were all lovely and I finally understood why so many waiters are actors, because good waiters must always be ready for performance. I saw it for myself. The swing doors burst open and out they came with a different posture, a different face, presenting me into the hands of my owner with a nod of officialdom and a sideways glace at the maitre d'.

'Mr Huston is a most wonderful director. I have to tell you he is wonderful. *Smaaaaart. Si.*'

'You worked with him, right?'

'*Si*, on *The Unforgiven*. He is what I am calling my lucky director, okay? To me, he is lucky.'

Marilyn giggled. 'You should see him at the crap tables. Luck ain't even in it.'

'Ah, *si, si*. John is *obstinado*, no – at the roulette, no, and the whisky?'

'*Obstinado*,' she said.

'I tell you, Maraleen. Without a doubt. He reminds me of John Steinbeck. You know Mr Steinbeck? I directed *La Perla* – yes, it doesn't matter. Long time ago I directed *La Perla*. Okay? He is the same kind of *macho*, *si*. The same *hombre muy obstinado*. Drinking. Ho.'

'You can talk to me about Steinbeck,' I said. 'I know half of *Travels With Charley* by heart. Charley the dog and the big man cross the country. Charley knows more about geography than the writer, no? And Charley is the artist lying in wait while the pines go black against the sky.'

'Isn't there a rumour, he's about to get the Nobel Prize for Literature?'

'*Es verdad*,' said the man, whose name was Emilio Fernández. He had a nice moustache and a very serious wife called Columba. She was an actress but her dark eyes told you she wasn't so willing to participate in all this excitement. It sometimes happens. She had decided Marilyn might be a threat to a male artist's integrity.

'You are soon working again with Mr George Cukor,' said Columba brightly. 'Is true?'

Marilyn half closed her eyes. 'I love George.'

'Is a bedroom comedy, no? Not hard to make political engagement with this kind of material?'

'I'm not so sure,' Marilyn said. 'It's set in a bedroom. What other kind of politics is there?' She shrugged and Mr Fernández let out an enormous laugh, while his wife pressed her lips together.

A young friend of theirs who had written the screenplay of a movie about a cockroach was very attentive to Marilyn and she liked his jokes. His name was José and he later sent her a forest of poinsettias. But all evening my excitement grew at the promise of Cantinflas, the modern Quixote who was dining at the other end of the table and making everybody laugh. I felt I had waited a long time to meet Cantinflas. They called him the Charlie Chaplin of Mexico. In fact he was much more than that: a verbal idealist, a picaresque underdog, the spirit of the nation. I kept looking along the table at him and seeing his thin moustache and wishing I knew him as a friend. But in a sense I had always known him, by osmosis, by intuition, this impoverished Everyman, this satirist, for whom politics and art were twinned. In a country of illiterates he took over the language; in a country of migrants he took over the city. He laughed at the law and made life spectacular. The eternal *pelado* had known my kind all his life, and then, in the midst of my reverie, he stood up at the end of the table and proved it. He spoke English as he had when he was Mr Fogg's valet in *Around the World in Eighty Days*.

'In Vaudeville, in Godville – we need our props.' He took up a small, crushed hat and the whole table erupted with applause as he put it on his head. The cheers continued as he took up a bottle and poured himself a drink, then another, holding the bottle and cocking the hat. He twisted his mouth from side to side as if a bee was on his nose and took up a leg of chicken from the plate. Marilyn clapped. We watched him eating the chicken, but there was something in our concentration that made it seem as if we were staring at a Velázquez. He ate greedily like a dog and knew it like a man. 'If work was precious,' he said with a mouthful of chicken, 'the rich would no doubt have hoarded it up for themselves.'

'Viva Cantinflas!'

The table shook with delight and uproar. He began to

smoke a cigar. 'In the great tradition of enormous welcomes,' he said, 'offered since ancient days by the denizens of Mexico with their benisons for the roughly transplanted – I mean, the weary sailor who expects courtesy for his Cortez-y, the noble plunderer who begs safe harbour – it has been our habit to accept them with hungry eyes before enjoying their oppressions. In short, ladies and gentleman, we join with the law-givers of our nation in welcoming America to our table. She comes in armour of harmony. About time, too, and no mistake in the hour of our death, Amen.'

The man beside me was actually crying with laughter. He thumped the table. There was something quicksilver and brave in the performance: Cantinflas had no notes and the routine was new, but nothing seemed ill-fitting and the words he spoke were fiery and nonsensical and they cheered everyone up. 'Her skin is like porcelain snow as on the peaks of our volcanoes. Our guest is not from the mansion house, my friends. She is from the house in the *barrio* next to the thieves' market, as I am – not the King of Siam, but a man – and by her talent alone she has made herself the Queen of Love and Intelligence.'

Everyone looked at Marilyn and she laughed that wonderful laugh of health and good times and better ones to come. 'Marilyn is here with us and she is a fact of democracy.'

'I love you Cantinflas,' I said. The people at the table were cheering and they seemed in that moment to be the people who knew best how to live, who knew how to be themselves. And they felt proud, most proud of Cantinflas and his words. Proud of his dissidence. One of the actors came to his side in the part of Hotel Manager. Cantinflas turned to him and shied like a horse.

'I am not ready to pay my check,' he said. 'A check is an imposition, an insult to the free man. I demand you countermand your demand if you call yourself a man.'

'Señor,' said the man playing the hotel manager. 'It is rumoured you have been speaking freely of freedom. The bill is doubled. I believe you used the word "democracy"?'

'I said "geography". I said Miss Monroe was the Queen of Knowing Where She Is.'

'Señor. There is no charge for the cognac. No charge for the chicken and the cigar. This is your bill for the use of expensive words.'

He looked at the bill and the comic's face snarled with feigned disgust. 'El Capitán! If my eyes are my eyes, it says here that the cost of our evening is four times the national debt.'

'That is correct, Señor. You have overspent. It is not cheap in this country to praise beauty.'

'Ah, ugliness! Ugliness,' said our hero. From the side of the room came the sound of violins, the kind of sad music heard in silent movies. Marilyn's eyes were wide with excitement and I nuzzled into her waist. 'It is the dog! I tell you, the dog!' Cantinflas said, pointing. I'm sure I must have blushed under my whiskers. Marilyn laughed and rubbed my cheek. 'The dog is the navigator. I believe he is the geographer.'

'How so, Señor?'

'Marilyn's dog is the dictator of optimism. I say he has slipped into Mexico to run a campaign for president. He has attached himself to this wonderful woman for the purpose of running our country.'

The table roared and Marilyn hugged me and I was almost dizzy with the attention.

235

'You are insane. This is a dog!'

'Indeed, a dog. A small white dog. A small dog belonging to *la chica modérna*. He is here as a guest of the Mexican film industry.'

'*Sí*. And your point, Señor? At this establishment we charge very heavily for nonsense.'

'And what do you charge for wisdom? Tell me, el Capitán. Is it or is it not the case that a female rhinoceros was elected to public office in Brazil?'

'That is right, Senor. Two years ago. I believe the candidate's name was Cacareco.'

'An able public servant.'

'Indeed. A rhinoceros. An able public servant if you happen to live in Brazil. Elected by the popular vote.'

'The popular vote! That phrase will be added to your bill, Señor.'

'And I put it to you, el Capitán. The people of Malawi returned a parakeet as district officer. The people of Poland once voted a pig head of police. He is said to have exhibited a sense of justice most natural and fitting for the people.'

'Please don't give me "The People".'

'It is certainly what I will give you, el Capitán. I give you the people. And I give you choice! And I give you democracy! Sir, I give you beauty! And I give you – with all the heavens in attendance, with history at our beck and call and the rebel spirit of Cuauhtémoc guiding our lightning – I give you the dog of Marilyn Monroe for president!'

The table erupted more than ever before and everyone stood up with glasses aloft and voices raised, the hubbub of good cheer infecting everything and Marilyn in love with the great joke and the spirit of Mexican reason. People gathered round

236

and stroked my ears and kissed Marilyn's hand and Cantinflas was mobbed by his friends. The waiters lined the back wall of the dining room and applauded. There was dancing and Marilyn and Cantinflas were like teenagers – Norma Jeane and Mario Moreno – dancing a snaky-hipped rumba and laughing their heads off. Later, Mr Fernández made a phone call and had them open the Ministry of Education, so that Marilyn and the rest of us could see the murals of Diego Rivera. (The painter was stupid about Trotsky, but what the hell. You can't expect all visionary people to be visionary in the same way.) Cantinflas and Marilyn and the young screenwriter grabbed bottles of champagne and led a procession across the square, then up the street to the ministry. The place was dark but someone found candles, and soon light flickered over their faces, over Marilyn's happy eyes, as they made their way down the corridors in search of Rivera's offering of a dream they could share, *The Day of the Dead*.

Marilyn and the screenwriter found a corner where they could take off some of their clothes. She was kissing him and he lay on top of her and soon she moaned in his mouth. He was fast. (Nice to see old people enjoying themselves.) Privacy's not really my bag so I lay at their feet and wanted to snuggle into their snuggle, and once they stopped moving I took my chance and spooned into their legs. '*Bueno*,' said the young man. 'A little heartbeat at my feet.' The next day the fellow sent the flowers to our hotel room and Marilyn replaced the card with another one before sending the bouquet on to Cantinflas.

Mrs Murray had spent those first days at the hotel making telephone calls. I don't know what was up. I would say she was more emotional than usual and you know how it is with religious people, they turn most vehemently to God when they seem least ready to accept his example. Marilyn understood. She didn't do the God thing but she did do the Mrs Murray thing. In any case, on the third day she rose again, the housekeeper, tripping down the stairs to breakfast with a list of retailers for Marilyn and a small bone for me. She got it from my good friend the bellhop. 'He isn't doing well with that bone, Marilyn,' she whispered after a while.

'No, Mrs Murray. I think he's probably had enough of bones already, in this place. We saw the Rivera murals by candlelight. Aren't they something? I sure wish we could take one home with us.'

'Beyond our budget,' said Mrs Murray.

Remember the bones in Central Park, the buried bones of old Manhattan that came to mind the day I went with Marilyn to see Dr Kris? A similar vision appeared to me as we drove through those beautiful, snow-capped mountains on the way to Toluca, a vision of canine forebears who had died and were buried in the hills. It wasn't a gloomy thought, either: the local enchantments had cancelled the gloom for me, if not the dread, and for the first time I looked at the wonder of the world happening and considered myself party to some of its darker secrets. The car chugged towards the market town, Mrs Murray whispering facts about pots and looms, and Marilyn stroked my coat as she looked into the same mountains and felt like one of the clouds rolling past in the blue sky. Mexico was a place where people and animals still lived together on the streets.

The market was big enough to get lost in. My friends bought tiles and ordered leather-covered chairs, they picked up a bowl painted with flowers, bought baskets and blankets, an Aztec tapestry featuring a reclining god. Most of the items were for delivery, but some of them were carted by Mrs Murray and the driver back to the car while Marilyn sat in dark glasses and a scarf drinking a long soda from a scuffed bottle. I felt like Berganza amidst the hubbub of the market, indeed I did, a good, old scavenging *pícaro*, and I even sneaked some fava beans and licked a dreadful iron spoon covered in gravy. Many of the things they were buying were not to my taste, as they say: all that scalloped furniture! 'Down boy,' said Mrs Murray when I tried to assail a leather bench with my paws as a way of signalling its inelegance. At the edge of a stall selling *patatas bravas*, two perfect Imagist cats – cats out of William Carlos Williams – came padding over the dusty ground and they were street cats, fairly louping with fleas. They snarled. Their mouths were dirty but they spoke well. First one:

> Just smelling
> fish
> makes me so
> hungry.
> They lie on that
> stall
> sweating salt

Then the other:

> My father was
> dozing
> on a Pepsi crate
> behind the
> old hotel.

He woke up
to laundry vans
parked in a row.
Late last night
I saw him
making graves
for all his
tiny broken
threads.

A group of communist friends had us to lunch. They were people Marilyn had known in Connecticut. It appeared Mrs Murray knew some of them, too. Mr Field was a director of the Institute for Pacific Relations and his wife, Nieves, who was lovely and patted me constantly, had once been a model for Rivera. They all talked about Cuba and the waiters kept appearing with more morsels and bottles of champagne. Marilyn put her glass down to me and let me lick up a few mouthfuls.

'Fizzy,' I said. 'Fidel-io.' appearing

The most interesting person on the shopping trip was a man called William Spratling. After a visit to Taxco the next day we ended up with him at his ranch, a place islanded in lush, green banana trees. In the memoir of his father, Jean Renoir tells how the old man, walking with him across a field, would perform a strange dance to avoid stepping on dandelions. Spratling appeared to have the same small habit of carefulness. He had been a professor of architecture at Tulane University and he also knew everything there was to know about the rights of man and the properties of silver. I liked him for the sausages. I liked him as soon as I met him, walking towards us with a cane, kissing Marilyn, his blue eyes glittering from years of charm.

During breakfast he spoke of his old friend, William Faulkner. He said Mr Faulkner was a man with a vision, a man in touch with every happy and bleak part of himself, a true writer, someone who could imagine the world in such a way that nobody who read him could live exactly as they did before. Years ago, in the early days, Mr Spratling had helped Faulkner write a book about Sherwood Anderson, but he preferred to talk about his friend's drinking and shouting days in Hollywood. 'Do you know, Marilyn, Louis B. Mayer had him under contract at Metro? Bill said he couldn't work on the lot and asked if he could work from home. LB said that was fine. Next thing LB hears, Faulkner hasn't been seen for weeks and that's because he was working from home – in Mississippi!'

'That's funny,' said Marilyn.

When someone tells a joke, a great number of Americans have a tendency to say 'that's funny', while Europeans have a tendency to laugh. Marilyn had always been firmly of the latter party, yet in that last stretch before filming began on *Something's Got to Give*, my owner began to slide away from her natural responses. I saw it first in Mexico, perhaps at the exact moment of the Faulkner story, the beginning of her slide towards abstraction, towards a place where all voices sounded like voices from the past. Nothing was new to her. Like a sleepwalker she haunted the daylight hours.

Mr Spratling had put on the first show of Mexican art at the Metropolitan Museum, and it comforted Marilyn, ennobled her, really, to have him show her the best places to buy silverware. He was good fun and his brilliance brought her out of herself. After a large shopping spree in Taxco and the Jardín Borda, the crowd returned to the city and Marilyn was taken on an arranged visit to a local orphanage. Mr Spratling and Mrs Murray took me the short distance to Coyoacán, and the closer I got the more nervous I became, history seeming to bleed from the walls of the buildings and from the sun itself that afternoon. It was as if some old belief, something personal, from the latent quarters of my own past, was coming together as we walked towards a building with towers. Mrs Murray picked me up and she stood in front of the building and wiped a tear from her eye. Mr Spratling spoke and I caught the name 'Mercader', the taste of Paris buns coming powerfully with the thud of memory. This was the house in which Leon Trotsky was killed. Mrs Murray let me down onto the road and I sniffed my way forward and stopped beside the gate, becoming sure I could scent a memory of fur coats lingering on the road, Siberian furs with linings stitched in Manhattan.

I looked at the windows, the dust on the road. Every object has its story and every being has his tale, and Trotsky, well, here was his house and the garden he tended. Inside the house, they would no doubt have his original desk and all the photographs, the inkpot and the dictaphone. But standing there, my head was filled with the power of his example. Wasn't he the god of small things and massive ideas, a cultivator of man's better instincts? That, my friends, is the greatest work of the imagination: not action, but the thought of action. (Trotsky and Shakespeare, I thought, what friends they would have been.*) I glimpsed the garden where

* Thinking about writers always reminded me of Charlie. That time

242

Trotsky must have grown his small lettuces. He showed us all creatures are servants and every creature is master of the servant in himself. I dropped a tear in the dust at Coyoacán, just as Mrs Murray blew her nose and walked back to the car saying the past is always the past, and nothing can change it. I followed her with emotions hot as the sun. 'It is men, Mrs Murray – you hear me? It is men not animals who are guilty of bestiality. It was noted before any of us was born by Plutarch's talking pig.'

'Nice and quiet now, Maf,' she said.

On the way to meet Marilyn, I was imagining how nice it would be to discover oneself in the form of a pottery dog, the kind much admired and much displayed by Mr Spratling. Those pottery dogs were a big deal in Colima culture, staring into the inevitable with their blank eyes and their ears pert for news of a reprieve. As the heat rose and the car pulled to a stop, I found myself wondering if Mr Freud had kept any of those dogs among the funerary ornaments in his famous study. The heat was radiating above the dusty road but I could see Marilyn up ahead. She was sitting on the steps of an old *cantina*, playing with a pretty Mexican girl in bare feet, the two of them laughing and clapping their hands. It began to rain and the rain felt like a great relief in all the dryness. The girls stood up and danced on the porch and the rain made them seem so young.

---

on the ferryboat, when he spoke with Marilyn about politics, I licked his hand and absorbed some lines about Trotsky written by his favourite writer. 'I was excited by this famous figure, the impression he gave of navigation by the great stars, of the highest considerations, of being fit to speak the most human words and universal terms.'

Fourteen

Of all the directors in Hollywood, I have to say George Cukor is the one I liked best. I loved the fact that George was a stylish storyteller but also a glorified interior decorator. Women were not blank canvases to Cukor so much as darling little dolls, waiting to have their dresses put on and their hair set in curlers, ready to have their mouths painted and their spirits tested. He was heartless of course and queer as a week in Tangiers, but George had a fine understanding of female self-consciousness, a never-ending insight not only into how women thought but into how they would like to be thought of. He was the best director of female talent the industry ever produced, a man with personal taste so good it was verging on bad, someone who knew how to furnish and dress a room, never forgetting – while wishing to forget – that he came from good, middle-class Hungarians who simply loved the theatre.

Cukor believed a woman is a project not an animal, a basket of pearls waiting to be strung. She is a girl from nowhere who is ready to be transformed into her greater, imaginary self, who adorns her surroundings and spells drama. He made films the same way he did his house – the most beautiful house in Beverly Hills, which stood like a lavender-scented villa on the

Côte d'Azur – and that meant comfort and discipline and a great depth of lightness. George believed it was the merging of opposites that dignified life, and, out of all his doubts, he had come to be very good at what he did, and quite imperial in Cordell Drive. For people, I've noticed, life's greatest satisfactions are always imperial: they have to involve the crushing of something, especially the crushing of one's smaller or former self. I loved his style. I loved his methods, the way he touched things and made them instantly gracious. Thus, he sat Vivien Leigh on a Regency fauteuil and began to rehearse her for her part in *Gone With the Wind*. Thus, he laid Greta Garbo on a satin bedspread under a painting by Vuillard, and holding her hand as if it were a porcelain bird, showed her how to manage her grief in *Camille*. And thus, again, he summoned Marilyn to an oval room beyond a scented belvedere, to a spot between two Venetian parcel-gilt blackamoors, and stroked her face with the backs of his fingers. They were standing under a painting by Georges Braque of some pears waiting to be eaten. The director told my friend she was a very great artist who would stun the world in *Something's Got to Give*. I just sat on the cold parquet floor and stared at a copper fireplace. I padded outside to let Marilyn get on with airing her worries. I tried to imagine what it would be like to live at George Cukor's house, and decided it would be hard, the kind of hardship endured by the orphan Lazarillo de Tormes, one of the original picaroons, who lived for a short spell with a man who painted tambourines. Lazarillo invented the art of running away.

The swimming pool was silent. Two rather facetious cats were lying on top of a parked car in the driveway, while a third skipped metrically down the edge of a turquoise awning to leap onto the flagstones. She mewled coquettishly and rubbed her shoulder against her cheek. 'All of us endorse your plan,' she said.

> It's clear you love the common man.
> A better democrat we've never met
> At least among the younger set.

The novelist Henry Fielding, friend of my childhood, friend of my childhood friends, once opened a book with the true observation that a good man is a standing example to all his acquaintance. That's to say, goodness is the greatest prompt for emulation, though I find this to be truer of dogs than of other animals. Fielding sets out his handsome theory in *The History of the Adventures of Joseph Andrews, and of His Friend Mr Abraham Adams*. My mother's owner, my own breeder, the Scottish fellow, often came from the tractor with whole passages of Fielding stuck in his head. (He was a fan of epic comedy, the art of the novel, the sport of digression.) Anyway, this business of example – of example's force – works on dogs but rarely on cats. Cats have a strong heart for the burlesque. They remember not the thing itself but the manner of the thing. In this sense they are very modern. When trying to emulate the dogs at Mr Cukor's house, the cats were apt to speak viciously as they skirted the plant-pots, speaking in classical forms without really adding anything to the conversation of the dogs. 'Go down to the pool, and mind your step, please,' the coquettish one said in a state of mental luxury.

> The boys are discussing a Sicilian cheese.
> It was stolen by Labes of Aexone,
> A villainous thug in Aristophanes' day.

The three dogs belonging to Mr Cukor were lounging around the pool discussing the nature of drama. It was often the way with showbusiness dogs, though in my experience canines have a tendency to chase the matter round and round with more vigour than their owners. Not more than Cukor, though, who chased such lore in his sleep. A low painted table stood by the pool bearing two glasses of tequila, their rims glinting in the orange sun, the stone statues of gods and emperors listening among the magnolias. The most talkative dogs were a pair of dachshunds, Amanda and Solo; the third was Sasha, a standard black poodle, seemingly irked, as if the other two had been ganging up on her. Sasha had come from Paris, a gift from Garson Kanin and Ruth Gordon, people who believed, as Sasha did, that movie legend was much more important than the sorts of legend peddled by the hacks of ancient Greece. As you know, I'm a dedicated student of non-human behaviour, and I'd say the two dachshunds, who were born somewhere in the Valley, were getting off on the fact they could be more high-minded than the self-important European, Little Miss Boulevard Raspail. 'Listen, dude, you gotta listen . . .'

'A look-eh. We 'ave a veesitor.'

The dogs turned their heads as I came down the steps feeling embarrassed that I had to take each step individually. I couldn't bound down like some gasping husky to meet them at the bottom. (We all have our handicaps.) The French one came forward. 'A veesitor, indeed-eh. Are you Marilyn's dog-eh?'

'Aye. That's me,' I said.

'Ee says, "aye". Scottish, no?' She turned and took two pretty steps to the pool, where she dropped a paw into the water and sighed. 'Scottish.' She turned. 'Did you know-eh

247

that nice animal – what's him? Greyfriars Bobby? Is in Edinburgh, no?'

'Grey Fired Who?' said Solo.

'Bobby, you eediot. I mean the dog who stayed close to the old man. The Disney film.'

'I didn't know him personally, I'm afraid,' I said. But I loved her for asking and was nearly dumb with admiration.

'A great story-eh. It makes Lassie look like an 'uman being. I'm not kidding.' I leapt up on a canvas-covered pool chair to watch them. It felt as if Sasha was getting her own back for something said earlier.

'Far out man,' said Solo. 'I was just telling Sasha here that justice is the name of the game.'

'He was trying to tell me,' she said. 'Failing-eh.'

'Doin' it, dude. Not tryin'.'

Sasha shook her head in a contemptuous way and looked at me as if I might instantly understand how juvenile they were. 'They're Californians,' she said. 'What could you expect-eh? They don't know 'ow to appreciate their own culture so they . . . do what? They quote Aristophanes all day.'

'Not true, man. We're cool with movies.'

She rolled her eyes. 'He was bred by two girls who worked at the City Lights Bookstore. You know the one I'm talking about-eh? In San Francisco? The girls came to live in Sherman Oaks and started breeding dachshunds. Listen to the way they talk-eh.'

'I like accents,' I said. 'I lived in Sherman Oaks for a while, with Mrs Gurdin. She deals in English dogs. You know her?'

'Oh everybody knows her,' said Amanda. 'Drives around in that big-ass van, dogs hanging out the windows? She's a little hopped-up. She's Russian, right? And she's got that paranoid husband who's always running his car off the road. Jesus. I mean, *Jesus*. You started in that house and now you're with Marilyn in Brentwood?'

'There was a lot of New York in between.'

'Ah, New York,' said Solo. 'I wish we could go to New York some time. That would be cool. Mr Cukor grew up there.'

'They have nice accents in New York,' I said. 'You guys have nice accents.'

'That's not an accent-eh,' said Sasha. 'It's an echo of stupidity.'

'Oh, pipe down, sister,' said Amanda. She looked at me with a degree of borrowed ease. 'She's just sore because Mr Cukor has gone and cast a dog – not her – in the new movie. She's in a rage.'

'I am not-eh,' said Sasha. 'The part, it ees not right for me. I don't jump-eh. I don't do tricks. Never 'ave.'

'We were talking about *Wasps*,' continued Amanda. 'You know that cool comedy? Did you have that?'

'Yes,' I said. 'A guy in England who used to come to visit was a critic. Cyril Connolly?' The guys shook their heads. 'He came to lunch all the time. He gave me a whole lot of the Greek stuff.'

'Yeah, man,' said Amanda. 'The play gives us something to chew on. Labes commits a felony. He might be a scoundrel, who knows? But man's vanity is the great destroyer of nations. That's what the play proves.'

'No, Mrs Dog-eh,' said Sasha. 'Bombs are the things which destroy nations. 'Aven't you heard this?'

'No they don't,' I said. 'I mean, they could. But the thought of bombs preserves nations. The thought of bombs keeps nations from exercising too much vanity.'

'We'll see about that,' said Sasha.

We could hear laughter through the trees, it came from the house and was getting closer. It was the humans. They would soon arrive to get their drinks. Sasha did a little French thing in her throat, somewhere between a growl and a whimper, full of contempt. 'The movies is where drama comes good-eh.'

'What do you mean, dude? Comes good?'

'Where the moral life is clarified-eh. I say it is the movies that make people see the meaning of friendship, the truth of love, the price of ambition. Movies, yes. We are in the right world, brothers and sisters.'

I thought of making a case for the novel, but I was young then. I merely smiled with pleasure at the spectacle of her enthusiasm.

'It is movies, little dog. Or television? I offer you Rin Tin Tin. What about Lassie-eh or the Greyfriars Bobby? My favourite is Toto, whose philosophical silence in *The Wizard of Oz* made 'uman wishes seem truly absurd, no? In that movie? I swear to God-eh. Toto stole the show with 'er thoughts alone.'

'You crack me up, Sasha,' said Solo. 'She's comparing herself to the movie greats. You know why: because she wants to be one of them.' Things went quiet for a moment and I heard footsteps.

'You know Toto was in one of Mr Cukor's movies?' Sasha whispered. 'She was in *The Women*.'

'I just gathered that,' I said. 'Up in the house while they were talking. I saw a photograph.'

'She *shone*,' said Sasha.

*

A few weeks later, one afternoon, I watched Marilyn pack the car at Fifth Helena Drive. She had errands in Palm Springs. That day, something made me imagine that she was changing into a version of the girl she once was. Her hair was pale and her skin beautifully clear; it was as if the world had bleached her with attention. We drove up Highway 10 and it might have appeared that she was nobody. We didn't feel like two creatures making for the desert, but rather like a pair of porpoises aiming for some blue and distant ocean, there to swim and turn and ride the great currents. Marilyn had always been political, but after Mexico it was her habit to see everything in political terms, everything from her face to her future. She was abstracted, as I said, unfocused, but that seemed to make her simpler, a blossoming girl.

She spoke to me over those hundred miles or so like someone sending her consciousness out over the land, over the trailer parks and the hamburger joints, to reach the little motels, their curtains closed. 'There's nothing wrong with sex,' she said. It would be nice, she thought, just to be a woman, a woman like any other, with talents to inhabit and share. Marilyn was sure she could become natural. One time in New York, she said that the best way for her to find herself was to prove to herself that she was an actress, but driving into the golden dusk that evening she changed her mind. 'I am trying to prove to myself I am a person,' she said. 'Then maybe I'll be able to convince myself I am an actress.'

She gave me half a turkey sandwich. It smelled of expectation and that's the nicest smell of all. We stopped next to a bowling alley. Marilyn was thinking about Dr Greenson, how he reminded her of a kind man who was a teacher at Van Nuys High. He was the same type: the sort of person you could trust with your uncertainties. The teacher once told her she could do anything in the world if only she put her mind to it. She tapped my nose and I barked with love. 'But I put my mind into tight sweaters instead,' she said. There was no top on the car and we could sit back feeling cool. The entrance to the Coachella Bowl was shaped like a pyramid; the boys in their leather jackets were passing round cigarettes at the door. I wanted to say I knew those kids, I knew their type, and saw that they would never know how free they were in their youth until their youth was over. I wanted to tell her about the young people in Dallas, the ones who took me to the hillside when she had to go off on the plane and divorce Arthur. I think she would have liked them, those kids jousting with the future. I lay on her lap. I wondered if Raymond had been made grocery clerk again this summer, or was he off with the Marines? Marilyn leaned her head back and the sky was mysterious, just like the sky in Texas as we waited for signs. She fell asleep and I thought it was probably the pills. I liked the sky anyhow, the thought of those chimps, those dogs, going in search of knowledge and making the universe a safer place to be. In one of his letters, Freud wrote that when next to his dog he often found himself humming the Octavio aria from *Don Juan*, about the bonds of friendship. 'The simplicity of life free from the conflicts of civilisation that are so hard to endure,' he writes. 'There is a feeling of undeniably belonging together.'

The hospital was a white building at the edge of the desert in Palm Springs. We weren't there for long, it was another stop-off on the way to Frank's, but looking over the emptiness to the San Jacinto Mountains made Marilyn think of those desert locations on *The Misfits*. It was a thought that made her cry and she did so quietly, like a child weeping at something they knew they could never change. But I'm sure the thought of Mr Gable also gave her strength for what she was about to do. She lowered the rearview mirror and used a tissue to wipe away her lipstick. She wanted to be immaculate. Lifting an envelope from the dashboard she stepped out of the car, wet her finger and held it up to the non-breeze. 'We're in the *agua caliente*,' she said cheerfully. I stood up with my paws on the steering wheel. I watched her walking over that dusty car park to the white building, every step an effort that could break your heart when you saw how beautiful she was and how massive the land around her. I believe she simply handed the letter to the receptionist. On the way back to the car she would stop and look into the distance, take a step, then stop again.

Dear Doctors,
A man in your care named Mr Gifford has been calling my home in Los Angeles claiming to be my father. Please ask the gentleman to refrain from calling me and if he has any specific concerns they should be addressed to my lawyer, Mr Milton Rudin.
    Sincerely yours,
    Marilyn Monroe

An hour later we arrived at Frank's. 'You know what, baby. Fuck the Actors Studio. Fuck Marlon Brando. And fuck Peter Lawford. Brother-in-Lawford my ass. He's a no-good, cheap hustler and a low-down English fag.'

On account of the Kennedys' bad treatment of him, Mr Sinatra was so angry he pushed a drinks trolley loaded with crystal glasses through some open patio doors. The glasses came to grief on a fat desert rock, the kind of rock that was everywhere at Rancho Mirage, dotted between a hundred cactuses. (It was one of the only things Frank had in common with Trotsky: they both loved cactuses.) The compound was on the seventeenth fairway of the local golf and country club, which gave the dry air an extra layer of boredom. When Sinatra was angry at someone he would rage at their entire being. 'Lawford is a faggot,' he repeated. 'You know his mother used to dress him up in little girl clothes? And now he's Jack's bagman on the West Coast. Big deal! Big deal! I'll tell ya honey, that boy's doomed.'

He was walking up and down the room kicking chairs out of the way. He looked at her. He brought down his fist on the polished lid of a grand piano. 'The fuckin' scumbag. The louse!'

'Frank.'

'Don't Frank me! Don't fucking Frank me!'

'Peter wouldn't . . .'

'He would. The jerk. He would. He did. The fucking creep. He did it.'

'I'm sure Jack wanted . . .'

'He did it. Don't Jack me! Don't fucking Jack me. I swear to God. I'll kill somebody.'

'Frank.'

'Fuck you! Fuck all of you. Fuck Lawford. Fuck Pat. Fuck the President. Fuck his cheap brother, his good-for-nothing sneak of a brother. Fuck them. And fuck you. And fuck Bing Crosby! The President wants to come to fucking Palm Springs. He wants to be over *there*? He was my friend! He actually wants to be at Crosby's? Shmucks. You know something, I feel sorry for them. I feel sorry for all of you. Two-bit hustlers and fucking sneaks. I'll tell you. You listening to me? Peter Lawford is doomed. I built a motherfucking helipad out there. You see it? You can walk over there. You want to see it? A helipad. A motherfucking helipad for Jack Kennedy.'

'He knows . . .'

'He knows? He motherfucking knows what? Don't tell me what he knows. Don't do it. Don't fucking do it. The President. I swear to God I'm going to kill somebody. The fink. You know what? I'm sorry for every one of you. I built a motherfucking HELIPAD!'

Marilyn stood biting her thumbnail. George the valet was staying out of the way, working with a broom in the kitchen in his white jacket. He had seen it many times before, the way the Kennedys could make Frank's self-assurance crumble. I wanted to go over to George and tell him all the places I'd been since I last saw him in Nimes Road, about New York, the parties, the people, and the trip to Mexico. All the adventures. I wanted to quote from *The Brothers Karamazov*. 'It's possible that there are no masters and no servants, George,' I wanted to say. 'But let me be the servant of my servants, and let me be to them what they are to me.*' I wanted to say this to George but he had stopped up his ears. You couldn't blame him because Frank had gone nuclear. I licked his hand and George pulled his mouth up into a frown.

'You know what? You're all sick people. Just sick people with no class. I did their campaign song. I organised fundraisers. Fundraisers! I ran their convention. *Ran it*. Booked everybody. Sang! I got every goddamn star in

* So says the Elder Zosima. He thinks God is always at home.

Hollywood to come out that night. I gave him goddamn *Chicago*. Jesus. *Bing Crosby is a fucking Republican!*'

Frank threw down a bourbon glass and put his hand over his heart. 'I'm going to have a fuckin' stroke,' he said. 'This is what you've all done. I'm gonna die right now on this goddamn rug. What – they're avoiding me? I'm some kind of gangster, all of a sudden?'

Marilyn lifted me up as if to protect me. There was a bottle on the breakfast bar and she poured from it into a fresh glass. 'Here, Frank,' she said. 'Why don't you take this?' He reached out blindly and took it like someone in a trance.

'What am I?' he asked. 'Some phoney? Some dweeb in the movie business, huh? Some nightclub shmuck? They think I can win the election for them and then . . . what? They embarrass me? They dump me? They make me lose face, huh? I'm what, an asshole to them? I'm some dago to them? Ol' Frankie-boy, huh. What am I, the loser?'

'You're not any kind of loser, honey,' said Marilyn. 'Frank. They're politicians.'

'FUCK THEM!' he screamed. He gulped from the glass and put his face up close to our faces. 'I gave you that little dog. I gave everybody everything. That's my problem. I gave everybody too much.' I could feel her hands trembling round my ribs.

'It was all a gift to yourself,' I said. 'That's the kind of giver you are. Leave her alone.'

Frank went on raging and spilling his guts, just like a man, just like a spoiled man. Complaining is an art that some men practise with self-annihilating zeal. Every word seems to make them smaller, greyer, sadder, when silence might serve them like medicine. Frank cut himself off from all he loved and cared about so as to express the full volume and crudity of his anger.

Grrrrrrrr.

'That dog has a throat problem. Take him to the damn vet!'

I looked up at him. 'You're an idiot, Frank.'

'Tell him to stop looking at me. I'll crush your head, you little fuck.'

I jumped out of my owner's arms and felt sorry for a moment that I ever left Scotland. Who was I, to guard an unhappy actress? Who were these people anyway, who could invent life on the screen but couldn't begin to live their own lives? I ran to the back of the living room and deposited a small puddle of pee onto an orange Hessian rug. I forgot to say that the Sinatra compound was unforgivably orange. Dogs can't quite see that colour, but Frank's mind was full of orange and the rage of orange and I picked that up. All the pleasures of interior decoration go into reverse when you find yourself, even in your imagination, in a very orange place: the walls were orange-verging-on-peach and the sofa was orange-verging-on-brown, while the paintings were as orange as a muggy evening in Madras and the carpet was dangerous orange, like the spurting of Mount Etna. I could feel every one of the tones. I am a dog of indigo moods, of cornflower hues, so for me the large rooms at Rancho Mirage were a horror at the top end of the scale. Sinatra once said that orange is the happiest colour, but his hysterical use of it made you realise that he lived in something close to a perpetual nervous breakdown. He liked orange and he liked red, the colours of alarm.

*

Marilyn always had a book in her handbag. She was always on the way to a discovery, to a large recognition that would change everything. And I suppose that kind of hope was the story of our journey. Good human relationships depend on an instinct for tolerating and indeed protecting other people's illusions: once you start picking them apart, taking down their defences, reducing their plan for survival, making them smaller in their own eyes, the relationship is as dead and gone as the Great Auk.* Marilyn might have spent her life searching for someone with the imagination to love her, and now she was faced with the ruination of all those hopes, Sinatra looking at her with pure hatred, saying, 'You're so damn stupid, Norma Jeane. You know that? You and Lawford and the President – you're all nothing. You hear me? *Nothing*.'

I went to Marilyn at the patio doors. She was weeping with a glass held against her chest and I rubbed against her legs. I could feel her knees trembling as she watched Frank dragging clothes from one of the guest rooms out to the pool area, golfing clothes and swimming togs that belonged to the Lawfords. He was shouting about calls made to Atlanta during the election and favours done for Joseph Kennedy. 'See this, Norma Jeane? See this, you two-bit whore,' he shouted at the patio doors, pointing to the bundle of clothes. He pulled out a Zippo and in two seconds there were flames rising by the pool side. Marilyn looked over as if the fire was a perfectly ordinary thing. I started barking and

---

* I am no academic, but I feel there is a hole in the great universities. Why is there no Faculty of Extinction? It is a subject of interest to man and beast, or maybe, like most creatures, I merely reveal myself to be a thing of my own time.

running in circles, while Frank, still shouting about loyalty and Washington, came out of other guest rooms bearing kids' hats, towels, and sneakers. Eventually the fire rose and threatened one of the sun-loungers, at which point Frank, now levitating with rage, kicked all the burning Lawford belongings into the swimming pool. The flames floated for a while and Frank stomped through the room, slamming doors and cursing the day he ever came to Palm Springs. Marilyn and I just stood at the patio doors, the smoke going up like ghosts. We walked out to the pool and my owner put her feet into the water and drank her champagne, the burnt clothes floating across the blue pool, like land masses on a charred map. We stared at them. It seemed like a billion years had just gone by in Frank Sinatra's pool, the dark continents floating to the centre and America, a small pair of bikini bottoms with strings scorched and trailing, drifted into place as the compound lights suddenly went out and it was dark.

Fifteen

We do not go to bed worthless and wake up wise, but we hope the night may bring some colour to our moral travels. Lying with Marilyn in her bedroom in Fifth Helena Drive, the bougainvillea would often seem to tremble in the darkness outside the window, the moon pulling at our blood as we dreamed. But she mostly slept alone. Into the night she would look at album sleeves or speak lines to herself, her eyes just dots of white in the dark and humid room. If I barked, even once, she plopped me outside the bedroom and closed the door. I would stand there quoting Euripides and scratching on the wood, mewling like a cat. 'One loyal friend is worth ten thousand relatives.'

The stuff from Mexico still lay around the house in cardboard boxes. One night it was unseasonably cool when Marilyn finally got to sleep, the curtains billowing from the window and the sound of a dog barking in San Vicente Boulevard. 'Shhh,' I said. 'She'll put me out.' She had taken sleeping tablets and she dreamed of Pierre Salinger. It was a press conference she had seen on television, Salinger holding the White House rabbit Zsa Zsa by the ears, telling the laughing reporters that the rabbit was sent to young Caroline Kennedy by a Pittsburgh magician. Zsa Zsa came with a horn and a beer opener. 'Mr Secretary,' comes the question. 'Do you know that this rabbit is a lush?'

'All I know about Zsa Zsa,' said Salinger, 'is that she's supposed to be able to play the first five bars of "The Star-Spangled Banner" on a toy trumpet.'

'Could we have the rabbit come over here and run through a couple of numbers for us?'

'I can ask her,' said Salinger.

Then it was Khrushchev. In her dream he looked like the producer Joe Schenck. The Soviet wanted more than anything to visit Disneyland. He said he would release the nuclear rockets if they stopped him from meeting Mickey the Mouse and Pluto the dog. Marilyn wanted to speak about Shostakovich and he wanted to speak about the space animals. He boasted about Laika and then about Belka and Strelka, saying the pupniks would honour the Soviet Union for a thousand years. Marilyn then dreamed the face of Mrs Kennedy cradling Pushinka, Strelka's pup, a present to her daughter from the Russian leader. She held the pup in her arms and it looked up at her. Marilyn stood by herself in a kind of desert, next to a hospital, or was it a fortified house in Coyoacán? In a garden, she saw a man tending his rabbits and cuddling them. The man turned around and smiled for the camera, just as the rabbit opened its mouth. 'It is as well that the potentialities of art', the rabbit said, 'are as inexhaustible as life itself, for those of us who do not simply adhere to the false beauties and vain art of the ruling class may come to believe that art is much richer than life, shedding a variety of light on what it has meant to be together in the world.'

For *Something's Got to Give*, Mr Cukor got the set-builders at Fox to make a replica of his house on Cordell Drive. It was the same right down to the Roman statues and the shuttered windows, the tables by the swimming pool and the jacaranda. As I told you some time ago, dogs don't have a natural capacity to separate fact from fiction – we only learn by attending to people's neuroses – yet the new version of Cukor's house really tested my faith in the power of actuality. In the end, even the dogs came to feel the house on Stage 14 was more Cukor's house than Cukor's house. It was more of a home and less of a stage set, except that the roof of the make-believe house reached upwards from the fake trees and the fake statues to end not in the starry skies of California but in a crowded grid of hot lights and cables. We tried to ignore that.

'Oh look. It's Hopalong Oedipus.'

'Funny, Dino. That's very funny.'

Wally Cox had injured his leg so his voice was even punier than usual. Dean Martin liked to rib him about his smart intellectual friends. 'Hey, Wally,' he said. 'You still friends with all them shrinks? Do you think they'd do me a deal? I need a whole truck-load of 'em over here. Will they do me a deal, Charlie?'

'That's funny, Dino.'

'Tell them I'm a golf bum from Steubenville, Ohio. Do they do cheap rates for that?'

'They'd probably charge you more, Dino,' said Mr Cukor crossing from the pool and clapping his male lead on the shoulder.

'That's sick, George. It's Nutsville in here.'

'You think this is Nutsville? You should see the laughs they're having in the old country.'

'In Italy?'

'That's right, Dino. On the set of *Cleopatra*. They've gone thirty million dollars over budget.' I wondered if that nice Roddy McDowall might be enjoying himself over there. I'm sure he likes a bit of chaos. Mr Martin grinned and turned to Mr Cox.

'Hey, Wally. Is that where all the shrinks are at? The expensive New York guys? They all in Cinecittà helping Liz with her make-up?'

'Funny.'*

Mr Martin could talk about make-up. His face was a brown olive ripening on the ancient coast of Liguria. 'Don't talk to me about budgets, Harvey,' he said in the direction of Mr Cukor. 'I got seven children. Ask Wally. Seven kids. I spend more on milk than I do on bourbon, Clyde. That's no joke. And Hopalong here, he won't give me one of his fancy shrinks. Isn't that just the meanest thing you've ever heard?'

Marilyn had flown Mrs Strasberg over from the East Coast to help her with her lines. But my owner didn't come to the sound stage most days, feeling sick, feeling low, and when she did come she was wired, I'd say, feeling anxious one minute and rebellious the next. Since coming back to LA, Marilyn's panic about who she was had become who she was. I am probably too ignorant of normality to notice when things are getting beyond repair. But Marilyn was off the hook during that last film, no doubt about it. Mr Levathes

---

* Mr Cox was a model of human freedom, at least of human freedom as it was understood by Jean-Paul Sartre. He was free to be and not to be, and, in the end, like Mr Hemingway and others, he proved his existence by ending it.

the studio lizard was always popping his head round the door of her bungalow and sticking out his tongue. 'You good for work today, Marilyn dear?' I wanted to bite him and I wanted to pee in his golf cart. One day I heard him speaking with an associate producer behind the set. He said, 'She's out of control but she's still bankable. Greenson says he can probably pull her though.' Sometimes I would just wander round the set looking for adventure and pestering the electricians for scraps of their sandwiches. Dean Martin was often to be found in the little road outside the sound stage, swinging his golf club and smoking. Mr Cukor had shot around Marilyn for weeks and now there was nothing to do but sit and wait for her. He brought his dog Sasha to the set in the hope it would calm his nerves. He lost sight of the dog in all the annoyances, but soon Sasha and I were outside the sound stage and running over the road to investigate the snacks situation. We ran past a phoney cowboy saloon bar, then slowed down near the front office, where Sasha nodded up at the windows. 'They will fire her, little dog. Listen to me, the studio will fire her soon.'

'They wouldn't,' I said. I was shocked. I was no longer able to see anything clearly.

'Soon. They will do it.'*

It was a very hot day and the lot was silent. 'People have rights,' I said. 'The workers have rights.'

'They also have duties-eh,' said Sasha, licking one of her paws and tapping the ground. 'They have a duty to turn up and twinkle.'

* I suddenly understood why Jean Renoir called this place 16th Century Fox.

'So you think they will fire her?'

'I heard them. They will do it. She is threatening to go to New York-eh, next week-eh, to sing at Kennedy's birthday party.'

'Aye. That's right. I heard Mrs Murray talking about it on the telephone.'

'At Madison Square Garden, *oui*?'

'Right.'

'If she does it-eh, they will fire her.'

'They'll fire her? They'll *poind her gear*?'

'Is a funny way of putting it, no?

'Robert Burns,' I said. 'You know his poem "The Twa Dogs"?'

'I never had that.'

'Caesar and Luath. The two dogs. The poet records their discussion about the behaviour of evil landlords.'*

We rounded a corner at the end of the road and saw the open doors of the refectory. We stopped and Sasha turned to me with a French look of sadness. She licked my ear. 'She is lost,' said Sasha.

'No,' I said. 'She is just beginning. It is her thirty-sixth birthday soon. We went to Mexico and found items for her new house: she is smart and political. In Mexico she was like a new person.'

'They are always being new,' said Sasha. 'And yet they are always being the same.'

* It was the favourite poem of my breeder, Mrs Duff. In her political heyday, she would often copy out the lines and send them to government officials. She imagined it might take the innocence of dogs to put them straight.

A cat came out of the refectory, his whiskers damp with milk. Two carpenters walked between us with a length of coloured glass and for a dazzling moment we all seemed like figures in a stained-glass panel. I thought of Duncan Grant's favourite panel, William Morris's *Sir Tristan is Recognised by Isolde the Fair's Dog*. It was exactly two years since those easy days in the garden at Charleston, and it was a different sun that shone down on the bleached pavements of 20th Century Fox.

The milky-faced cat was no Tristan, but I was reconciled to his fame. Sasha was not. 'You know that's Orangey over there-eh?' she whispered. 'He won a Patsy for *Breakfast at Tiffany's*.'

'He got a statue?'

'*Oui*,' said Sasha. 'His second one.'

'How lovely,' I said. 'He must be very talented.'

'I think he over-acts,' said Sasha. 'He can only play one part – himself.'

'Ah, well.'

'You try to be too nice, Maf. *Mon Dieu*. Once you start believing in cats, it's time to give up!'

'No, Sasha,' I said. 'We never give up.' I stomped my paw. 'We move on. New adventures. New people. More snacks.'

'Snacks, yes!' said Sasha. She looked up and sneered at Orangey. 'Monsieur,' she said. 'I see you are content to be a bourgeois pig. Look at this milk. They give you extra at the commissary, no?'

Orangey just smiled. I wondered whether cats weren't really the most intelligent of creatures. Sufficient unto themselves, they turned solitude into a great and sustaining thing, while dogs and men, in order to be happy, needed

266

each other. The famous cat seemed a paragon of poise and self-awareness, licking his ginger moustache, taking several gentle steps across the road while quoting William Butler Yeats. 'Minnaloushe creeps through the grass,' he said,

> alone, important and wise,
> and lifts to the changing moon
> his changing eyes.

A while later we were retrieved from the kitchens by a second assistant director who was swearing. He intended to be a great *auteur* one day and didn't care for chasing a couple of mutts around the lot for an hour. Back on set, Marilyn was available for work. The big news now was not Marilyn's lateness or Marilyn's absence but the horrific unprofessionalism being displayed by the dog Tippy, who was supposed to recognise Marilyn's character when she returns from a desert island. I might be alone in thinking *Something's Got to Give* was quite a nice script; admittedly, it was not *The Brothers Karamazov*, but it was perfectly minxy and funny and not without style. Marilyn hated it, though, and I guess she felt a failure coming back to that after *Anna Christie* and the Trillings and her young publishing friend Charlie, the intelligent beings of New York.

But if it's prima donna you want, see under: Tippy. The willing Marilyn, despite a temperature of 101, was platinum and smiling by the pool, trying take after take, but the outrageous Tippy just wouldn't perform. 'I told you-eh,' said Sasha. 'She is not right for the part. This dog has no feeling for the character. *Phoof*. Mr Cukor was smitten by her bright coat – always the *décor*. He thinks of the *décor* before he thinks about her talent.'

'She is pretty bad. They're on the twenty-third take.'

'Ego,' said Sasha. 'I'm afraid it is just the ego. Toto would never have behaved like this.'

'Sasha, Toto was the character in *The Wizard of Oz*. The dog's real name was Terry.'

'It doesn't matter.'

I pawed the ground. 'I think it does matter,' I said.

Sasha wasn't listening to me. 'Look at this one,' she said. 'This Tippy, how she snaps at the trainer. Tsk. Tsk. What a waste of fur.'

Playing Ellen, my owner just put down her little United Airlines bag and knelt before the dog. The motivation was pretty simple: the dog hadn't seen Ellen in five years and she recognised her, even though her children in the pool did not. But Tippy kept missing her cue and she refused to invest in the scene. 'I wonder what Lee Strasberg would say about *her*,' I said to an obviously glowing and vindicated Sasha.

'Come on. Come on. Speak boy! Speak!' said the trainer, with Cukor shaking his head.

Marilyn laughed. She seemed pleased to know someone else was fluffing their lines. Cukor's patience was frayed to nothing. It was obvious he felt humiliated by Marilyn's absences, and now he felt cursed by Tippy, the dog resting its head vacantly on his star's shoulder and lolling its useless tongue, while the hours rolled past. 'Some animals-eh, they simply don't have the guts,' said Sasha. 'They don't know how to *give enough*, you know-eh?'

'Aye,' I said. 'It's a shame.'

'No, it is shameful,' said Sasha. 'The dog has no bravery. No heart.'

Cukor finally got a take he could use and Tippy wandered

over to our water bowls without an ounce of embarrassment.

'How was it?

'Wonderful,' I said. 'You really carried the mood of the scene. Beautiful piece of work, that.'

'Inspired,' said Sasha. 'The whole thing depended on a certain restraint, no? And you had that.'

'Thanks guys,' said Tippy. 'It took a few goes, but what the hell? It's worth holding out for it, right? It's worth holding out for The One. I based the whole thing on *The Two Gentleman of Verona*. You know Launce's dog, Crab, the one not shedding tears or saying a word? Yeah, man. It was heavily based on Crab and I think I nailed it. I really worked through the emotions. It started with thoughts of rain. I remember rain on the roof of the kennels the night my grandmother died. I knew rain was the key. It was all in the silence. I just had to get back to that and I remembered Launce's lines.'

'Bravo,' I said. 'It worked wonders.'

'In the scene-eh,' said Sasha. 'The motivation was beautiful. You might win a Patsy.'

'Oh, don't, guys,' said Tippy. 'I just can't, you know, I can't allow myself to think about that.'

Next time we looked over, Marilyn was on one of the sun loungers having each of her sinuses checked by the studio doctor. Paula Strasberg was at her side in a black cape, whispering into her ear. Whitey Snyder was hovering with a lip brush. Pat Newcomb was there with a frown and a sheaf of telegrams from New York. And towering over us all was the simulacrum of Cukor's house, the house with the white shutters. Marilyn caught my eye. She opened her mouth to say something but nothing came, and I felt she might be looking for a distraction that could replace the many distractions in her immediate circle. There were always phone calls to Dr Greenson, and this day he turned up on the set and we stood outside with him waiting for the car. He was arguing the studio's case. 'Maybe it's just me,' he said. 'I'm just being me.' Marilyn looked him in the eye.

'I was once me,' she said.

'We're working on that.'

'Good news,' she said.

In the society of the future, Trotsky wrote, all art would dissolve into life. That is how the world would know good philosophy had triumphed. No need for dancers and painters and writers and actors: everyone would become part of a great living mural of talent and harmony. Ever since I bounded from the gate of the farm in Aviemore and jigged down the road in Walter Higgens's van, I know that I had been looking for the great operatic moment, the supreme fiction, a place where politics and art would show themselves united however average the day. We didn't know much but we knew one thing, that earth is so constituted that heaven could never better it.

You find things out. Pups ask me what happens in life and I say you find things out. That day back in my youth, when Mrs Bell went down to the wine cellar and struck a match for one of her Gauloises and asked me to swipe out the flame with my paw, I think I was too young to work out that she must have been thinking about her dead sister. (Virginia had trained each of her dogs to perform the same trick for her.) During that day's lunch at Charleston, Mr Connolly's mentioning of Virginia had brought Vanessa up short, confronting her, all of a sudden, with echoes and portents. And something of the same atmosphere filled the limousine that took us away from Pico Boulevard the last time I was on the set of *Something's Got to Give*. Marilyn told her driver to give everybody the slip and head for the freeway. 'Take us to Forest Lawn, Rudy,' she said. 'I feel like walking. You know how you sometimes want to just walk and walk and get everybody's worries out of your hair?' The car was a neat refrigerator, a perfect place to be if you're going to live in California. A book about Mexican gardens sat under the rear window.

And so to Glendale, to the other side of Griffith Park from where I'd started my Los Angeles life, to watch the light fading over the San Fernando Valley. Rudy parked at the gates and I walked up Memorial Drive with Marilyn, noting how the names of all the roads and lanes made the cemetery sound like the regions of the moon. The Vale of Peace, The Court of Reflections, Morning Light, The Garden of Victory. By the time we reached the part of the hill she was looking for, I had worked out that this was the place people's remains came when they died. The fallen eucalyptus leaves crackled as we walked over them. I sniffed the ground and had a pee. Marilyn took a slip of paper out of her purse: in pencil, in her own hand, it simply said, 'Murmuring Trees, Lot 6739'.

The breeze at Forest Lawn journeyed visibly over the graves, taking light and shadow with it as it made its way up the hill. And the graves appeared to respond to us, a woman and her dog out for a stroll in the early part of a summer evening. What a fund of consciousness there was in that silent park. My owner sat down on the grass at the top of Murmuring Trees and lit a joint given to her by one of the make-up assistants back at the studio. She crossed her ankles and blew out smoke.

We saw God's Acre. The Old North Church. The Court of Valour. I suppose the names were meant to seem restful, and yet, from where we sat, the place teemed with anxiety about God's absence. (He is never at home.) The lanes were meant for everlasting hope, and since I've got such respect for the made-up, the invented, the seriously confected, why not celebrate God as totem of the great fabular instinct? Why not indeed. Sitting on the grass at Forest Lawn, I finally believed in people's belief in God: he may not be supreme, or even particularly animated, but he must have at least as much reality as Snoopy or Fatty Arbuckle.

There wasn't a spot of rain at Forest Lawn, which made me wonder why the lawn stayed so lawn-like, given the temperature and the wind that came from the mountains. We were both on the same level, down on the lawn and happy to be with each other. Marilyn had her funny cigarette and she began speaking again the way Emma Bovary spoke to her dog, Djali, as if it were an act of faith to believe in a dog's silence. She was talking about the little girl who was a friend of hers at school, a year older than her and the most talkative girl in the class. Alice was a person of the future: her blue almond eyes and her black hair were made for love, the tinder in her quiet voice always ready to catch fire and burn up the great world. She was an ordinary Los Angeles girl whose mother worked as a cutter for Consolidated Film. 'I guess she was always laughing,' said Marilyn. 'One of those girls you think's gonna make life easier for everybody, just by laughing all the time.' My fated companion blew out the smoke and pinched her tongue. 'Dr Kris once told me about a letter she got from Anna Freud,' she said. 'I distinctly remember a phrase Kris quoted from it: "One never really loses a father if he was good enough." '

Marilyn stared into the valley. Animals who avoid death are also avoiding Darwin. I knew that perfectly well. What was that thing Mr Connolly said in his cups? Yes. 'Life is a maze in which we take the wrong turning before we have learned to walk.' Very good. (And four legs are better than two if wrong turnings are what you're about.) I have to admit there was plenty of Darwin for me to pick up along the way, but I didn't like the way it sniffed of everything dying. What is evolution, after all, but the tale of our ultimate extinction? I chose to live my adventures and examine them only where it might prove entertaining to myself and others. Later I understood that the whole game is a struggle for survival. Look at those graves going down the slope at Forest Lawn, each one standing for a different attempt at endurance, a signature stab at permanence that ends here with a small iron lozenge glinting in the sun. You know what Charles Darwin was reading as he sailed on the *Beagle*? He was reading *Paradise Lost*, the great scientist finding on the cusp of his discoveries that our lives are spent not quite living in the garden but trying to remember it. I had one of my little visions, looking into the haze of the San Fernando Valley. At first I saw all the buildings and freeways stripped away to reveal the bare beanfields, then I saw the buildings stack up again and fall in some future quake.

Marilyn took out a compact case and brushed her eyebrows. She popped a couple of pills. 'I feel this is going to be a good summer for us, Maf,' she said. 'When we get this lousy picture finished, we'll go back to New York.' I wagged my tail and paddled into her lap, licking her hands that weren't so smooth any more. I think she was stoned as she giggled and got to her feet. We walked down the grass and she stopped to look at some recent plates under the trees. 'Beloved Husband and Father, Edwin M. Dawson, 1903–1958.' A few steps along: 'Irene L. Nunnally, Beloved Wife and Mother, 1904–1960.' We walked down to the older section, past a multitude of ordinary graves, our shadows reaching ahead of us. Marilyn took out the slip of paper again and looked at the number written down. Eventually we came to the place she wanted:

ALICE TUTTLE
BELOVED DAUGHTER, 1925–1937
'OUR BABY'

'She was my best friend,' said Marilyn. She spent a while stroking the lettering on the plaque, the same finger going round each word as if she meant to inscribe something personal into its iron law. She spoke to the grave. 'It was asthma,' she said. 'It just came on. Then it was all over.' Marilyn said she had meant to bring flowers but she didn't have any and she touched the plaque and she touched her mouth before fishing in her clutch bag and placing ten dollars in a small glass vase covered in dust. The grass seemed very green, like studio grass, but the breeze was real. A moment arrived when Marilyn didn't want to be there any more and she scooped me up. 'Goodbye, Alice,' she said and we walked down to the road. The further we got from Murmuring Trees the more like Marilyn she became, her walk different, her breathing deeper, as the gates came into view. My owner hugged me and looked into my eyes. I was still thinking of Milton as we came to the edge of Forest Lawn. 'Millions of spiritual creatures walk the earth,' I said. 'Unseen, both when we wake, and when we sleep.'

'Good dog,' she said.

It was a week later when Mrs Murray decided every garment in the house must be washed. My owner had gone to New York. I can't explain why I always felt close to the domestics; it wasn't on the whole a matter of politics, more of smell, the little things of temperament and the kitchen. All the windows were open and the bees were gossiping from flower to flower, a contagion of greyness out on the sunny porch. 'Big bonanza for the beatniks of Berkeley,' said one of the bees, landing on a garden hose. 'Zukofsky and the Business of Zen.'

'Isness not business,' said another bee, backing into a flower.

'Sorry?'

'Zukofsky, stupid. The gig is called "Zukofsky and the Isness of Zen".'

I wonder if I was the only person to notice how much Mrs Murray was beginning to look like me. It happens very often to people who spend a lot of time with dogs. Mrs Sackville-West, for instance, was said almost to be the spitting image of Pinker. Lionel Trilling is known to have parted his hair in imitation of his Afghan hound, Elsinore, and they say John Steinbeck was often mistaken for his poodle Charley as they crossed the country in a pick-up truck called Rocinante. In the same way, Mrs Murray had begun to look exactly like me or some similar dog. She happened to be carrying me one day from the sun room to the kitchen when we passed a Mexican mirror: she paused there for a second to contemplate the heavenly angels ranged in her mind against suffering and

275

sin, and when I looked into the glass I could have sworn we were not looking at ourselves at all but at Monet's *Portrait of Eugénie Graff* with her small terrier. It was not simply that my friend Eunice looked a lot like Eugénie, Madame Paul, the owner of the pâtisserie in Pourville, but each looked a lot like the respective dogs in their respective arms, an echo that almost put me off my bowl of Friskies.*

But the day grew cold by the evening. That was the problem with the Spanish hacienda style: by day it seemed correct and bright, but by night time, unless there were fairy lights and briars and distant guitars, the house appeared closed to the joys of the Hispanic world. My mood was always created by the houses where I lived, that was the price of having been owned by artists and make-believers, their imagination clung to the walls, and so too did their absences. It would be one thing to say that Marilyn was in my thoughts, but that wouldn't cover it. I could taste her essence everywhere. Wandering through the rooms, I felt the trace of Chanel No. 5 was very strong and it brought her close again. All her things made a strong impression: an inscribed copy of 'The Wee Small Hours', a single, beautiful shoe by Ferragamo, the Russian novel by the door, not quite finished. My friend would return to Brentwood in a few days, and I'm sure I would be waiting for her with happy eyes in the hallway or by the pool.

---

* Madame Paul, in a letter to her sister, observed that Claude Monet had a very sweet tooth – '*aimait les sucreries*' – but that his painting of her and the dog would not be hung in the shop. 'We shall ensure it finds a proper place in the laundry room,' she wrote. 'I am in love with the achievements of art, and feel sure that Monsieur M. has caught us exactly. My husband is of a different opinion. I believe he is mortified to learn that Foulette and myself are made from the same materials.'

Mrs Murray had placed clothing over every surface. The television was very loud in the corner. There were shirts on hangers billowing from the windows, dresses over the cold standard lamps; there were tights along the fireplace and mirrors sheeted in satin scarves. Every object seemed to find its vantage point in the living room. 'All created things are an image of things in heaven,' said Mrs Murray, twisting the TV aerial and directing it south. She was mumbling things from her Bible and eating a Tootsie Roll at the very same time. She turned to me and I hopped up on an armchair and she gave me the end of the Tootsie Roll and I licked my chops. She sighed and gave me one of her looks. 'There's something you ought to know, Maf Honey,' she said. 'And that is that animals do not go to heaven.'

'What a relief,' I said. 'We can believe without having to pay the consequences.'

'What you barking for?' she said. 'I'm only telling you the truth. No need to take it out on me, little . . . Snowball.'

She smiled through her old winged glasses. The door was open onto the terrace, and I could hear the cicadas *veep-veep-veeping* their defence of John Stuart Mill against the charge of human arrogance. Next minute the TV kicked in and soon we could see her on the stage in a white stole and a dress made of stars. On the little Magnavox TV, she appeared more than ever a person entirely removed from ordinary life. Every creature is an effusion of something rare, but she was beyond reach at the centre of her ghostly aura, the night crowding around her as she sang 'Happy Birthday'. My fated companion looked as if nothing real had ever touched her, no small regret, no other person, no Alice Tuttle. She was unearthly. I was sure for a moment I saw the boychick Charlie in the crowd. The camera went on to a row of smiling faces, young people who cared about the future of society, and I'm sure one of them was Charlie. We saw President Kennedy walking to the stage. Opera music began to play. The screen went fuzzy and the music got louder. I thought for a second the extra-terrestrials might be sending a message, but it was just Kennedy speaking on the telecast, the screen fuzzy and the music larger than life. Mrs Murray seemed oblivious to everything in her armchair. She darned one of Marilyn's favourite socks and mumbled the words to an old hymn.

The bougainvillea had dropped some of its petals into the swimming pool. I sat on the terrace, enjoying the evening. My owner might be half a continent away, the insects might be lost in arguments, and Mrs Murray might be working quietly in the Mexican armchair, but we were all here together beneath the blue forests of the sky. Constellations of beasts were glinting up there – Ursa Major, the scorpion, Canis Major – just as they had for Ptolemy nearly two thousand years ago. Then Lizzy appeared, the cat belonging to the orthodontist over the wall, and she seemed fully in step with the strains of Wagner coming from indoors. The cat spoke slowly and was reflected in the swimming pool.

> The sun is spent, and so are we,
> Who hop among the ruins seeking light.
> Enjoy your summer, *mes amis*,
> The day must end at the burial site.

I went up to the wall of vines and put my paws up, but the cat didn't run or fret and she leaned down playfully. She saw I knew something. 'Your adventures have taught you much,' she said. 'Even your adversaries might agree. You are older, Maf.'

'Artists are always young,' I said. 'In their work, they are always young and their dreams are always new.'

'Good dog,' she said.

With the music playing, it occurred to me that the pool might be the deep blue water of the Rhine, and over its surface maidens might appear to sing an elegy to the memory of their lost gold. Their laughter rang from the violins in the house. And then the ravens spoke of vengeance and Siegfried was killed, as we always knew he would be. I looked up and imagined I saw a fierce red glow in the sky, the flames mounting as Brunnhilde rides her horse into the funeral pyre and all is done and gone. Everything cleared and the swimming pool was nice again, a little pond in California. Wagner once told Cosima that she must share everything with their beloved spaniel, Peps. 'Tell Pepsel everything that comes into your mind,' he wrote. 'I find when I begin to work that I need the dog to come and watch over me.'

Mrs Murray was snoozing over her work as I walked past her in the living room. The television was now a field of snow and the clock ticked in some other universe, so I walked past the hanging garments and found my favourite place at the back of the house, on Marilyn's bed. I lay down sleepily and scratched my borrowed collar. It's true I was often banned from the bedroom, sometimes kept to the guest cottage for being too talkative, but that night I was free to lie on my owner's bed and sniff the exact and everlasting scent, the cotton freshness that seemed so right as I closed my eyes and breathed the secrets of her pillow.